Steve Yarbrough

Safe from the Neighbors

Born in Indianola, Mississippi, Steve Yarbrough is
the author of four previous novels and three collections of stories. A PEN/Faulkner finalist, he
has received the Mississippi Authors Award, the
California Book Award, the Richard Wright
Award, and an award from the Mississippi Institute of Arts and Letters. He now teaches at Emer-
son College and lives with his wife in Stoneham,
Massachusetts.

PRAISE FOR STEVE YARBROUGH'S *Safe from the Neighbors*

"Very few writers understand the complex history and maddening social order of the Mississippi Delta. For Steve Yarbrough, though, it's home turf. He is wickedly observant, funny, cynical, evocative, and he possesses a gift that cannot be taught: he can tell a story."
—John Grisham

"Steve Yarbrough is a masterful storyteller—one of our finest—and *Safe from the Neighbors* is a masterpiece. . . . This is a spellbinding, powerful novel."
—Jill McCorkle

"Yarbrough's lines can stop you in your tracks."
—*The Florida Times-Union*

"One of Yarbrough's talents is his cinematic ability to paint the Delta South—its people and places—without any of the predictable stereotypes. His writing style is so natural and straightforward and bristly with suspense that you hardly notice his abundant insights into the complicated history of the region."
—*Oxford American*

"*Safe from the Neighbors* . . . is over far too quickly. . . . Exceptionally well told."
—*Free Lance-Star* (Fredericksburg, Virginia)

"Emphasizes how the past is never really dead and how little we truly know about the people and neighbors with whom we grow up. . . . Excellent."
—*The Decatur Daily*

"*Safe from the Neighbors* is a novel of unusual richness and depth, one that's as wise about the small shocks within a marriage as it is about the troubled history of Mississippi. Steve Yarbrough is a formidably talented novelist, shuttling between the past and present with a grace that feels effortless."
—Tom Perrotta

Safe from the Neighbors

Safe from the Neighbors

STEVE YARBROUGH

Vintage Contemporaries
Vintage Books
A Division of Random House, Inc.
New York

FIRST VINTAGE CONTEMPORARIES EDITION, FEBRUARY 2011

A portion of this work originally appeared in slightly different form in *Ploughshares*.

Grateful acknowledgment is made to Farrar, Straus and Giroux, LLC for permission
to reprint an excerpt from "The Funeral of Bobò" from *A Part of Speech*
by Joseph Brodsky, translation copyright © 1980 by Farrar, Straus and Giroux, LLC.
Reprinted by permission of Farrar, Straus and Giroux, LLC.

The Library of Congress has cataloged the Knopf edition as follows:
Yarbrough, Steve.
Safe from the neighbors / by Steve Yarbrough.—1st ed.
p. cm.
1. History teachers—Fiction. 2. African Americans—Civil rights—Fiction.
3. Mississippi—Fiction. I. Title.
PS3575.A717S34 2010
813'.54—dc22
2009022311

Vintage ISBN: 978-0-307-47215-1

Book design by Robert C. Olsson

www.vintagebooks.com

Printed in the United States of America

For Ania W

The perpetual activity of forgetting gives our every act a ghostly, unreal, hazy quality. What did we have for lunch the day before yesterday?

—Milan Kundera

The Sixteenth Section

The Seventeenth Section

"JUST LOOK WHAT HAPPENS TO POETS," I used to tell my honors class on the first day of school. "Half the time they go mad. And you know why I think that happens? Too much truth distilled to its essence, all surrounding evidence ignored or discarded. And I'm not faulting them for that. They're just doing what poets are supposed to, and they've left us some beautiful works of literature, some of which have lasted for hundreds of years.

"When you pursue truth the way a historian does, though, you'll find that it seldom travels without escort. There are all kinds of accompanying data. And causation, in particular, is usually a complicated matter. Let me give you an example of what I mean.

"In 1944, the day after the Allies landed in Normandy, a woman who lived down in Belzoni gave birth prematurely to quintuplets, and all of them died within the hour. The Jackson and Memphis papers had already reported the invasion, and this poor woman had reason to believe her husband was there. Like women all over Mississippi—all over America—she was terrified, scared to death her guy might've died on a beach thousands of miles from home. Now what effect do you think her fears could've had on her pregnancy?"

A hand or two always went up. "Maybe it got her so scared it threw her into labor."

"It certainly could have. Things like that do happen. And so since there would've been no reason for her husband to storm those beaches if the Nazis hadn't been entrenched there, you might consider accusing Adolf Hitler of having helped cause the deaths of those babies, along with all those other deaths he helped cause, millions upon millions of deaths in hundreds of battles or in concentration camps spread across Europe.

"But you might look for other 'causes' as well. For instance, when I was a student up at Ole Miss, where I learned about these dead babies while working on an oral history project, I discovered this lady's father had lost his job in 1931 and stayed unemployed until 1942. The whole time she was growing up, she didn't have enough to eat, so by the time she got married she'd been malnourished for years, just like a lot of other Americans at that time, including my mother and father and quite a few of your grandparents. We're talking about the Great Depression, and who usually gets blamed for responding inadequately to that?"

Another hand in the air. "Herbert Hoover?"

"That's right. We won't worry about whether that's fair or not. We'll just add his name next to Hitler's." I usually started to move around the room at this point, walking over to the window to look out at the athletic fields where the Loring High football and baseball teams held their practices. With my back to the students, I'd say, "Of course, it turns out this woman had smoked all the way through her pregnancy and, according to some, drank hard liquor, too. It was illegal in Mississippi back then, but you could get booze from bootleggers, and more than a few people thought she did, though they weren't sure how, given that she was poor and broke. These days, knowing a lot more about the effects of smoking and drinking on fetuses in utero, we might want to add her own name to the list of folks 'responsible' for this. We might put her mom's name up there, too, because when she found out her daughter was pregnant, she told this troubled young woman to get out of the house, that she and her husband couldn't feed any more mouths."

I'd always turn around and face them before making the next statement. "Depending on whether or not you subscribe to a religious worldview—and I know most of you do—you might even want to add God's name to the list we began with Adolf Hitler. Because the temperature in the Delta on June seventh, 1944, was a hundred and four degrees, and nobody had air conditioners then. Women's bodies are already under plenty of stress during pregnancy, and immediately prior to delivery, this particular young woman displayed the symptoms of heatstroke."

The last suggestion never failed to make them uncomfortable: twenty-five bodies changed position, shifting in their seats, shuffling their feet. Nobody cared if you laid a few more deaths on Hitler's doorstep, and as for the young woman herself, well, she should have known better than to smoke and drink. But most of the kids in my classroom, black and white alike, had been washed in the blood just like I had, and while the blood had long ago washed off me, they were still covered with it.

"You know what you could do, though?" I'd say, stepping over to the board and picking up a piece of chalk that I started bouncing off the palm of my hand. "You could do what a good historian does. Note all the available facts, create as full a picture as possible, then conclude that on the day after D-Day, between two and three in the afternoon, five babies born to a nineteen-year-old woman named Mary Ethel Benson—whose husband, Charlie, was in France, where he'd win the Medal of Honor—died in Belzoni, Mississippi."

From the looks on their faces, you could see I'd sold them my argument, just as I'd sold it to myself.

In 1860 there were 7.24 slaves for every free person (all of these being white) in Loring County. And even though a lot of African Americans left the Delta in the 1920s and again in the years after the Second World War, the racial balance has remained remarkably stable. In 2006, the county was 70 percent black, while the town of Loring itself was 68 percent.

You could see this history reflected in the faces, bodies, apparel and accoutrements of the students arrayed in the bleachers for the opening assembly of the fall semester. About 70 percent were black, most of them dressed in standard-issue Wal-Mart clothes. The white kids, on the other hand, wore designer jeans, with the girls favoring what my twin daughters, both at Ole Miss now, had taught me were called "cap-sleeve T-shirts," "double-layer tanks" and "peasant skirts." They carried brand-new JanSport backpacks, and the majority had driven their own cars to school, whereas their black classmates either walked or rode the bus. You could tell that many of the black kids, and a few of the white ones as well, had starch-heavy diets, though our free-lunch program tried to serve healthier fare. Except for a few athletes, who tended to flock together regardless of color, the races didn't mix much at assemblies. The white kids clustered high up in the bleachers, reversing the order that prevailed in movie theaters when I was a boy.

Our principal, Ramsey Coleman, walked to the lectern, directly under the basket at the far end of the court. He's a likable guy who took a lot of flak a few years ago for looking like Johnnie Cochran, folks asking if he'd found any bloody gloves lately. Like me, he'd recently turned fifty and had grown up in Loring.

While he welcomed everybody back and enumerated the exciting developments that had taken place since the spring semester—"we bought six new HP laptops for the computer lab, got new uniforms for the football team, replaced all the windowpanes y'all shot out and filled the holes in the walls with bulletproof plaster"—I found myself wondering what it would be like coming to school knowing I wouldn't see either of my daughters in the hallway between classes or eat lunch with them and their boyfriends (when they had any) like I had almost every school day for the last four years. A lot of things had just changed, and though Jennifer and I had known it was coming, I don't think we really understood how we'd feel when we drove off and left them up at Oxford. Each of us cried coming home, but while you might imagine their absence would draw us closer, if anything it seemed to push us farther apart. At first that surprised me, but after a few days it was starting to make sense. Up until a certain point, we'd done things together as a family, but then the girls got older, life got busier and we drifted into a kind of unspoken agreement that I'd do some things with them— teaching them to drive, listening to them complain about my colleagues or taking them fishing, back when they still enjoyed that—while she'd do others, like helping them buy clothes, showing them how to cook and reading their English papers. We couldn't share each other's loss because for a long time now we hadn't shared each other's pleasure.

"Two teachers left us over the summer," Ramsey was saying. "Don't act triumphant, though. Y'all didn't scare 'em to death—they just got better-paying jobs." Most of the kids laughed. Ramsey was fond of saying that only 2 percent of the students were really troublemakers, but since he first made that statement the phrase *Two Percent Club* had begun showing up on walls and in toilet stalls. Last year, somebody had spray-painted it on one of the buses after busting out all the windows, misspelling *Percent* as *Procent*.

"Mr. Pratt," Ramsey went on, "finished his doctorate and got hired to teach zoology up at Delta State."

Somebody hollered, "He never were nothin' but a old *gi*raffe."

Ramsey jotted a note on his legal pad. Once assembly ended, whoever had made the remark would be hauled into the office. Ramsey laughed a lot and told jokes, but there were better people around to have mad at you.

"Fortunately, we've secured the services of Mr. Marcus Billings, a graduate of this very school whom Dr. Pratt personally recommended. Stand up, Mr. Billings."

Mark Billings stood and waved. He'd been my student seven or eight years earlier, and I distinctly remembered having called on him to answer the question of how many U.S. senators each state has. Looking stricken, he finally ventured, "Ten?" Ramsey had told me he'd hire him despite, as he put it, "certain deficits" in his Delta State transcript. Mark's main qualification seemed to be his willingness to accept the job.

The other vacancy had occurred the previous week, when we were up moving the girls into their dorm at Ole Miss. Our French teacher learned that her husband, an executive at one of the ConAgra catfish plants, was being promoted to the company's Omaha headquarters, and Ramsey left a panicked message on my cell phone, wondering if I had any suggestions. But before I could call him back, I received another one saying he'd found the solution.

Which, as it turned out, was "Mrs. Maggie Sorrentino," a trim, dark-haired woman in her early fifties. She wore a pair of white slacks and a purple silk blouse, gold bracelets on each of her wrists and a thick gold necklace. Earlier, pulling into the teachers' parking lot, I'd noticed a recent-model Mercedes, one of those sporty jobs that probably cost more than my house. It had North Carolina license plates, so I figured a rich relative must have paid one of my colleagues a visit and let whoever it was drive the car to work.

"Mrs. Sorrentino," Ramsey continued, "studied French at a very special institution named Duke University. I imagine y'all have heard of it? They do amazing things there with basketballs. Unlike one or two of our players, *they* can even write their names on 'em."

When the assembly was over and everybody began to file out, I found myself walking down the hall beside the new French teacher, whose classroom was in the same wing as mine. Up close, I could see she wore a lot of eyeliner and that her lipstick matched her blouse. She must have doused herself in perfume— the odor was that strong, but I liked it. "I wanted to introduce myself," I said. "I'm Luke May. I teach American history and a special honors class in local history."

"Local history?" she said, as if she doubted any such thing existed.

We stopped outside my classroom. "We focus on the history of Loring County and the Delta, though we also talk about the rest of the state. Reconstruction, the Progressive Era, the Depression, civil rights and so on. A lot of things happened here. You might be surprised."

For an awkward moment, as she started to shake her head, I thought she was going to walk away without saying anything more, though nobody in her right mind would behave like that towards a colleague trying to welcome her to a new job.

"Luke," she finally said, "you don't remember me at all, do you?"

While we stood there, the eyeliner and the purple lipstick faded away, and a little girl's face took shape.

I'VE NEVER READ MUCH FICTION. What bothers me about
most novels is how much of the world they exclude by focusing
on the inner lives of one or two characters. I'm also troubled by
the whole notion of a "plot," in which one event leads to
another in a manner that, more often than not, seems overly
simplistic. Nevertheless, shortly after my daughters graduated
from high school, I retreated from reality and embarked on a
novel-reading binge.

Many of the books I read that summer had been recommended by Ellis Buchanan, whom Jennifer had invited for dinner that Monday evening. A native of the east Mississippi hill
country, he'd moved to Loring and bought the local paper in the
fall of 1960. In other words, he arrived in the Delta in time to
witness the most turbulent years of the civil rights movement,
and then managed to cause a lot of trouble for himself and his
family by advocating voting rights for blacks and suggesting
that segregation was both immoral and economically unsound.
He constantly received threatening phone calls, and somebody
eventually hurled a firebomb into the building where the *Weekly
Times* was published, though it happened on a Friday night,
when no one was around. At Loring Elementary, it was understood that his son and daughter shouldn't be invited to join

activities on the playground. You'd see them sitting there in the sandbox together or bouncing up and down on the seesaw.

Ellis was almost eighty now. His wife had been dead for twenty years, his children never came back after they graduated from college, and he'd sold the paper in 1990. Mostly what he did these days was read, listen to classical music and tend to his roses, and once a week he came to the high school and spoke to the journalism class. He was still handsome, as Jennifer frequently said. Tall and silver haired, he rarely appeared in public without a tie and was wearing one that evening. "So what did you think, dear," he asked her as I poured him a second glass of the Oregon Pinot Noir he'd brought along, "of the Brodsky collection?"

Jennifer teaches freshman English up at Delta State, but her passion is poetry. She writes every day, and once or twice a year somebody, usually a small journal, will accept a poem. Back in the early '90s, the *Southern Review* published one—the biggest splash she'd ever made.

Ellis was always pushing collections at her, but his taste ran towards work a lot more restrained than what she was drawn to. He loved Frost and Robert Penn Warren, while she preferred Sylvia Plath, Anne Sexton and a lot of younger poets whose names I'd never heard until she mentioned them. And once she did, I usually forgot them.

"I don't know what to think about Brodsky," she said. "But I've got a feeling he's been badly translated."

"The translations seemed just fine to me."

She tossed her long curly blonde hair, revealing sharp cheekbones. At a time when most of our women friends were growing bigger and bigger, she kept getting thinner. I couldn't figure out why, since her diet hadn't changed. "You're entitled to your opinion," she said, "though I have trouble when *cheese* is forced to rhyme with *energies*."

Ellis feigned outrage. "I don't remember any rhyme like that."

She lifted her wineglass and sipped from it, soaking in every second of his attention. Sometimes, when they were sitting there like that, I almost felt as if my presence were indecent, that I should have got up and left them alone together. "Listen to this stanza," she said, "from 'The Funeral of Bobò.' " She stepped over to the sideboard and picked up a large red-and-gold hardcover.

> *Farewell, Bobò, my beautiful and sweet.*
> *These tear-drops dot the page like holes in cheese.*
> *We are too weak to follow you, and yet*
> *to take a stand exceeds our energies.*

She closed the book—the halves thudding together—and laid it triumphantly before him.

He eyed it for a moment, then crossed his arms over his stomach. Smiling, he said, "Yes, that's definitely a bad translation. Brodsky wrote in Russian, where there's no word for cheese because they lack the energy to produce it."

Several hours and three bottles of wine later, the evening reached its conclusion, as so many of these evenings had, with Ellis glancing at his watch and expressing shock. "My Lord—can you believe it's almost midnight?"

Under ordinary circumstances, Jennifer, who usually has to grade around one hundred twenty papers each week, is rarely able to remain awake after 10:00 p.m. But a visit by Ellis Buchanan, no matter how often one occurred, was nothing ordinary. "It's early," she said. "Let's drink one more glass of wine. It's good for your heart."

"I have no heart. That's how I've managed to live so long. If you don't have one, it can't wear out. You should get rid of yours before it's too late."

My wife was drunk. "That's why I write poetry," she said. "I'm trying to lose it on the page."

Our guest rose. Unlike my father, a tall man who'd become stooped at a certain point in his life, Ellis had retained his full height and, except for a few wrinkles, didn't look much different than he had twenty years ago. "I'm going to get out of here," he told me, "before this young lady suggests I'm a man of virtue. I'd hate to be reduced to a set of good impulses."

"I'll walk you home," I said.

He laughed. "Afraid that in my doddering senility I'll lose my way?"

"After all we've had to eat and drink, I need some exercise bad."

"I think he's lying," he told Jennifer, then bent to kiss her cheek. "He's scared I'll be found wandering around somebody's catfish pond in the morning with a dazed expression and two or three cottonmouth bites."

"If those cottonmouths bit you," I said, "you wouldn't be wandering anywhere. You'd be dead."

"Mr. History," he said, using the nickname one of my students coined a few years ago. "Wed to fact like an innocent young bride."

Outside, crickets chirped in the velvet air. That afternoon it had rained, and the yard was soggy. Still, you'd never think of warning Ellis to watch his step. It went without saying that he knew right where he was going.

In high school I'd worked as his intern, helping him do the pasteup and then carrying the sheets down the street to the printer, and before long he was taking me with him to news conferences. Through him, I'd met some major figures in the civil rights movement, like Aaron Henry, as well as the finest governor this state ever had, William Winter. You can find some of the worst people in the world in Mississippi, but also some of the best, and the quickest way to tell them apart is to look where they stand on race. Ellis Buchanan was one of the best. He'd done some good things for me personally, too, helping me win an Ole Miss scholarship so I wouldn't have to take out loans or depend on my father, who'd been urging me to attend Mississippi State and study agriculture, then come home and help him farm.

Walking to his house that night, he asked how my parents were doing. My dad didn't have much use for him and would avoid him if it looked like they might meet on the street. And as for my mother, well, she hadn't been able to speak to anybody for quite some time. "His blood pressure's through the roof," I said, "and he's having problems with his feet. They're always swollen. And poor Momma doesn't know where she is, which I guess may be a good thing."

"That isn't likely."

I looked at him. "You've never become forgetful, have you?"

He laughed. "Well, now that's hard to answer, isn't it? Because if I had, I wouldn't know it."

"I'm not talking about anything extreme. I mean when you forget somebody's name, when you know it but just can't quite dredge it up."

"I'm not in the habit of dredging."

"You used to be. I seem to recall that when you were a journalist, you did a fair amount of it."

"Did I? That must be one of the things I've forgotten."

A certain portion of Ellis's emotional capital had always been invested in irony. That probably helped him survive his wife's death—she'd had lung cancer and suffered badly towards the end—as well as the '60s and early '70s, when his politics put him on the outs with almost everybody in the white community. Later on, as the town tried to rehabilitate itself, he became its unofficial spokesperson—the guy who could explain to the outside world that while Loring, Mississippi, had a long way to go, it'd already traveled a great distance.

"On the subject of forgetting," I said, "I met someone today I haven't thought of in years."

"Really? And who might that be?"

"Her last name's Sorrentino now."

"She's Italian?"

"No. She was originally named Calloway, Maggie Calloway. She seemed hurt that I didn't remember her. We were friends when I was small—I'm guessing I was no more than four or five when we met, but I can't say for sure. The thing was, she moved away. I don't know exactly when this happened, but you'll probably remember. Because her father shot and killed her mother."

As a young man, Ellis had played basketball at Ole Miss, and he still carried himself with the grace and certainty of an athlete. That night he never broke stride. "October first, 1962," he said. "Does that date ring a bell, Mr. History?"

THE HOUSE WHERE I GREW UP burned about twenty years ago. It was situated a few miles north of Loring, near the intersection of two country roads, only one of which was paved when I was a boy. The one we lived on wasn't, and my dad considered it a major triumph when he managed to embarrass the county board of supervisors into grading it and adding several loads of fresh gravel. Normally, the supervisors didn't pay much attention to men like him, but he'd been persistent and, in the end, won out.

The house and the surrounding acreage belonged to the sixteenth section, which was rented out to farmers to support the local schools. In our county this land was put up for auction every five years, which meant that people like my father and my maternal grandfather, who until his death was Dad's partner, had to enter sealed bids, and when the time to open these bids rolled around a certain number of relationships inevitably got fractured.

Some of my earliest memories involve the barbershop owned by Mr. Parker Sturdivant, a cotton farmer who cut hair only on Saturdays, and I was always terrified that my turn might come when his chair was empty. Bald himself, he showed no respect for anybody else's hair and would keep the clippers whirring until he got through with whatever story he'd started telling when you sat down. More than once I climbed out of his chair in tears, and I wasn't the only boy who did. Like most of my friends, I preferred Mr. Sturdivant's employee, a guy named Andy Owens, who had wavy red hair and supplemented his barber's salary by delivering the Memphis paper. Though the papers were dropped off at the local bus station by a southbound Greyhound around 2:00 a.m., people usually got them late on Sundays because Andy always drank the night away and frequently stopped for naps on his route the next morning. You often saw his truck parked at the edge of a country road, papers piled high in the passenger seat, Andy's head resting on the steering wheel. It was understood that if you were on your way to church and still didn't have your *Commercial Appeal*, it was okay to open the door and slip one out.

Sturdivant's was the spot where men gathered to swap lies, sometimes stopping by even when they didn't need a haircut. They talked about the fortunes of the Loring Leopards or the Ole Miss Rebels, chewed tobacco and shot brown streams of juice into tin cans and Dixie cups, moaned about rain or the lack of it. Cross words were never exchanged. My own tears notwithstanding, I associated the place with laughter.

They were laughing in there one morning about the uses to which the word *public* had lately been put. My friend Eugene Calloway and his father were under the clippers, Eugene a heavily freckled boy of five or six, Arlan a slim, prematurely gray man in his midthirties, who swept his hair upward in the style of such country singers as Porter Wagoner and Faron Young. Eugene, perched on the vinyl-covered board Andy placed across the arms of the barber's chair for boys like us, cast an eye at his father, probably wondering if Mr. Sturdivant was going to mess up and cut off too much. His dad, as everybody knew, was particular about two things, his clothes and his hair.

"Heard one of 'em the other day standing in front of Western Auto saying the town needed more 'public' parking spaces," Mr. Sturdivant was saying. "And then another one, that big old horse-faced fool they call McCarthy—"

"Mc*Carty*," my father said.

"Who cares?" said Mr. Sturdivant, who didn't like his stories interrupted. "He's just McNigger to me."

That drew a laugh from most of those assembled: my father, Eugene and his dad, Andy, three or four other men. I probably wanted to laugh, too, but I doubt I would've. My mother had grabbed me by the ear when I called the man who sacked our groceries at Piggly Wiggly "a nigger." So I asked why she didn't pull my father's ear for saying it, since he said it all the time, or Grandpa's, since he did, too, and she told me that what they said was their business but what I said was hers.

"Anyway, McWhatever looks back at the other one and says, 'Yes sir, deed we do. Deed we do. And we be needing more pub-lic *park* space too.' "

Everybody laughed again. One of the other men said, "They think if you call something public, that means it's theirs. They don't know it's still ours."

Eugene's dad said, "It's not ours, either. It's the govern-ment's."

"You got that right. Get right down to it, there's not much the government don't own, is there?"

"Not much," Eugene's dad said, shaking his head.

"Hold still, Arlan," Mr. Sturdivant ordered. "I can't style hair on a moving target."

"You're not styling it, Parker. You're just mowing it." He looked at the mirror mounted on the opposite wall. "And I do believe you're about to leave me a tad bereft."

Mr. Calloway, I'd noticed, loved words that started with *be-*. *Bereft, bedazzled, befuddled, beguiled.* I'd heard him say all those and more. Because I was so taken with the way he talked, I'd asked Dad one time if my friend's father had gone to college. He said, "Arlan Calloway went to the college of tough luck." Mr. Calloway grew up poor, he told me, and everything he had he'd gotten by actually going out and working for it. That impressed me at the time because the Calloways had a lot more than we did. They lived in a modern brick house with a small pool in the backyard, and had two television sets and a stereo. Mr. Calloway drove a new truck and his wife a new car.

Mr. Sturdivant stuck the clippers into the holster on the side of the chair, then combed Mr. Calloway's hair straight up into the air until it resembled pictures I'd seen of the Matterhorn. After turning him loose, he motioned to me. "Guess it's your lucky day, Luke. Time I get through with you, you'll look just like Yul Brynner."

On the booster board I closed my eyes, unwilling to look at my image in the mirror. I heard Eugene hop out of Andy's chair and my father settling in there. As always, rather than leave immediately, the Calloways would sit and watch us get our hair cut, then Eugene's father and mine would walk out into the parking lot together. Besides having been friends when they were kids, they were both members of an organization called the Citizens' Council.

"How about that Meredith boy?" one of the men said while I sat there with my eyes closed.

Mr. Sturdivant was running the clippers dangerously close to my ear. "He's something, ain't he?"

"That boy better learn to sing 'Dixie.' "

"He ain't gone go to Ole Miss. Ever comes to it, I'll be standing right beside Ross with my shotgun."

I recognized Mr. Calloway's rich baritone: "Ross Barnett is nothing but a fake. I wouldn't be surprised if him and JFK are in cahoots."

I waited to hear what the others would say. I knew they were talking about our governor and the president, whom my father had voted for even though he was a Catholic. At that point in Southern history the Republican Party had three strikes against it: the Civil War, the Great Depression and Little Rock Central.

My father was the first to raise an objection: "Arlan, I think Ross knows what he's doing."

Mr. Calloway laughed. "I never said he didn't, James. I'll wager he knows exactly what he's doing. It's you and me and the rest of this beleaguered assembly that's in the dark."

This comment seemed to forestall further debate—in the barbershop, he wielded that kind of authority. For a while nobody said anything, then one of the men cleared his throat and asked, "Y'all think the Leopards got a bat's chance against them boys from Leland?"

By the time I escaped the chair, my head felt about ten or fifteen degrees cooler. I knew I shouldn't look at the mirror but couldn't stop myself. Mr. Sturdivant had given me a pair of white sidewalls.

Though the barbershop would later move downtown, it was out on Highway 47 in those days, sandwiched between Delta Electric and Loring Auto Parts. On Saturdays the parking lot filled up. People cut their engines wherever space existed, which in practice meant that you'd often emerge to find another truck parked behind your own. As odd as this may sound today—when life in small Southern towns has picked up speed, everyone eager to rush home and access the world by clicking the Explorer icon—if somebody blocked you in back then, you'd stand around and wait, talking to whoever else was out there, until the owner of the truck behind yours stepped out of whichever business he'd been in. Then you stood around a little longer and talked to him, too. To do otherwise would've been unneighborly.

Somebody had parked behind our truck that day. Over the

last year or so, since I began piecing these events together, I've often wondered whether things might have developed differently if Dad had simply said goodbye to the Calloways, climbed into the truck and driven away. I say this because I've learned that in Loring County in 1962, you only found out who was bidding against you for a piece of sixteenth-section land if his bid was higher than yours, or if, prior to the announcement of the results, he took it upon himself to inform you, which most people were understandably reluctant to do.

Since we couldn't leave, the Calloways didn't either. While our fathers talked about the fishing over in Lake Lee, Eugene and I drew a ring in the gravel, then squared off back-to-back and began to grunt and push, each trying to drive the other outside the circle. Eugene was a good bit heavier, so it's reasonable to think he prevailed, though in fact I don't remember. What I do recall precisely is the moment when I once again heard that word.

"It's *public* land, James, and I've got to do this for me and my family. If I can't expand, I can't borrow. Banks lend on the basis of how many acres you're farming. Benighted as that kind of thinking may be, that's how they are. You know that just as well as I do. In the end, what's going to ruin us all is labor costs. Time's coming when we'll be paying folks six dollars a day to chop cotton. Only answer I see's increased mechanization, but who's got the money to buy new equipment?"

My father, as I have said, was a tall man, a shade under six-foot-four. He eventually put on a lot of weight, his belly began to pull his back and shoulders forward, and when he walked he always looked as if he were just about to step through a low doorway. But at this point in his life he was still thin. Lanky, people said.

Though a couple inches shorter, I'm no midget. So I can tell you that when a tall man's unwilling to meet a shorter man's gaze, he's got three options. He can look past the crown of the other guy's head, as if he were studying the horizon. Or he can glance from side to side, like he was on the witness stand and trying to avoid the eyes of the DA. Or else he can stare at the ground—knowing just how pitiful it looks when somebody his height does that.

My father availed himself of all three, first pondering a distant Texaco sign. Then cutting his gaze from left to right and back. Finally hanging his head, his cheeks turning from pink to red to purple while Eugene and I stood silently by, aware that something had just changed between our fathers but not fully understanding what it was.

"No hard feelings, I hope," Mr. Calloway said. "I sure won't have any, regardless how it all plays out." Then he offered his hand.

For a moment I thought my dad would refuse to shake it. There was plenty I didn't know, but I intuited that refusing to grasp a man's extended hand was a decision of enormous import, one with the power to alter lives—of the four of us standing there, and of my mom, Eugene's mom and his sister, Maggie.

What I couldn't imagine was the degree to which certain gestures—shaking hands, smiling and saying good morning, opening a door for another person, slapping somebody on the back or throwing your arm around his shoulder—could hide, for a time, the riot that raged inside.

It was almost as if my father willed the blood to flow out of his cheeks, his color returning to something near normal. He raised his head, reached out and shook Mr. Calloway's hand. There in the lot outside Sturdivant's Barbershop, on a sunny September morning in 1962, he said, "Arlan, we just won't let it come between us."

And at that Mr. Calloway grinned and slapped Dad's back.

BY A CERTAIN POINT, sex between Jennifer and me had become—to risk a pun—grindingly predictable. This development coincided with the growth of our daughters, whose bedrooms were across the hall from ours. When they were small, they fell asleep early. We still had our evenings left, and usually made the most of them, having a drink or two on the couch while watching a movie, then heading off to bed, where things progressed pretty much as they had in the backseat of my old Galaxy on various back roads in the vicinity of Oxford. But as the girls grew older, they were the ones who stayed up, listening to music, talking on their cell phones or banging around in the bathroom, and this made Jennifer reticent. If I touched her suggestively in bed, she'd usually whisper, "Let's wait till morning." But when morning came we'd be in a hurry, and if we did make love it was often rushed. After a while it turned into more of a duty, and I think both of us stopped looking forward to it. Finally, we more or less quit.

I imagine similar circumstances prevail for many married couples, though it's hard to say because people don't talk about this subject unless sitting across a desk from somebody getting paid one hundred seventy-five dollars an hour to listen sympathetically and nod every thirty seconds. What I can say for certain is that one afternoon when I was about twelve, I discovered the key to my father's closet, where he kept most of his guns, and when I opened it, intending to mess around with a Japanese rifle he'd brought home from the war, I came across a box of Trojans. He had eight of them, all wrapped in red cellophane. The next time I saw the inside of that closet—a couple of years later, when he handed me the key and told me to bring him his shotgun because a cottonmouth in the backyard needed killing—the box was still there, its contents providing evidence that my parents hardly had a sex life.

I laughed at the time and told myself he must be really clumsy if his wife wouldn't let him touch her. I never stopped to wonder if maybe they weren't both just tired—not only of each other, or of working hard for next to nothing, but of life in general.

Were it not for her writing, I might have wondered the same thing about Jennifer. No matter how worn out she might seem when she came home from school, she'd spend an hour or two at her desk before dinner. The study is just off the kitchen, behind a set of French doors. These were always closed when she was working on a poem, but I could still see her in there when I walked by. Most of the time she was just staring at the computer screen, her elbow occasionally propped on the desk, her chin resting in her palm, her eyes closed, her lips moving silently. I assumed she was trying out a line, seeing how it sounded before writing it down.

She wrote first thing in the morning too sometimes, and she was doing that when I got up the day after Ellis came over for dinner. Her classes started later than mine—ten o'clock most days—and she usually spent her extra time grading papers, but since the fall term had barely begun she wasn't yet being bombarded with bad freshman essays.

I tapped on the door. At first she didn't react, just sat there in her bathrobe frowning at the screen. So I tapped again, harder.

This time she looked up and frowned. "Yeah?"

I cracked the door open. "Working on a poem?"

"I *was*."

I'd love to say that the abruptness with which Jennifer responded to me when nobody else was present had its origins in her difficult artistic temperament. Unfortunately, that would be a lie. She hadn't always been like that, but when our marriage was starting to sour I often was. I wanted to sit in my armchair every morning and read the Memphis paper, and sit there at night with big biographies of Southern demagogues like J. K. Vardaman, Theodore G. Bilbo and Pitchfork Ben Tillman. I'd react with annoyance when she interrupted me, wanting to discuss some problem one of the girls was having or to tell me about some administrator up at Delta State. Once, when I was engrossed in a Huey Long biography I'd probably already read three or four times, she pulled it out of my hands, stuck a finger in it to mark my place and held it against her breast. "Did you hear what I just asked you?" she said. I must've stared at her with a confused expression—I didn't have the faintest idea. She gave the book back. "You aren't interested," she said, "in any life that isn't over."

Now, seeing her sitting there looking pissed off, I was tempted to slam the door and break every pane of glass in the damn thing. This sudden rush of anger, if I'd taken time to consider it, should have puzzled me. Things had been like this for a long time, and I hadn't thought of breaking anything before. "I was just wondering," I said, doing my best to sound calm, "whether you've had any breakfast."

Winston Churchill is supposed to have once told Lady Violet Bonham Carter, "We are all worms. But I do believe that I am a glow-worm." For whatever reason, Jennifer made an instantaneous decision to treat me like a glow-worm that day. She quit frowning, reached for the mouse, clicked out of whatever file she'd been in and said, "I'm not hungry, but I'll keep you company."

While I made a pot of coffee and popped a frozen bagel in the toaster, she perched on a stool near the refrigerator and told me about an e-mail she'd gotten first thing that morning from Candace. She and Trish were in the same dorm but had different roommates, and Candace was concerned about the girl living with her sister. She'd gone by there the night before to see if Trish wanted to walk downtown, get a latte and hang out on the balcony at Square Books. Her roommate said she'd gone to the library, which would explain why she hadn't answered her cell phone, but Candace noted that the room smelled of pot and the girl's eyes were the color of blood oranges.

She was from Jackson. We'd met her when we moved Trish in, and I hadn't been too taken with her. She had the kind of gothy look I've come to associate with bright kids who don't do their homework, make snide comments about people like Lincoln or FDR and are always infatuated with the likes of Lee Harvey Oswald, Charles Manson and John Wilkes Booth. "I had a bad feeling about her to begin with," I said. "I hope to God Trish isn't there in the dorm smoking pot all the time."

"Well, you always told them to let you know if they wanted to try it."

"No, I told them they ought to leave it alone, but that if they did decide to try it, they should do it at home."

"I seem to recall you even said you'd get it for them."

"Hey, I'd rather find some than have them get it from somebody else."

"What'd you intend to do, buy it off one of your students?"

Since I knew they'd never take me up on the offer, I'd never really thought about it. "I was just trying to make the point," I said, "that if they wanted to do something they shouldn't, they didn't need to slip around. It's the hiding and lying that make it so attractive."

Jennifer let me pour her a cup of coffee, though she'd been trying off and on for the past year to give it up. I poured myself a cup, buttered my bagel, and we both sat down at the table. We agreed that one of us—me, most likely—would talk to Trish before the day was over and make sure she understood that smoking pot in a dorm could get her in trouble. "And as for the other girl," I said, "she needs to exhale into that little refrigerator they rented and close the door on it."

Jennifer burst out laughing. I loved it when she did that. She tossed her hair, and the faint lines at the corners of her mouth deepened into valleys. "That's what you used to do, isn't it?"

"I'm not saying if I did or didn't. I'm just saying it hides the pot smell."

"What else did you hide back then?"

"Nothing, not after I met you."

"Really?"

"Not a single thing. I was a can, and you opened me up."

"My, what skill with metaphor."

I crunched my bagel. "Comes from living with a poet, I guess."

"So I'm a poet?"

"You write poems, don't you?"

"Sure. And every now and then, the *Potato Quarterly* publishes one."

"From what I know, the *Southern Review* was founded by Robert Penn Warren and isn't into vegetables."

She sipped her coffee. "Well, do I have to point out how long it's been since they took anything of mine?"

I knew how long it had been. Even when we were mad at each other, I hated seeing her with a rejection in hand, and some weeks she got as many as eight or ten. It seemed to me that anybody who loved poetry as much as she did deserved a little success, but that's not how the world works.

I'd always admired her perseverance. I was devoted to teaching—still got excited when a student won a scholarship to the kind of school I never could've dreamed of attending, and it happened more often than you might think—but I'd long ago lost the ambition to write about an event that occurred in Loring around the turn of the last century, when because of a racial incident Theodore Roosevelt closed down our post office. I'd done all the research, but never got very far with the actual writing. Determined to tell readers what really happened, to compose a narrative free of any bias whatsoever and let them draw their own conclusions about the motives and character of those involved, I wrote more than fifty-odd pages that stuck to the facts and avoided conjecture. But when I stopped to reread them, I knew immediately that nobody else would ever voluntarily do so. The average laundry list was more compelling.

"You had something in that journal over at MSU last year," I said. "I imagine that's a pretty good magazine."

She grinned. "*Jabberwock Review*. As in *jabberwocky*. You know, nonsensical speech or writing? Thanks for helping me make my point." She raised both arms, stretching and yawning, and when her bathrobe slipped open I saw she wore nothing beneath it.

The timing was awful. It was already 7:20, I hadn't showered, and for me school started at eight. What I'm saying is that any rational person would have concluded that our efforts were every bit as doomed as Pickett's Charge, but I advanced onto open ground with greater gusto than those lost Virginians. After all, I knew it couldn't cost me my life, just a little bit of dignity, and most of that was already gone.

I reached across the table and, before she could stop me, put my hand on her breast.

"Oh," she said, color rushing into those cheeks that were naturally so pale. "Well."

A couple of minutes later, in bed, she said it again as I slid inside her and started to move. "Well . . . now how about *this*?"

Her breath was hot in my ear. Rather than lying there stiffly, more victim than participant, she locked her legs around me like she had when we were younger, her heels riding the backs of my thighs.

Our alarm clock had two settings, A and B. A was for me, and during the week, I always kept it set to go off at 6:45. B was for Jennifer, and since she'd gotten up early I figured it probably wasn't set now at all. I was wrong, of course. About two minutes into playtime it sang its siren song, and the effect on me was both immediate and catastrophic.

"Ignore it," she begged. "Oh, please ignore it."

If Pickett's men had retreated as fast as my erection, they might have lived to die another day.

"Oh, no," she groaned.

Behind my eyelids, a film began to play: a woman lying on a couch under a ragged quilt of the type my mother used to sew, her head resting on a regular pillow rather than one upholstered in the same fabric as the cushions. Her mouth was open, her teeth perfectly white. Her hair was auburn and a little bit frizzy. Where the quilt fell away from her body, her right breast lolled to one side, the nipple big and brownish. As I stared, she opened her eyes. For the longest time she did nothing, just watched me watching her, and then, with no haste at all, she reached out and pulled up the corner of the quilt. From the distance of more than forty years, I heard her say, *Luke . . . What's the matter, honey? Having trouble sleeping?*

"There," Jennifer whispered. "Oh, there."

"ACTUALLY, my degree's not in French," Maggie Sorrentino told me, "but in international relations."

People say asinine things when they're feeling like asses, and I felt like one that day. I don't think it was caused by what happened when the alarm went off—that, after all, had ended on a high note—but by my reaction to Maggie's presence. Everything about her suggested that she was beyond the means of people like me. "You studied French to become more international?"

Her voice, when she answered, was unnaturally quiet, as if she were working hard to restrain it. If she hadn't been smiling, I would've thought my stupid question had angered her. "I guess I initially studied French because the man I wanted to marry was studying French. Of course he studied international relations, too, which is how we met."

We were sitting together at a table in the school cafeteria, off to one side by ourselves. Apparently, everybody else had also noticed her car the day before. Park a piece of equipment like that in the faculty lot of a public high school, especially in a place as poor as Loring, and it's going to create a certain amount of distance between you and your colleagues, as will the kind of jewelry she wore. The one piece missing was a wedding ring. Yet when he introduced her, Ramsey had called her *Mrs.* Maggie Sorrentino.

"Your husband," I said, "did he move back here with you?"

"My husband's dead."

"I'm so sorry."

"Oh, believe me, I am, too."

"When did that happen?"

"Almost eighteen months ago. He had cancer of the esophagus, though he never smoked and barely drank. People tell me it's unusual to develop that unless you're a heavy smoker and drinker. But then it's unusual, too, at the age of fifty, which is how old he was when he found out about it."

"What did he do for a living?"

"The last few years of his life, he taught public policy at Duke. Prior to that, he worked for CNN."

"You lived in Atlanta?"

"Close by. And then, as I said, we moved back to North Carolina."

"Do you have any children?"

She'd brought her lunch in a brown paper sack. So far I'd seen her consume a granola bar and three or four celery sticks, her mouth barely moving while she chewed, and the whole time she kept looking right at me. Now she withdrew a small carton of Dannon yogurt and said, "Maybe you could ask me something else."

I'd thought about her and Eugene and their parents a lot over the past day. Ellis had provided the crucial bit of information that caused my synapses to fire: namely, that her mother had been killed the night riots erupted at Ole Miss after the courts ordered the enrollment of a black student named James Meredith and folks poured in from all over the South to defend segregation, eventually forcing JFK to send in a huge number of troops. Ellis also told me that Arlan Calloway, though arrested for murder, was never indicted. When I asked how that could be, he said, "Supposedly, he shot his wife in self-defense." He took Maggie and Eugene away, and his parents, who'd lived there most of their lives, left as well.

Finding her response to my question about children plenty strange, I decided that maybe she herself would prove rather odd. But I went ahead and asked, "So where did you and Eugene and your dad go when you moved away from Loring?"

She spooned some yogurt into her mouth and acted as if she needed to ponder this before replying. Something I'd learn about Maggie—and something I'd come to like—was that it violated her nature to answer any question quickly. "First," she finally said, "we went west. All the way to Needles, California. My dad bought a gas station that went broke. Have you ever heard of anybody who couldn't sell gas in Needles? Half the people who come there are running out of it, and the other half are scared they're going to. But there were a lot of established stations, and in all fairness to my father, the last guy to own ours had gone broke, too. That's why he agreed to sell.

"After that happened, we picked up and headed back across the country to Virginia. That's where my grandparents had moved, and where my grandmother was originally from. My father got a job at the Radford Arsenal, helping produce propellants for submarines. He died there, in fact, during my first year of college. One day a bunker exploded. They never figured out exactly what happened, nor did they ever find a trace of either of the men who'd been inside, one of whom was Dad."

"Jesus."

"I imagine you'd like to know about my brother?"

By now I was scared to ask. Her dad had shot her mom, then been blown to smithereens, and her husband had died of cancer. And there was still the question of children, which she'd told me not to pose.

"Nothing bad happened to Gene," she said. "Just lots of

good things. He's a successful real-estate agent in Fort Worth, and he and his wife have four daughters between the ages of fifteen and twenty-five. Those girls—well, they're all gems." I figured maybe she'd pull some pictures from her purse, but she didn't. Instead, she ate another spoonful of yogurt and, while continuing to look at me, tipped her chin up ever so slightly. "You're probably wondering," she said, "why I'd come back to this particular place. Given what occurred here, I mean."

You have to understand that Loring, Mississippi, isn't the kind of town people come back to, for any reason whatsoever. It is, in fact, the kind they leave. Very few of those I grew up with are still here, and most of them own large chunks of land that have belonged to their families forever. New arrivals are almost always drawn by the promise of low-wage jobs, either in the catfish industry or at the Wal-Mart Supercenter or the big Dollar General distributorship that opened a while back. Around here, true wealth comes coated with glue, and it's always stuck to the same sets of hands. "I guess I am curious about that," I said. "Though I don't know how I'd react if something similar happened in my family, because it didn't."

"Well, I'll tell you. A couple of months ago, I sat up in bed one morning and noticed how perfectly gorgeous the day was. I'm not trying to brag, but I own a nice house in the countryside between Durham and Chapel Hill, and I lavished a lot of care, during the last few years, on my garden. My bedroom there has a big window, and I looked out at the sunlight flooding my roses and heard the water trickling from the fountain my husband had built for me and it was all just perfect, except for one thing: I suddenly felt that if I spent one more moment in that house, surrounded by all that beauty, I'd go completely mad. I checked into the Carolina Inn that afternoon, stayed there for two nights while I arranged to have the place looked after, then I packed a couple of bags and started driving.

"I went to Radford and visited the cemetery where my

grandparents are buried, then drove aimlessly across the country, intending to end up in Needles, where I'd turn around and come back. I kept stopping in small towns, and some of them made a big impression on me. Especially one in Kansas. I ate a sandwich in this general store where they sold all kinds of things related to farming, including seed. I listened to what people were saying, but none of it made any sense, and I finally figured out why. It was because they all knew so much about one another that they'd lapsed into a kind of shorthand. It might as well have been a foreign language. And I realized that nobody on the face of the earth knew me well enough to do that.

"I finally did go to Needles, where our gas station had been turned into an espresso stand, a faux Starbucks that was doing booming business—probably because there wasn't a real Starbucks nearby. And it just fascinated me that my dad's undoing could be the source of someone else's success.

"When I started back east, I knew I had to see Loring. So I got here a couple of weeks ago and checked into that motel across from McDonald's. I guess I expected to stay just a couple of days before going back to North Carolina. I wanted to see the house I used to live in, and to see if I could find out where my mother's buried. The first morning I went out and bought the *Weekly Times* and spotted an ad for someone who could speak French well enough to teach it. The ad sounded sort of desperate, so I found myself thinking, Why not? I went in and applied for the job, and when Ramsey gave it to me I rented a house."

In the face of such honesty, I experienced a range of emotions. And as odd as it may sound, given that personal tragedy had provoked her actions, envy was one of them. I couldn't imagine being able to leave home like that and go wherever whimsy led me. This seemed to me the kind of thing only a young person would do, though I hadn't done anything of the sort when I was young. So for the second time that day, I made a grossly inappropriate comment. "Well," I said, "if you were trying to escape beauty, you've come to the right place."

That afternoon, retrieving a book from my car that I'd promised to loan one of my honor students, I ran into Ellis Buchanan, who'd parked in the space next to mine and was carrying a beaten-up hardcover of *All the President's Men*. He brought the same book with him at the beginning of each school year, for the first of his regular Tuesday-afternoon lectures to the journalism class.

"Going to make a few points about the freedom of the press?"

"No." He shut his door. "Making the point that the press has never been less free than it is right now."

"I admire your sentiments, but for your own personal edification, you might want to refresh yourself on the Alien and Sedition Acts."

"I'm beyond edification," he said before going inside. "When you're as old as I am, you will be, too."

A FAIR AMOUNT OF WHAT I KNOW about my father I learned
from my maternal grandfather when I was a boy. He'd known
Dad all his life, by virtue of having sublet land from my other
grandfather, who died long before I was born.

According to Grandpa, for many years, on the first of March,
Dad had to wait outside the office of Herman Horton, the president of the Bank of Loring, for the purpose of securing that
year's "furnish"—the money he and others like him needed to
borrow each spring in order to plant their crops. The queue that
formed there was known as the begging line, and according to
my grandfather as the end of February drew near my father's
mood always soured. Nobody could stand to be around him, so
great was his fear of being turned down. When he finally made it
inside, he was never offered a cigar, as Arlan Calloway and a few
select others were, and Mr. Horton didn't inquire about his family. The sole recognition of his individuality came when Horton
intoned, as he did every year, "March again. And here comes
May."

"Yes sir. Here I am."

"How much do you mean to hit me up for this year? And
before you answer, remember that I hate it when a man over-
reaches."

At that point, even though Dad had already whittled the figure down to the bare minimum he thought he could survive on, he'd knock off another two or three hundred dollars. After he handed over a list of proposed expenditures, Horton would study it for a few minutes, then shake his head and say, "Looks to me like you plan on buying too much fertilizer. You know what the best fertilizer is, May? Piss in the field before sunrise and piss in it again after sunset. Plain old hard work."

Dad always got the furnish, but before he left the banker invariably observed that people who didn't own any acreage and had to rent sixteenth-section land ought to give up farming and find a job pumping gas and fixing flats. One year, Grandpa said, my father somehow found the courage to respond. "Mr. Horton," he said, "I like farming." And old Herman, who frequently performed at the Loring Little Theater, replied, "I like acting. But they tell me Spencer Tracy does it better."

To go back even further, I know that my dad's own father was a hard man who hewed to the notion that people never got tired, unless they had a weak character. Grandpa said he worked all his children like mules, with a predictable result: each of them got out from under his roof just as fast as possible. In the case of my father, World War II provided the escape hatch, and his height served as a passport. One morning in the summer of 1944, a few months shy of his eighteenth birthday, he simply disappeared. "The military wasn't looking too hard right then at things like birth certificates," Grandpa told me. "Uncle Sam was running short of men. So your daddy talked his way into the United States Navy."

Though he saw both Hiroshima and Nagasaki a few months after they were nuked, Dad never told me much about them, just mumbled that they were both a mess and changed the subject. I was already in my thirties when I finally asked, and told myself he probably figured that since I hadn't been interested enough in his wartime experiences to question him back when I was a student and otherwise eager to interview every veteran I could find, the time for that talk was long past.

One bit of information he did volunteer, however, was that in December 1944, at the Great Lakes Naval Training Station, on a night when the temperature dropped below zero and a fifty-mile-an-hour wind came howling in off Lake Michigan, he was ordered to walk guard duty in front of an empty barracks. As impossible as it might sound, the watch officer found him standing asleep in a doorway around 3:00 a.m., stiff and stunned. His punishment, enacted the following night, was to spend the entire evening shoveling snow in similar weather. The next day he started feeling hot, and by dinnertime was running a fever that soon soared to one hundred four. He ended up in the infirmary with a bad case of pneumonia, the scariest moment of his life occurring when he woke up to find two navy doctors hovering over him. "Good Lord," he heard one of them say, "looks like we're going to lose this poor boy from down south."

That remark, I think, provided the caption for the remainder of his life: a poor boy from down south.

His house, a little bungalow with Sheetrock siding, was near the elementary school. He and my mother moved there a couple years after I left for Ole Miss. When he realized I'd never come home to help, he gave up farming altogether—a fortunate decision. Most small farmers in the Delta had already gone under by that time, and virtually all the rest would before long. He took a job maintaining county school buses, though by now he'd been retired for more than fifteen years.

The place wasn't much to look at, but one thing that used to catch the eye of passing motorists was his tomatoes. Every February he planted his seed in the mulch bed at the side of the house, and once the threat of frost had passed he transplanted them in the front yard, where they grew big, red and juicy. Quite a few folks knocked on his door wanting to buy a sackful, but he always just gave them away. This year, for the first time, he hadn't planted any, and as far as I knew nobody except Jennifer and me ever came to the door anymore.

We parked in his driveway that night, and I grabbed the picnic basket from the trunk. She'd baked a hen, then painstakingly pulled all the meat off the bones and cut up the bigger pieces, making them easier to feed to my mother and easier for Dad to chew and swallow. He'd lost a lot of his teeth and was having trouble with most of the ones that remained.

We found them in the den, where they almost always were, no matter what time of the day or night we came over, the TV tuned to the Weather Channel with the volume turned all the way down, Dad on the couch with his bare, swollen feet propped up on the coffee table, my mother at his elbow in her wheelchair, a padded restraining device called a Lap Buddy holding her in place. A few months before, after my father fell asleep from exhaustion, she'd gotten out of the chair and taken a couple of steps before falling and breaking her hip. That led to three months in Loring Rehab, and for a while it looked as if she'd never leave. Now she was back home, staring at the floor with a puzzled expression on her face.

"Look who's here, Momma," Dad said. Her head didn't move, so he reached over and cupped her chin and raised it, forcing her to look at us. "She knows who y'all are," he assured us, as he did every time we showed up. "She just can't say it."

I believed I saw something in her eyes, but it wasn't recognition. It seemed to me more like embarrassment. We spend most of our lives writing our own personal histories, and my mother's stood out from those of the people she'd grown up with. To the best of my knowledge, the word *nigger* had never slipped from her lips, and I was fairly certain she'd voted for Jimmy Carter and Bill Clinton. Unlike my friends' mothers, who instilled in them the belief that honesty was the highest of virtues, she taught me, at an early age, that it was sometimes all right, even necessary, to lie as she did, in the context of explaining why, after a shopping trip to Memphis, we weren't going to tell my father that we'd spent the afternoon outside the gate at Graceland, hoping for a glimpse of Elvis. She loved rock and roll, even in the late '60s and early '70s, when it was associated with drugs and antiwar protests, and she'd listen to it on the radio whenever my dad left the house. In this meat-eating culture, she lived off vegetables, and nothing made her madder than Dad's attempts to make her eat something she didn't want. At breakfast he often stabbed a slice of bacon and laid it on her plate, and she'd pick it up with thumb and forefinger and fling it on his.

Now she chewed whatever he managed to put in her mouth, and hearing any kind of music at all made her moan, unless it was the sound of her own voice humming something Dad claimed to recognize as an old folk song. She couldn't recall how to walk and would eventually forget how to swallow and, if she didn't die of pneumonia, would finally starve to death.

Of course, I could've been just as wrong in my assessment as I thought Dad was in his. There might in fact have been nothing at all in her expression, and that possibility was what made it so hard for me to see my mother. She looked just like any number of other old people who'd lost themselves completely.

"I smell something good," he said. "What'd you bring us, Jenny?"

Jennifer hates being called Jenny and has never let anybody else do it. "I baked you a chicken, and there's some green beans and mashed potatoes and some corn bread, too, though it may be a little too sweet."

"I doubt that. I could use a little sweetness along about now, and I believe Momma can, too." When he let go of her chin to push himself up off the couch, her head dropped again and she began humming and kept it up as I wheeled her into the kitchen.

People in the Delta, whether black or white, educated or igno-rant, almost always pronounce *ruined* as *rurnt*. I'm no linguist, so I don't know if this results from our well-known reluctance to employ two syllables when one will suffice or simply the desire to find a harder sound that more accurately reflects the verb's meaning. Regardless, that's how we say it, and my mother said it that night.

In the kitchen, having rolled the wheelchair up close to the table, I watched Jennifer tie a bib around her neck and dish out some food. She passed the plate to Dad, and he scooped up a lump of mashed potatoes and raised the spoon slowly towards my mother's mouth. "Open up now," he said. "Come on."

She looked at Jennifer, who'd sat down directly across the table from her, and the trace of a smile crossed her face. Then she laughed and said something unintelligible, and while her mouth was still open Dad stuck the spoon in there, leaving the white lump on her tongue. For a second, before her jaws began to work, I thought she'd spit it out, and again I recalled my des-perate hope, when the girls were babies, that their applesauce or green peas wouldn't end up oozing out before they swallowed.

While my wife watched my father feed my mother and offered encouragement, I took the top off the garbage can in the corner, lifted the bag up and pulled the drawstring tight, then carried it out to the street and put it in the container for pickup. I stayed out there as long as I could, bending over and pretend-ing to police the driveway, in case the neighbors looked out the window and wondered what I was up to. I finally went back inside, grabbed another garbage bag from the utility room, and walked into the kitchen.

Gobs of mashed potatoes lay all over the floor, alongside a spoon and shards of glass. If a person with Alzheimer's sees an object or a hand coming towards his or her face, what's left of the reflexes will sometimes take over, and for that reason my father always tried to sit beside my mother and feed her from an oblique angle. This was easier if something in front of her could hold her attention, which was why Jennifer sat directly in her line of vision.

Today, apparently, it hadn't worked. Dad was standing at the sink soaking a towel to wipe his pants off, and Jennifer was scrounging through the cabinets looking for a dustpan.

My mother looked at me and smiled shyly, as certain female students will when they haven't read their assignments and don't have a clue what's going on but are pretty sure it won't be held against them. "Rurnt," she said. "All rurnt."

Did my father hear her? The water was running in the sink, so it's possible he didn't, though he was closer to her than I was and his hearing had always been acute. He turned the tap off and vigorously rubbed his pants leg while I lined the garbage can and squatted down with the dustpan so Jennifer could sweep up the mess.

Dad made another attempt—more successful than the last—to feed my mother, so I mopped the floor, wrung out the mop and put it back in the utility room, then returned to the kitchen. It looked as if Momma had eaten all she was going to, so Jennifer glanced at her watch, said she needed to get ready for tomorrow's classes and stood up to leave.

While Dad was rising out of his chair, probably hoping for a peck on the cheek, I mentioned that Nadine Calloway's daughter had just returned to Loring from North Carolina and asked if he recalled what had happened to her mother. And it was as if an unseen hand had settled onto his head, pushing him right back down.

Driftwood

SHE WAS NEVER MRS. CALLOWAY TO ME. Just Nadine. Several inches taller than her husband, she had auburn hair and in my recollections is often wearing jeans, though I'll admit you almost never saw those on women in the Delta back then and she's got on a dress in all three of the pictures I would eventually be shown of her. Nevertheless, as we proceed beyond my comfort zone—into something that might be more, or maybe less, than strict history—she sports a pair of stiff blue Wranglers, the kind you wouldn't be caught dead in today until you washed them several times, and a long-sleeved white blouse in the cowgirl style, with fake pearl buttons down the front and on the cuffs. Boots would go with this outfit, but instead she wears red Keds.

The sneakers are the only element that makes sense. In 1949, as a senior, she led the girls' team from Hard Cash High to the Mississippi state basketball championship. By the time she enters the life of my family, the town of Hard Cash no longer exists, having voted itself into oblivion to avoid taxation. In other words, a certain part of her past had already been wiped out before I knew her.

She's not the type of person you expect to forget. This is partly due to her imposing height—taller than any other woman in town, she's sometimes referred to as the "Jolly Green

Giant"—but also to her tendency to hug every man, woman and child, not to mention her ability to shake her head and say "shit" without making you think she's just done something awful. There aren't a lot of people around here who can get away with that kind of talk, and most of those who can are men like Mr. Sturdivant and the crowd that assembles in his barbershop.

The first time I become aware of her, she's standing on the front porch of a country store where my mother often stops to buy me an Orange Crush. She's hugging a girl with one arm and a boy with the other. I've never seen any of them before, and the kids capture my attention to a degree that Nadine can't, not in this initial encounter. The girl's older than the boy and a little taller. His hair's the same color as his mother's, but hers is "cold black," as I would have phrased it then. Superman's hair is cold black, Batman's too.

The boy and I start sizing each other up, as boys always will, each looking to gain an advantage over the other. If his mother let go of him, maybe I could lure him over to the edge of the porch and trip him off it. I did that one day to my cousin, who was visiting from Jackson, and he fell right into a mudhole, got it all over himself and was headed for a whipping from my aunt until he pointed a finger and hollered, "He twip me! He twip me!" So I got the whipping, from Momma, but the pain and embarrassment were hardly commensurate with my pleasure in seeing my citified cousin covered head to toe in country mud.

The problem with trying to trip Eugene, however, is that his mother won't let him go, and even if she does, his sister will keep an eye on him and on me as well. I can tell she's a tattler.

"Arlan's going to take over from Buck," Nadine is telling Momma, who's sitting in a rocking chair underneath a big ther-mometer shaped like a bottle of Barq's root beer. That's where she always sits while waiting for me to finish my drink so we won't have to pay a deposit on the bottle. Lots of women sit there, though men never do. "Buck's heart's been acting up, and the doctor's told him that if he keeps getting out on that tractor in the hot sun, he's going to keel over and die. So this just seems like the time for Arlan to come home. He's been wanting to go back to farming. He thinks the world of James and is glad to be your neighbor again. As for me, I've heard a lot about Loring. Of course we used to play y'all in basketball."

"Used to beat us, too," Momma says. "But then it seems like us Loring girls have always been puny."

"Who's this young man here?" Nadine asks, nodding at me. "He wouldn't be y'all's son, would he?"

"I'm afraid so. He's got a little meanness in him, like his daddy, but I expect most of it'll be drained off in another thirty or forty years. That's generally how long it takes with men in the May family."

Before I know it, the tall woman is hugging me, too, pulling my face into her stomach, my nose grazing one of those imitation pearl buttons. I can neither see nor free myself, not with that Orange Crush in my hand, but I know she had to let go of her own kids to grab me and I'd bet they've both moved some distance away.

"Hello, Mr. May," she says. "My name's Nadine. And these two ruffians with me are Maggie and Eugene." Then she lets go and is squatting down in front of me, eye to eye on my level. "You like basketball?" she says.

I barely know what a basketball is. But Grandpa's been teaching me to punt a football, though he's no good himself and half the time he misses it completely. "No ma'am," I say. "Like football, though."

"Well, I'm not supposed to play that because I'm a girl. But I'll tell you a little secret, if you'll keep it between you and me."

It won't be a secret, and we both know it. My mother's still sitting there. The boy's over at the corner of the porch trying to prime the pitcher pump, and the girl has backed off a few feet and is watching her mother and me. "Yes ma'am," I say. My face is hot, but I don't know why. I never will, at least not for a long time.

"I've got two brothers I used to play football with," she says. "And you know what? I beat the tarnation out of them. They couldn't catch me, and even if they did they never could bring me down. So just remember that if you ever need somebody to play football with."

I tell her I will, but by then I'd say anything to make her stand up and let me alone. Rising to her full height, she reaches out and musses my hair, at the same time telling Momma that she needs to go inside and buy some cheese and crackers and baloney and Dr Peppers for her husband and his dad, who are crawling around in the dirt at their headquarters setting the plows on a cultivator. Then Momma says she needs to go in and return my bottle, which she pulls from my hand even though there's still a little drink left in it.

As soon as they disappear into the store, I take off towards the steps, intending to bound down them and jump in the car and hide my hot face. But something happens and suddenly I'm flying through the air, starting to tumble, my ultimate destination the same mudhole my cousin ended up in.

Nobody saw her trip me, but I don't say a word, just lie there breathless on my back looking up at the porch where the girl with the cold black hair stands watching.

More than forty-five years later, she was eyeing my phone, which lay on the table next to the paper sack that held the remains of my lunch. "You've got a message," she said.

It's one of those black Nokia fliptops with a red light that pulses when somebody's left you a voice-mail or sent a text. I opened it to find a missed call from Trish and a message, too. I keep the phone on silent when I'm at school, and the girls know they're not supposed to call unless there's an emergency, though for Trish that term's broadly defined. I figured it was nothing, but you never know. "Excuse me," I said, and put the phone to my ear.

Whereas Candace rarely gets excited, her sister's seldom calm. She spits words out as if they tasted bad, then strings clauses together, one after another, until you can't even remember how the sentence started. And she was in classic form for this message.

The "emergency" was her discovery that today was the last day students could buy football tickets at reduced prices, so she needed me to transfer two hundred forty dollars to the bank account she shared with Candace. That wasn't in the budget Jennifer and I had agreed on for the month, though I'd figured the subject would come up sooner or later. It had taken until now only because Ole Miss kicked off the season on the road the previous weekend and hadn't played a home game yet. Also, this was a Wednesday, when Jennifer had a night class and wouldn't get home before ten. She'd kept that schedule for years, so it was probably no accident that Trish had waited until now to call. I'd have to decide without talking to their mother, unless I could reach her by phone, which wasn't likely.

"I need to call my daughter," I told Maggie.

"Do you want me to leave?"

"No, you can hear it."

So I phoned her, but even before I could say hello she blurted, "Daddy, I'm sorry to bother you, because I know you're at school and I'm not supposed to call unless it's something serious, which in this case it is, since if we don't get our tickets today—"

"I'll transfer the money when I get home."

"Couldn't you do it sooner?"

"Nope, sure can't. We're not supposed to use these computers for personal business." I knew that before agreeing to this she'd make it sound as if I'd just told her we couldn't pay her tuition and she'd have to come home and work at Wal-Mart, so I said "Bye now" and pressed END CALL.

Maggie opened the plastic container she'd brought her fruit in and laid a banana peel, an apple core and a yogurt-streaked spoon inside it, then clamped the top back on. "Children are expensive, so I hear."

"Yesterday you told me not to ask if you had kids."

"Because I didn't want you to."

She wasn't smiling, but she wasn't frowning either, so I forged ahead. "But why's that subject off-limits?"

"In other words, you're ignoring my request?"

"I guess so. You can tell me to buzz off, though, and I will."

She laughed. "*Buzz off*—now there's an expression I haven't heard lately."

"Well, I teach history," I said, "so I guess it's normal that some of my terminology might sound anachronistic."

"You're using terminology on me?" Somehow she managed to create the impression that her eyes had grown a lot larger, and they were plenty big to begin with. "Why, I don't know what to think."

I figured she'd probably registered my stupid remarks the day before and decided it might be fun to coax me into making a few more. I was trying to come up with a suitable reply when Ramsey Coleman sat down at our table and opened his lunch box.

The lunch box is actually an old mailbox that he attached a handle to. He loves putting discarded items to odd use. He once made a flowerbed out of a junked refrigerator, and he feeds his dog from a "bowl" that was originally a Loring Leopards batting helmet. Thus his nickname, Mr. Salvage, which sometimes gets changed to Mr. Savage when he loses his temper.

"Mrs. Sorrentino," he said, "how are you this fine day?"

"I'm all right. And you?"

"Couldn't be better. Could *not* be better." He pulled out a sandwich wrapped in wax paper and grinned at me. "What about you, Luke? Since those girls of yours took off for Ole Miss, you been whistling 'Dixie' or singing the blues?"

The exchange with Maggie had left my face feeling flushed. "Mostly," I said, "I've been writing checks."

"The check-writing blues? I believe that's somewhere between mean and lowdown. Lasts a long time, too."

"You're not doing much to lift my spirits."

He slapped me on the back. "I'm not your preacher. I'm your old pal, Buddy Black Man." To Ramsey, nothing is funnier, or more serious, than race, and he put his sandwich down to chuckle at his own joke.

After that, the three of us sat there together for a few more minutes, Ramsey asking Maggie how her classes were coming along and, at one point, trying out the French he'd learned at Jackson State. Then I told them I had to get ready for Local History class, and Maggie glanced at her watch and said she'd better be going, too.

Leaving the lunchroom, I must have resembled those guys you see in the 20 K walk at the Olympics: stiff legged, moving as fast as I could, feeling the effort in my shins. I'd just put my hand on one of the swinging doors when Maggie said, "Luke, could you wait just a minute?"

I stepped into the hall and held the door open until she came through, then let it swing shut.

"I was wondering," she said, "if you know anything about cars?"

"A little. Why?"

"This morning, driving to work, I saw a dashboard light come on but don't have any idea what it means."

"What it means," I said, "is a trip to Greenville."

"I'm sorry?"

"Nobody in Loring can fix a car like that. Whatever's wrong with it, you'll have to take it over there to get it worked on.

There's a shop on Eighty-two that can handle German imports. The closest dealer's down in Jackson."

"But could you at least take a look after school and see if you can tell me what the problem is, so I'll know what to say when I call?"

The bell rang and the lunchroom doors popped open, smacking into a wall already pockmarked by repeated impact. Kids began pouring out while she stood there looking at me as if the only thing that mattered in the world right then was my answer.

"Sure," I said, "I'd be happy to have a look."

In Local History that afternoon I reminded my students that the purpose of the class was twofold. "We want to examine the major events that occurred here in the Delta and around the state, looking at how they influenced our lives and then placing them in the context of events that unfolded nationally and internationally at the same time. Anybody here ever heard of James Meredith?"

In a regular class, most kids wouldn't be able to name our current governor. But these were honors students, and a number of hands shot up.

"Rosella?"

"He's the man that integrated Ole Miss."

"When?" *Who*, *what* and *where* are easier than *when*. In the age of the Internet, everything is now.

"The Fifties?"

"Close—1962. And how did it occur? Did he just stroll into the Lyceum and register?"

"No sir. There was a huge riot and some people got killed."

"Right again. A *humongous* riot. The president of the United States—John F. Kennedy—had to mobilize almost thirty thousand troops in order to safely enroll a single African American student at the state's leading university.

"Now, this event got attention all over the world—it was front-page news in all the major European papers as well as those in Asia and Latin America. Remember, in the Cold War, the Soviet Union and the United States constantly tried to convince everybody else that their way of life was superior, so this race war was a huge propaganda coup for the other side. What happened at Ole Miss might even have played a role in the Soviets' decision to challenge us a few weeks later during the Cuban Missile Crisis. At the same time, the Meredith event directly affected people right here in Loring. Do any of you know a gentleman named Charles McGlothlan?"

They *all* knew Charlie, who was the man your momma went to if your older brother ended up in jail for dealing drugs and needed somebody to negotiate a plea bargain. One or two of them might even have known that back in 1967, not long after opening his practice, he led a famous boycott that got national attention when a crop duster dipped down over Front Street and sprayed pesticide over the protesters.

"In 1959," I said, "three years before James Meredith and the U.S. Army integrated Ole Miss, Mr. McGlothlan graduated from high school with straight A's and applied there himself. Of course, back then Loring had a white school and a black one, and once Ole Miss got his transcript they could tell which one he'd gone to and immediately sent him a letter saying he was unqualified. His only options were the traditionally all-black schools like Alcorn and Valley State, so he enrolled at Alcorn. But when it came time for law school, as a result of what Meredith had done, Mr. McGlothlan *was* able to attend Ole Miss, where he became the second African American law graduate. He came back home, opened his practice and started up a community-assistance program that worked to reduce poverty and also helped people register to vote."

I often used Charlie as an example in my classes, knowing full well that the parents and grandparents of many of the white kids had given them a completely different version of the McGlothlan story—nothing more than an opportunistic troublemaker who'd exploited racial discord to make money. And as for Meredith, if they'd told them anything at all, it was probably that after championing integration and stirring up all manner of mischief, he'd changed his tune, turned into an archconservative, gone to work for Jesse Helms and become a supporter of the Klan leader David Duke. I could tell from their faces that some of them didn't like hearing any of this. But teaching history often involves making people learn something they'd rather not know.

The previous night, when I'd asked my father about Nadine Calloway, I knew immediately that he'd hoped never to hear her name again. What I didn't know was why. Since like a lot of local people he wouldn't discuss the Citizens' Council, and since her husband had been in it with him, maybe it was nothing more than that. But I didn't think so. He brushed aside my question by mumbling something about how unusual Nadine was, then changed the subject. In other words, he behaved exactly as he had when I finally got around to asking him about Hiroshima and Nagasaki.

While Maggie watched, I slid behind the wheel of her Mercedes. The first thing that grabbed my attention wasn't the soft leather seats or the wood trim on the dash and doors but the concentrated scent of her perfume. For a moment I lost track of my surroundings, as though I were drunk.

I finally stuck the key in the ignition and turned it, and the next thing I knew Hank Williams was singing "My Bucket's Got a Hole in It."

I must have looked shocked, since she said, "What'd you figure me for—smooth jazz?"

"Yeah. Either that or classical."

"My father loved this music. I hadn't heard it for years until I saw that CD at a gas station in Texas." She gestured at the control panel. "You can turn it off."

I touched the button, and the music died.

She leaned close to me, pointing. "It's that light there. See, it says to check the engine? But the car's running just fine."

"A check-engine light usually means it's an emissions problem."

"Is that serious?"

I started to say that on a car like hers, everything was serious. But then it dawned on me that if you could buy the car in the first place, probably nothing was. "Have you gassed up recently?"

She nodded. "Yesterday afternoon."

"Where?"

"At Mr. Quik."

That station's strictly self-service, and Maggie wasn't the type. I switched off the ignition, then walked around to the passenger side, opened the gas flap and checked the cap, which was definitely a little loose, so I screwed it down tight. "Keep an eye on that light," I said. "There's a good chance it'll go off in a day or two. But if it doesn't, you'll need to go to Greenville and have them look at it."

"Okay," she said. "Thanks a lot."

"No problem. Next time you pump your own gas, make sure you screw that cap down all the way. Otherwise, the computer will signal there's a problem that doesn't even exist."

"Right, and thanks again." She started to get in the car, then turned to look at me. "The question about children? Well, back when I was still young enough to have any, I didn't want to. I guess I was afraid I'd let them down. And by the time I realized I'd made a mistake, it was too late."

I waited to see if she'd say more. But instead she waved, got into her expensive car and pulled away.

THE LORING PUBLIC LIBRARY has a number of quirks, chief among them its willingness, even now, to accommodate the requests of prominent citizens. When I was growing up, one such person was Clinton Finley, who owned the Chevrolet dealership and served as mayor from 1953 until 1975, when he died of a heart attack.

At some point in either 1973 or '74, he walked into the library and asked to speak to the head librarian. Nobody's sure what he said, exactly, but the following morning he and his daughter drove over in a pickup and removed all the issues of the *Weekly Times* from the civil rights era. Nobody knows what became of them. And by and large nobody cares, because anybody interested in what the paper published during those years can go over to Ellis's house.

His living room has a picture window, and I could see him through it. He was sitting on the couch, nicely dressed as always, in a pair of charcoal-gray slacks and a short-sleeved knit shirt, deeply engrossed in a book. The air conditioner was droning away on a concrete slab near the corner of the house, so I couldn't tell if he was listening to music or not, but I'd have to bet he was.

As it happened, I was right, since when he answered the doorbell I could hear the sound of a string quartet. "Mozart?" I asked.

"Not exactly, but you're close."

"Haydn?"

"There's hope for you yet."

He'd left the book open on the coffee table, next to a glass of white wine that stood on one of the ceramic coasters we'd given him a few Christmases ago. Noticing me eyeing the wine, he said, "My Lord, I've forgotten my manners entirely. Let me get you something to drink."

He disappeared into the kitchen, and I took a seat in the big leather easy chair at one end of the coffee table. I felt at home in his house and had for a long time. But whenever I sat down in his living room, I remembered how it affected me the first time I saw it. I was seventeen, and he'd invited me over for dinner, which he always did at least once for each of his interns. His walls are lined with bookshelves, and he told me later that when I walked in that night back in 1973, something happened to my face: my mouth didn't exactly fall open, but it nearly did. I'd never seen so many books in anybody's house. I didn't even know an individual could own that many.

And a lot of them were pretty amazing. First-edition hardcovers of Winston Churchill's entire six-volume set *The Second World War*, leather-bound editions of all Dickens's novels, the collected works of Robert Frost and a signed copy of John Kenneth Galbraith's *The Affluent Society*, into which had been tucked a note, handwritten on stationery from the Peabody Hotel: *Mr. Buchanan, I enjoyed our conversation. The South needs more people like you. As does the rest of the nation. JKG.*

"You know him?" I'd asked.

"I *met* him once," Ellis said. "That's not quite the same thing."

"Still." Handling the book gingerly, I put it back on the shelf. "You've got them alphabetized, I see."

"When you need something, you want to be able to lay your hands on it."

"How come you don't separate fiction and poetry from non-fiction?"

He smiled at my question, which he later told me he regarded as evidence of a naïve bent towards compartmentalization. "A good book," he said that evening, "is a good book. They like to be together."

He now returned from the kitchen carrying a glass of wine that he put in front of me, then sat down on the couch and gracefully crossed his legs. "That's a pretty good Pinot Gris," he said. "It's entirely too hot to drink red."

"I came to bother you," I told him.

"Impossible. Unless you plan to devour every last bottle of wine in the house. Then, much as I value your company, I'd have to acknowledge feeling put-upon."

I laughed. "Just the one glass. Actually, I got interested in what we were talking about the other night."

"Joseph Brodsky?"

"No, the Calloway killing."

"Oh," he said. "Well, I told you about all I remember."

"Yeah, but I'm sure you covered it."

"Of course I did. It was big news locally. Elnora Napier actually wrote the articles, though."

Mrs. Napier, who'd been dead for close to thirty years, wore a number of different hats, handling advertising for the paper and writing stories from time to time, and also hosting a radio show every Friday at noon, on which she read the names of everybody who'd been born, died or hospitalized in Loring during the past week. "Could I take a look at them?" I asked.

"Sure," he said. "You know where the key is. But turn the window unit on or you'll come back parboiled."

In the kitchen, I took the key off the peg near the back door, then went outside. Ellis's study is in a detached building that once served as his home office. He'd written most of his articles and editorials out there, and it's where he's kept his archive since selling the paper.

Inside, it must have been a hundred and ten degrees. But I knew I wouldn't be there long, so I didn't bother to turn the air on.

The leather-bound volumes were shelved along the west wall, six months' worth of papers in each one, the dates neatly labeled on the spine. I'd spent a lot of time going through them some years ago, looking most intently at Ellis's coverage of Freedom Summer and the boycotts Charlie McGlothlan led later on. But it was probably fair to say that at one point or another, I'd had my hands on each volume—if the police ever needed to dust them for fingerprints, they'd find more of mine than anybody else's, probably including Ellis himself.

I found the one for July–December 1962 and pulled it out, squatted beside the bookshelf and flipped through to the issue of October 4.

Anybody who's spent time examining old newspapers is apt to develop a healthy respect for hindsight. Events now considered earthshaking often weren't perceived as such in their immediate aftermath, whereas the most trivial happenings sometimes seemed riveting for those who lived through them. The lead article in the Loring *Weekly Times* on October 4, 1962, didn't concern the recent invasion of north Mississippi by the United States military, the enrollment of the first black student at Ole Miss or the death of a local woman at the hands of her husband. Instead, it recounted how two members of the volunteer fire department had rescued a cat named Tom Collins that was trapped high up in a cypress tree on the bank of Choctaw Creek. Ellis wrote the article himself and also took a picture of the cat, cradled in the arms of its tearful owner. There was no mention of the Oxford crisis anywhere on page one, just a grossly inaccurate wire-service report at the top of page three.

Ellis's lead editorial, moreover, called for the resurfacing of Loring Avenue, which was so full of potholes that three different motorists had suffered blowouts there in the last week alone.

Elnora Napier's article was also on page three, directly beneath the one about Ole Miss. Miss Napier had her scruples, reporting only what was known and avoiding speculation.

This past Monday, shortly before daybreak, officers from the Loring County Sheriff's Department were summoned to the home of Arlan and Nadine Calloway, RFD Route 2, approximately six miles northwest of town, in the vicinity of Fairway Crossroads. Sheriff Mack Caukins informed the *Weekly Times* that when law-enforcement personnel arrived, they discovered the body of Mrs. Calloway, 31, on the floor in the kitchen.

"She had marks on her face and torso," Sheriff Caukins said, "consistent with shotgun wounds."

He noted that Mrs. Calloway had no pulse by the time officers arrived, and that Arlan Calloway, 36, told them his wife had brandished a kitchen knife in his face and tried to attack him, and that he used his gun in self-defense.

On Tuesday morning, officers appeared once more at the Calloway home and Arlan Calloway was taken into custody. He is presently being held in the Loring County Jail. Sheriff Caukins announced that an investigation is ongoing.

There was nothing else on the incident in the October 4 issue, but I did discover that a can of Red Bird potted meat was going for eleven cents at Piggly Wiggly, whereas a pound of ground beef cost a quarter, that the Loring Leopards had lost to Leland 26–13 the previous Friday, for the fourteenth year in a row, and that Flannery's Truckstop had just installed showers that drivers could use for free each time they filled up. A long time ago I had learned to respect information, in and of itself.

You can't hope to make sense of what happened if you don't understand the environment in which it happened, and you can't do that if you're too busy to care what a roll of toilet paper cost.

By October 11 the Calloway story had moved onto the front page, where it appeared beneath an article by Ellis that detailed the malfeasance of an alderman who'd treated himself to an all-expenses-paid weekend in Memphis—this piece took up the top half of the page and ran over onto page two. Ellis had another on the bottom of the page, about the phone company's plan to replace its operators with a rotary dialing system over the next eighteen months. In the bottom corner, Miss Napier began by recapitulating the previous week's account and then explained that on the afternoon of October 5, three days after being taken into custody, Arlan Calloway had been released.

> Sheriff Caukins announced that law-enforcement officials have concluded that Arlan Calloway acted in self-defense, as he stated earlier, and that no further action on the part of his department is necessary. Attempts by this reporter to reach Mr. Calloway for a statement were unsuccessful.
>
> Mrs. Calloway was buried on October 6, near her childhood home in Sharkey County. In attendance were her brother, Wesley Bevil, 37, of Shreveport, Louisiana, and her aunt and uncle, Mr. and Mrs. Ernest Crawford of Rolling Fork. She leaves behind her husband and two children, Eugene, 6, and Margaret, 9.

That was it. I flipped through the rest of the issue—ground beef had gone up to twenty-seven cents and the Leopards had lost again—and then returned the volume to the shelf, locked the study and went back inside.

Ellis was still drinking wine and listening to music, though now the string quartet had given way to the "Moonlight

Sonata." My shirt was wet with sweat from the study, and the refrigerated air inside the house made me shiver. I sat down at the end of the coffee table. My glass was standing right where I'd left it, so I lifted it and took a swallow.

Ellis looked at me. "Find what you were searching for?"

"I found Miss Napier's articles."

"Yes, but not what you were searching for."

"A man shoots his wife with a shotgun he just happens to have handy sometime around four or five in the morning, and a few days later the sheriff turns him loose and announces it was self-defense? How'd he arrive at that conclusion?"

"You'd have to ask him. But of course you can't, since he died the following year."

"But word must've leaked out at the time, since it always does."

"There *were* rumors."

I waited.

"Somebody told Elnora they had a witness."

"To the shooting?"

He nodded at me over his wire rims.

"Who was it?"

"Well, as you know, the Calloways did have two kids."

That wet shirt began to feel like an ice jacket. I tried to imagine what it would feel like to watch your father aim a gun at your mother and pull the trigger, but a moment or two wasn't long enough. A year or two wouldn't have been long enough. "You're saying one of them saw it?"

"No, I'm saying that was the rumor making the rounds."

"Was it the boy or the girl?"

"Some said one, some said the other. Mack Caukins never said a word. When children were involved, he kept his mouth shut."

I knew Ellis about as well as I knew anybody outside my immediate family, and also I could trust him to keep his own mouth shut if I asked him the question that had lodged in my mind the previous evening. "Was my father ever questioned about Nadine's death?"

"Your *father?*"

"He and Arlan were good friends. But the other day I remembered that Mr. Calloway once entered a bid on our land, back when we were living on the sixteenth section."

"That used to happen all the time."

"Yeah, I know it did. But last night, when I mentioned Nadine Calloway to Dad, he looked like I'd just kicked him in the balls."

Ellis leaned over and picked up his wineglass, took a sip and seemed to roll it around in his mouth for a moment before swallowing. Then he set the glass back down. "If I had to guess," he said, "I'd say your father was just shocked to hear her name again. Maybe he'd thought he never would. Who knows? Or he might've forgotten she ever existed. Remember, he's as old as I am. And I can tell you from personal experience that when the vast majority of people who once meant something to you are gone, day-to-day existence gets a little surreal. Maybe hearing her name popped him out of one zone and dropped him into another one that seemed far more vivid than the one he inhabits now."

Then he changed the subject—something he's always been good at—and asked how I'd spend my Wednesday evenings from now on, since that used to be the night I cooked for the girls. I told him I'd probably get myself some carryout at China Buffet, eat an early dinner and read for a couple of hours, then go over to Jackson Park and walk off my meal. He laughed and said if I got bored, I could always come by his place for the kind of stimulating conversation we were having right now. And if I chose to bring a bottle along, he'd have no choice but to help me empty it.

When I finally got up to leave, I noticed his copy of the *Mem-*

phis Commercial Appeal on the ledge in front of the fireplace, and that made me think of Andy Owens, who used to deliver the paper and, when we were lucky, cut my hair and Eugene Calloway's. "You remember Andy Owens?" I said.

"Andy Owens?" He rose and laid his hand on my shoulder, and together we moved towards the door. "Seems like I recall the name but can't quite place him. Somebody who used to live around here?"

Friday afternoon, the first week of classes finally over, I went home thinking maybe I'd take Jennifer over to Greenville and splurge on a big steak dinner at Mann's Eatin' Place. We'd done that from time to time back when the girls were younger, getting one of my students to babysit, then stuffing ourselves with a slab of beef before strolling down the levee and having a drink at one of the casinos. What I remembered most about those evenings was how often we made each other laugh. One night I tripped on a cobblestone and rolled halfway down the levee, and when I got up, with my jeans in shreds and my knees and elbows bloody, we both laughed so hard that somebody called the Greenville police, believing we were incredibly drunk and perhaps insane.

For a while now I hadn't thought of myself as a guy who did things like that but as somebody who chained himself to the desk to review his lesson plans and then, to have a big time, sank into his armchair to read. Still, what happened between Jennifer and me the other morning proved there might be a few surprises left.

I walked through the kitchen and found her sitting in front of the computer, with her face bright red, her head in her hands, her cell phone in front of her on the desk. If this had been a painting, the artist might have called it *Up-to-Date and Out-of-Sorts.*

"What's the matter?" I reached for her, but she batted my palm aside.

"Two hundred and forty dollars," she said, "for a bunch of fucking football tickets?"

"Oh, I guess you checked the bank account."

"Yeah, I *checked* it. You know why? Because when I went to pay for the groceries at Piggly Wiggly, the transaction got denied."

"There should've been enough in there to cover that."

"You forgot to take off the car insurance. The automatic withdrawal went through this morning, so now we've got a grand total of twenty-two bucks in checking."

"Then I'll transfer some from savings." What I said next is something that in retrospect was really stupid and would've annoyed me just as much. "When you've had time to think about it," I told her, "you're going to realize this argument was about nothing."

She stood and propped her hands on her hips, slinging that blonde hair out of her eyes. "In the context of a marriage," she said, "that's just a chickenshit way of saying it's about everything."

And so it was. In the debate that followed, each of us adhered to advice James Carville reportedly gave Bill Clinton during the 1992 campaign: Stay on message.

Her main themes? Due to having grown up in relative poverty, I raised our daughters to think money fell from the sky, and because of that she'd be driving up to Delta State and its retarded administrators and freshmen until she turned seventy, just to pay off all the loans we'd taken out. To forestall my objection that I'd be working just as long, she reminded me that I liked my job whereas she loathed hers.

The gist of my position, on the other hand, was that whenever either Candace or Trish wanted something their mother considered frivolous or inessential, they always approached me first, so I was constantly being put in this miserable position.

Plagiarizing Lennon and McCartney, she countered that money couldn't buy me love.

Because I recognized the inarguable nature of that insight and felt the ropes and turnbuckle gouging my back, I said, "Even if it could, I'm not sure how much yours would be worth."

The pleasure I felt when she burst into tears and stalked out of our study lasted at least two or three seconds, before the wave of shame washed over me.

Instead of eating a steak at Mann's I was back in my room at the school that night and enjoying a Big Mac, fries and a diet soda. For a while, I listened to the Loring-Indianola game on the portable stereo I keep in there to play my students stuff like Martin Luther King Jr.'s "I have a dream" speech, but we soon fell so far behind that I lost interest and switched it off. After finishing my dinner, I turned on my laptop.

Every now and then, when I've gotten interested in something I don't know much about, I type in strings of words on Google to see what comes up. *Nadine + Arlan + Calloway + Loring + Mississippi + 1962* produced few results, none of which bore any relationship to the event I was interested in. When I typed in *Arlan + Calloway + Radford + Virginia*, though, I found a small article that had been published in the *New River Valley News* in 1996, under the heading "Twenty-Five Years Ago This Week":

A bunker exploded yesterday at the Radford Arsenal, authorities said, resulting in the deaths of two men. Sam Martin, public affairs officer at the facility, said that Arlan Baker Cal-

loway, 45, and Johnnie Lee Sturgis, 28, both of Radford, were
working in the facility when the explosion occurred. No
cause, as of now, has been identified, according to Martin.

That was all. Arlan Calloway had been reduced to his demise.
When I typed his name in along with *Needles + California*, nothing relevant appeared. I messed around a little bit longer, trying
unsuccessfully to find any reference to the Nadine Calloway I'd
known as a child. I couldn't find anything for a Wesley Bevil in
Shreveport, or anywhere else in the United States, either, and
nothing came up for Ernest Crawford in Rolling Fork. There
were a few references to Maggie Sorrentino, including a listing
on PeopleFinders with her address in North Carolina, her home
phone number and an offer to sell me a "one-time search report"
on her for $7.95, which would list her birthdate, previous
addresses and known relatives. I also found an article from the
Durham Herald-Sun that named her and all the other members of
the local library association.

For a couple of days, I'd been thinking off and on about Ellis's
inability to recall Andy Owens. He hadn't gotten his hair cut at
Sturdivant's—due to his politics, he wouldn't have been welcome in there—but since he was a newspaperman with a prodi-
gious memory, it seemed strange that the guy who delivered the
Memphis paper for so many years could've slipped from his
mind.

I myself had no idea when Andy left Loring, or where he
went: one day he just wasn't there anymore to cut my hair. So I
returned to PeopleFinders and typed in his name. Something
like one hundred twenty-five different listings came up, beginning with an Andrew A. Owens, who lived in Murray, Kentucky.
In most instances, an age appeared next to the entry, as well as
the names of people associated with that particular Andrew
Owens. My impression was that the Loring Andy had been
about thirty-five in 1962, which would make him almost eighty

if he was still alive. He'd probably been married—I seemed to recall his mentioning a wife during one of those sessions when the men were complaining about their spouses—but I wasn't even sure about that.

Only one Andrew Owens lived in Mississippi, down on the Gulf Coast in Pass Christian, but if he hadn't been blown away by Katrina, he'd only be twenty-six years old, too young, I figured, to be our Andy's son. Anyway, I checked the list of associated names and found an entry for Robert C. Owens, also of Pass Christian, age fifty-five, in all likelihood this particular Andrew's father. I played around a bit longer and came up with two Andrew Owenses of about the right age—one in Pine Bluff, Arkansas (no middle initial, seventy-seven), and another in Christiansburg, Virginia (Andrew N., eighty-two). Pine Bluff is just across the river, about forty miles south of Little Rock, and I'd been there a few times. I couldn't place Christiansburg, though, so I got on MapQuest and discovered it was in the western part of Virginia, just north of Interstate 81. Then, as I was about to click out of the map, I noticed the name of a nearby town: Radford.

I sat there for a moment staring at the map. The towns were no more than seven or eight miles apart.

I clicked the BACK button until the browser returned to the *New River Valley News* article about Arlan Calloway's death. Then I went to the newspaper's homepage and found a search box. *Andy Owens* produced no results, and neither did *Andrew Owens*.

At Ole Miss, I once took a class with a professor who said, "If the historian isn't careful, he or she can start to resemble the district attorney who, having to stand for reelection, becomes a little too willing to find connections where none exist." The fact that somebody named Andrew Owens had lived close to Arlan Calloway in two different places probably meant nothing at all, especially since both *Owens* and *Andrew* are among the most common Anglo-Saxon names.

. . . .

I turned off the laptop, went out, and got in my car to go home. But driving by my parents' place I saw Jennifer's Corolla parked in the drive beside my father's van. I'd turned my cell phone off to keep her from giving me any more grief about the football tickets, so I knew immediately that Dad must have phoned the house. I pulled in behind her and jumped out.

An awful odor permeated the hallway. I heard moaning and figured Momma must have freed herself from the wheelchair and fallen again. She had a pin in her right hip, and when my dad brought her home from the rehab center, against the advice of both her regular doctor and the surgeon who'd operated on her, they'd warned him that if she fell again and that pin broke, she was going to suffer indescribable pain.

She was in bed, rather than on the floor like I expected, and was completely naked, her mouth wide open, her hands clawing at my father's face while he leaned over the bed trying to hold her, whispering to her like she'd probably once whispered to me back when I was a baby. On the floor beside the bed stood a bucket, and over in the corner lay a bunch of shit-streaked sheets and bedclothes. There were big brown blotches on the mattress, and Dad's shirt was soiled, too.

I heard footsteps coming from the bathroom, and then Jennifer brushed by me. She walked over to the corner and picked up the smelly linen, and when she looked at my father bending over my mother, trying to give her the only kind of comfort available to a person who'd been betrayed by both body and mind, you didn't have to be clairvoyant to know what she was thinking. Where do you find love like that?

THE TWO HUNDRED and forty dollars turned into thirty pieces of silver, material evidence of my betrayal. But even as she stopped speaking to me unless it was absolutely necessary, she started going by my parents' house every morning before class and most afternoons, too, helping Dad to change the diaper Momma now had to wear and to give her a bath. They were eligible for Home Health, but he was frightened by the medical bureaucracy, as he termed it, and believed that if he let its representatives into his house, they'd try to force him to put her back in the rehab center. So for all practical purposes, Jennifer was their nurse, even though nothing was more precious to her than time.

I went there every day myself, usually after dinner, but was a lot less useful. Generally, what I did was wash dishes, carry out the garbage and pick up Dad's bills, which I paid online when I did my own each month, so he wouldn't have to write checks. Once or twice I sat with my mother long enough for him to take a shower. Every now and then she'd raise her head and look at me, and I'd fool myself into thinking she was about to experience a moment of lucidity, but as far as I could tell that never happened.

Dad never really went to bed anymore, just slept sitting in a recliner near Momma's bed, the various medications he took for high blood pressure and diabetes lined up on the floor beside the books piled there, mostly stuff he'd been rereading for sixty years—Ernie Pyle's *Brave Men* and Richard Tregaskis's *Guadalcanal Diary*—but a couple more recent titles as well, like Stephen Ambrose's book about Eisenhower.

One evening, I noticed a green spiral notebook at the bottom of the stack, a BIC ballpoint clipped to the cover. When I was twelve or thirteen, he'd caught me reading a journal of sorts that I'd found tucked away behind his tackle box in the smokehouse. After snatching it out of my hands, he cuffed the side of my head and swore that if I ever said a word about it, he'd whip my ass so hard I'd have to shit standing up. What I'd been reading was intriguing: *I get to thinking about that girl in Manila sometimes and wonder how it would of been if me and her could of said more than just a few words and I had not of made a fool of myself by pointing like I did.*

Recalling that, I didn't pick up the spiral notebook, but when he came back from the shower, still toweling his hair, I casually pointed at it and asked if he'd been doing a bit of writing.

He balled the towel up and dropped it into the clothes hamper, then leaned over and pulled out the notebook and glanced at it before laying it on the dresser. "Yeah," he said, "I been making a few notes."

"On what?"

"The kind of stuff you historians get wrong."

"I'm not a historian. I'm a history teacher."

He laughed. "That's like saying 'I don't speak English. I just teach it.'"

"Not exactly."

"Well, the difference, whatever it is," he said, "must be too fine for an old fool like me to grasp."

· · · ·

The CHECK ENGINE light on Maggie's Mercedes never went off, and when she mentioned that at lunch the following week, I told her she'd better call Import Auto in Greenville and make an appointment. Whoever she spoke to over there said she ought to have it towed, so after school I hung around with her in the parking lot until the tow truck hauled it away, and then I drove her over to the Greenville airport, the closest place to pick up a rental. While we waited for the clerk to complete the paperwork, she asked if I'd like to stop by her house for a drink.

I'd been planning to invite her to dinner, maybe with Ramsey and his wife and Ellis, but I figured I'd better wait until Jennifer calmed down. Her attitude had shown signs of softening in the last day or two, and the previous evening she'd walked into the living room with a student's paper and said, "Listen to this from one of my little Republicans. 'People that are down on Don Rumsfeld need to remember he was secretary of defense twice before, in the Reagan administration and also for President Bush's father, and this means he knows what he's doing.'" She stopped reading. "Is that right?"

"That Rumsfeld knows what he's doing?"

I wouldn't say she gave me a half smile, it was more like a third, but it was still a lot better than the habitual frown. "No, that he was secretary of defense twice before."

"Just once," I said, "under Gerald Ford."

She turned and left the room without saying anything else, but I knew my stock was rising and might soon be worth as much as two hundred forty dollars.

There at the Hertz desk, when Maggie invited me over, I didn't see any reason why not. It was Wednesday, so Jennifer had her night class, and I wouldn't have to explain where I'd been. Besides, having a drink with a colleague didn't constitute a crime. I'd done it before, though in the past the colleague had always been male. In fact, it had always been Ramsey.

They gave her a full-size Buick, and I followed her back to the highway.

It's twenty-six miles from Greenville to Loring, a straight shot through the heart of the Delta, cotton fields on both sides of the road until you cross the Loring County line, and after that you start to see a few catfish ponds. I'd been driving that road, or riding on it while somebody else drove, for almost half a century, and during that time the scenery had hardly changed at all—except for those ponds, which were dug about thirty years ago. A cotton field in 2006 looked pretty much the same as it did in 1962.

I don't know why my life began to seem so monotonous as I drove that stretch, as flat and featureless, as devoid of color and distinction, as one of those ponds. But a pond teems with activity the eye can't see, whereas the surface was pretty much all there was to me. I was just a guy who'd never write a book or lead a boycott or take a stand against community mores or assault a beach or walk the streets of a bombed-out city. I was Mr. History. I read it and I talked about it, without ever once having done anything unusual enough to make it. Not even locally.

The house Maggie rented isn't actually in town but about a mile south of Choctaw Creek, surrounded by tall hedges intended to shield its inhabitants from the eyes of those laboring in the adjoining fields. The original owners had been wealthy farmers, but their luck ran out in the '60s, and the bank finally took over. Since then it had been rented out again and again and by now was fairly rundown—the paint peeling off, the veranda sagging, the front steps beginning to crumble.

She parked the Buick in the carport, and I pulled up behind her and got out.

"Inside," she said, "it looks a good bit like the Munsters' house. My own furniture's still in North Carolina."

"You know who used to live here?"

"No, though I'm sure I came here at some point when I was a child. I remember the pool."

"I remember it, too, but that's because the folks it belonged to started renting it out for parties in the late Sixties, when they needed money. You were gone by then."

"Who were they?"

"You couldn't put this in a book and get anybody to believe it. Their last name was spelled L-A-U-S-S. Pronounced *Loss*."

She touched my arm. "Carol Lauss! I haven't thought of her in ages."

"Karen, actually. She was their daughter."

"What happened to her?"

"Works at the Health Department. Both her parents are dead."

She unlocked the back door, and we stepped into the kitchen. It was big and had probably been state-of-the-art at one time, but now all the appliances looked old, the linoleum countertops and floor dated.

"What would you like? I've got beer and wine in the fridge, and I think there's a bottle of VO in here somewhere that came with the house."

"The VO sounds good, if you can lay your hands on it."

She opened the door on a cabinet above the sink. The VO was there, all right, along with twenty or thirty of those little amber-colored bottles that prescription medication comes in. They weren't lined up neatly, either, just piled together like some monument to Eli Lilly. She stood on her tiptoes, and when she reached up her blouse pulled loose, revealing a strip of flesh, along with a good bit of black lace. She turned around, holding the bottle, and for a moment just stared at me. Then she smiled and said, "Want some Xanax?"

There wasn't much point in pretending I hadn't noticed the stash. "Looks like you're well stocked."

"Oh, if it's a tranquilizer or an antidepressant, chances are I've got it. All of those prescriptions, incidentally, were filled a year or so ago in North Carolina. Most of them I never even tried, though maybe I should've."

"If you don't use them, why bring them along?"

"Well, you never know when you might need to be uplifted or subdued. At least I'm prepared."

I dropped my voice and said, "I don't want a Xanax. But I'll sure take the whiskey—assuming you're prepared to let me have more than one drink."

"Oh, I'm pretty much prepared for anything."

"Anything?"

There's a guy I work with, an assistant coach, who I can't stand. He drives to school in one of those pickups with struts that lift it about five feet off the ground, and there's a weathered sticker on the tailgate that says HONK IF YOU'VE NEVER SEEN A SHOTGUN FIRED FROM A MOVING RIG. According to some students who play football, he always starts sobbing in the team huddle before the opening kickoff and then, even though he's the faculty adviser for the Fellowship of Christian Athletes, turns foulmouthed, urging them to kick the living fuck out of those goddamn cocksuckers. None of that, however, is why I dislike him.

No, it's because whenever you go into the teachers' lounge and find him in the presence of a female faculty member, he's invariably flirting with her. He'll drop his voice and say, "Is that a promise? Or a threat?" He wants them to think he's got one thing on his mind, and he wants you to think so, too, and I do. And every time I see him acting like that, I start imagining how I'd feel if I ever caught him talking to one of my daughters.

So I couldn't quite believe it when I heard myself sounding just like him.

She stood there with her back to the kitchen counter, staring at me, and I had the sense that if I was behaving exactly as she'd expected, I'd still disappointed her somehow, lessening myself in her eyes. "Ice?" she finally asked.

"Straight."

She sloshed about two inches of VO into a water glass and handed it to me. Then she pulled a bottle of Chardonnay from the refrigerator and filled her glass right up to the brim. We took our drinks into the living room, which was empty except for a couch and a coffee table and a chair she told me she'd rented from Front Street Furniture, and sat down at opposite ends of the couch.

Our recent lunch conversations had skirted the subject of her mother's death. Consequently, while I knew that her husband had invested wisely in dot-coms and then wisely sold before the bubble burst, that they'd traveled all over the world, skiing in the Alps and climbing in the Andes, I knew much less about the time she'd spent here in the late '50s and early '60s. Every now and then I recalled something—like being in a car with her and her brother and their mother, going to vacation Bible school at Fairway Baptist—but then I'd start doubting the memory. Nadine, I was fairly sure, hadn't been a churchgoer. I do remember they kept alcohol in the house back then, though Loring County, like the rest of the state, was bone dry. Baptists didn't drink—or if they did, they hid it.

As if she knew what I was thinking, she said, "You know, I never did forget you. Not once in all these years."

"I'm that memorable?"

She sipped her wine. "I'm not saying you *are*. Just that you *were*."

"How so?"

"You were such a pissed-off little kid."

That didn't really jibe with the view I held of myself, in which I'd always been reasonably happy. "Well, I seem to recall that I almost broke my neck once because you tripped me end over end off the porch up at the old Fairway Crossroads store. That's hardly something a well-adjusted child would do, so maybe you were the pissed-off kid."

"No. I did it because I didn't like the look you gave my brother. And I didn't like it when Mom hugged you."

"Why?"

"She held on to you for too long."

"Jesus. Are you that jealous now?"

"I don't have anybody, or anything, to be jealous of."

"Were you when you did?"

"Oh." She shook her head. "When I had a fit of jealousy, Luke, you wouldn't have wanted to be anywhere nearby." She was wearing a nice pair of leather sandals. She set her wineglass on the coffee table, then leaned over and slipped her left heel, and then her right, out of the straps. Leaving the shoes on the floor, she drew her legs up onto the couch.

She was an excellent psychologist, and precious little escaped her. Ever had or ever would. Now, she saw something in my face that I wasn't aware was there. "Know what I once heard your father tell my mother?" she asked. "After one of those meetings our dads used to attend?"

The gatherings in question were always held on Monday evening. My father sometimes complained about missing *The Andy Griffith Show*—the only TV program he really enjoyed, and a mainstay of the Monday night schedule in those days. They usually took place at someone's home—often Mayor Finley's—but at least one of them, I've discovered, was right in City Hall.

The Citizens' Council had been formed back in 1954, in response to *Brown v. Board of Education*. The founders might not have been the best or the brightest, but they had sense enough to know that the violent images that would eventually be beamed out over the airwaves—from sites like the Edmund Pettis Bridge—could only arouse the nation's disgust and spell the end of official segregation. They were determined to use economics, rather than sheer physical intimidation, to maintain the status quo.

According to my father's membership card, he joined in the spring of 1959, shortly after Arlan Calloway returned to Loring with his family. By then the vast majority of white men in the Delta were already members, so I don't know what significance, if any, his relatively late decision to sign up might have. I don't know, that is, if it indicates he never was a true believer and joined only because not to do so, at that point, would have been financial suicide, especially since Herman Horton was one of the organizers. For all I know, he might have feared he was so low down on the social ladder that he would've been rejected. If that's the case, it could be that Arlan Calloway shepherded him into the fold.

At any rate, they always went to the meetings together. Sometimes Mr. Calloway dropped by our house to pick my father up, though he never came inside, just pulled into the driveway and hit his horn once or twice. Mostly, though, my dad went down to his place, leaving his pickup parked in their yard. As far as I know, they never went to town in Dad's truck, probably because Mr. Calloway's was much newer and had air-conditioning.

Many times, after a meeting, my father would marvel at something his friend had said or done. I can recall hearing him tell Grandpa that another Council member—the father of a boy in my class—had made everybody mad by refusing to fire one of his tractor drivers. I don't recall what that man's sin was supposed to have been, but odds are he'd been caught talking to a voter-registration activist. When his employer, who himself wielded no small amount of influence in the community, said, "I hate to do it. I just really do hate to," Mr. Calloway replied, "I hate to, you hate to, he, she and it hates to, too, but he, she and it have to, and so will you."

"That Arlan," my father concluded, "he's resourceful. And that turns him into a *resource*."

More than forty years later, sitting there on the couch beside Arlan Calloway's daughter, whose bare calves were drawn up onto the cushions just inches away from my hand, which I could suddenly find no use for, I said, "My father? Your mother? What are you talking about?"

So she told me, and I have to admit that she evoked the scene well.

It's early summer, and she's been in bed with Nancy Drew when she hears her father's truck pull into the driveway. She lays her book aside and bounces out of bed, like she always does when her daddy comes home. He's usually got something for her, a piece of candy or a hug, and either one's as good as the other.

That night, for some reason, he doesn't cut his engine, just sits there in the driveway, the motor idling while the passenger door opens and my father gets out. He's left his own truck parked there and heads over to it. Then her dad puts his pickup in reverse and backs into the road. Later on, she'll hear him say that somebody had been siphoning gas from his tractors and he was going to check on things.

She presses her face against the window screen, not understanding why her father's leaving. It's a small thing, but of the sort that could puzzle a girl her age. While she watches my father open the door on his truck, she hears another door open and the porch light comes on.

Her mother steps into the yard, into that circle of light. She's wearing a pair of white shorts and a long-sleeved blouse with the sleeves rolled up, and there's a drink in her hand, as there so often is at this time in her life. She takes a couple of steps towards my father, who's standing there with his hand on the truck door.

"Hey, James," she says. "Y'all been out stirring up trouble?" She's against those meetings, as she's told her husband many times. She's told her kids the same thing, arguing that change is going to come whether people like it or not, so they might as well welcome it with open arms. And she's got her own arms wide open now. "Come here," she says, "and give me a hug."

So my dad meets her halfway between the truck and the porch, and they wrap their arms around each other, and the girl with her face pressed to the window hears my father say, "Lord, if you ain't something."

"THE FIRST HUMANS were whittled out of driftwood," the man who used to run our Western Auto liked to say. He'd pause, then slyly add, "According to Norse legend, anyway."

Considered an educational resource, Mr. Coldfield made those comments every year as the first graders from Loring Elementary were herded through his home. A tall, scholarly looking man who wore black-rimmed glasses, he spent Sunday afternoons walking the banks of the Sunflower River or wading around in Choctaw Creek, hoping to find another odd-shaped piece.

Driftwood was his passion. Though perfectly pleasant, he had neither wife nor child and enjoyed only the most perfunctory relations with his neighbors, pretty much confining himself to "Hello, how are you?" and "Nice day today, isn't it?" About half the folks in Loring had been inside his house but nobody—except first-grade teachers, as far as I know—ever entered it more than once.

To Mr. Coldfield, these weren't simply pieces of wood. I recall standing in his living room, sweat trickling down my back and a fly buzzing in my ear, while he gestured at one of the many items on display, a cypress knee he'd pulled out of Lake Washington. Smooth surfaced and about three feet high at its tallest point, it was really two distinct masses that curled together near the top of the growth. He asked us what it looked like.

It looked like a cypress knee to me, and because that fly was driving me crazy and I was bored and eager to get back outside and roughhouse with Eugene Calloway, I piped up and said so.

Shaking his head with what may have been pity, Mr. Coldfield said, "That's not a cypress knee, Luke. There on the left? That's the hand of a young woman. And on the right? The hand of her sweetheart. Could be they're joining hands for the first time, or maybe the last. Or it could just be a regular day in their lives and they're out for a walk in the pasture, where the only eyes watching belong to a Black Angus. Nobody knows their circumstances but the wood itself, and you know what I love about wood?"

Until then, neither Eugene nor I figured he was crazy. He acted normal enough when he was selling you a baseball bat or a fishing pole.

"The thing I love about wood," Mr. Coldfield said, removing his glasses and polishing them on the front of his shirt, "is that it never talks. But if you sit and watch and wait long enough, it may show you a thing or two."

I've thought a lot lately about the various ways in which we reveal ourselves to others. Ramsey Coleman does it with jokes. If he's mad at you, his sense of humor, which is always sharp, can turn into an ice pick. He got angry at me once, years ago, for signing a petition against his requirement that each faculty member work the ticket booth at one sporting event per year. I'd just started teaching my Local History honors course, and when I mentioned at lunch one day that I was disappointed by my enrollment, he said, in front of another teacher, "I don't know why I ever agreed to let you offer that class. It probably won't fill up unless we retitle it Fuck Films." Jennifer's deepest feelings emerge only in her poems, which can make Emily Dickinson's seem lighthearted. My daughter Candace, on the other hand, will sometimes phone and say, "I'm lonely, Dad," or "I'm bored," or "I'm worried because I don't know what I want to be." Her direct approach seems to me, on the whole, the most healthy, if the least inventive.

Maggie fell somewhere in between Candace and Jennifer. She said a number of things in a straightforward manner. Other things she never said at all. This made reading her difficult, like trying to parse *The Decline of the West*.

That first time I went to her house, I left before seven but was about as drunk as I'd been since college. Though I thought about dropping in on Ellis, my tongue was pretty loose and there was no telling what I might say. So instead I drove on home, pulled a can of Bud Light out of the fridge and had started to chug it when the jingle a friend's dad had sung for us the night we graduated from high school rang in my ears:

> *Never fear*
> *Whiskey on beer.*
> *But beer on whiskey's*
> *Pretty risky.*

I poured out the Bud and stood the can on the counter, then ransacked the fridge for something to eat, removing the lids from all the pots I found in there—some cream of broccoli soup, a little beef bourguignonne left over from the previous evening, a big clot of mashed potatoes—before deciding I wasn't even hungry. So I brewed a pot of coffee, filled a large mug and went back to the living room, where I made myself sit down in my leather armchair and pick up a book, the title of which I don't remember. It might have been a good one—probably was, because I don't have a lot of money to spend on books and read countless reviews online before buying—but it quickly lost the battle for my attention.

Earlier, when I asked Maggie what she was telling me about

my dad, she said, "I'm just telling you that on one specific evening forty-four years ago, he expressed the opinion that my mother was really something."

"And then?"

"He got in his truck and drove off."

"And after that?"

"I went back and finished reading about Nancy Drew."

"I mean——"

"I know what you mean." She took a sip of wine. "Please don't view this as criticism, Luke, but you have a tendency to want answers when there might not be any."

"You intend that as praise?"

She had a nice smile—very tight, controlled, whereas lots of smiles dissipate by spreading across a face. "I intend it," she said, "as an observation."

I turned up my VO and took a good slug. I almost never drink whiskey and couldn't imagine why I'd asked for this instead of beer or wine. "There's always an answer," I said.

"Really?"

Nothing creates obstinacy like being forced to maintain an indefensible position. Just look at the career of Robert E. Lee. "Always."

"And you teach history? Sounds like math to me."

Neither of us said much of anything for a while then, just sat there drinking. When I think about that afternoon—as I do all the time—I see her living room as an almost empty stage. And it occurs to me that if the setting is stripped of props, people can't help but behave differently than they otherwise might. With no magazine to pick up and peruse, no music to hum along to, no painting on the wall you can talk about to prove you made it through art appreciation, there's nothing you can do except face what you're feeling about the person sitting there beside you.

At some point I got up, carried both our glasses into the

kitchen and refilled them, as though the house were mine instead of hers, and when we'd drained those I made another run. And then I put them on the coffee table, sat down on the couch and urged myself not to do what I'd just about decided to.

She warned me off, holding out her hand. "No."

"No *what?*"

"No, not now."

We're all surrounded by the borders we've drawn for ourselves, and crossing them is a major event, akin to a foreign excursion: you have to acquire travel documents, pay exorbitant ticket prices and, unless you're exceedingly lucky, probably find yourself stranded for an indeterminate period in a place where you can't communicate with another living soul. The question I put to Maggie that afternoon, as I see it now, constituted a passport application. "When?"

"Maybe later," she said, pulling on her sandals and standing up, leaving me no choice but to stand up myself. "But then again, Luke? Probably not. Okay?" Before pushing me towards the door, she stood on tiptoes and gave me a quick kiss.

I've traveled vast distances while sitting in my armchair. But I've never covered more ground than I did that night, with a forgotten book in my lap and a cup of cold coffee on my knee.

Maggie said she never had children because she was afraid she might let them down. A reasonable person would probably conclude that somebody had let her down, and the obvious choice was her dad. But I wasn't so sure that's how she saw it.

I didn't know why her mother once spent the night at our house, but she had, and for the last couple weeks I'd been thinking about the night I woke up and went into the living room to find Nadine asleep on the couch. And how, once she finally realized I was staring at her, she'd slowly pulled that quilt up to conceal her breast.

I didn't know if the next recollection associated with that one was accurate or not. I'm sitting at the breakfast table, in the house we lived in then, on the sixteenth section, a few miles north of Loring. My father, sitting next to me, is eating like he always does, his jaw making that familiar clicking noise. There's still some food on his plate, a piece of bacon, maybe, or a biscuit, or an egg fried stiff, just the way he likes them. He eats the same thing every day, and so does everybody else who lives on a farm in the Delta in 1962. We don't experiment with chocolate-chip pancakes, and Pop-Tarts won't be invented until the following year. Granola bars do exist, just not in Mississippi.

Nadine steps into the picture. She's wrapped in a man's bathrobe, a beige terry-cloth thing that Dad won't wear because he says it makes him feel like a sissy. Momma, who gave it to him, should've known better. The only time he's not dressed in regular clothes is when he takes a bath or gets in bed.

Nadine's hair has been carefully brushed, so it's not frizzy like it was at night, and she's holding the big yellow bowl my mother serves grits from. That's what's in it now, and she's troubled that we haven't eaten every last bite. Hovering over me, she says, "You want a little more, hon? So you can grow up tall like your daddy?"

I don't want to displease her, because by now I like her better than anybody I know, including Eugene. I've thought about her a lot, and because of what I saw when she was lying on the couch and her lack of haste in concealing herself, I'll think about her even more. But I'm full as a tick, so I smile and say, "No thanks, ma'am."

"What about you, James? You got any room left?"

My dad chews away and finally swallows, his Adam's apple bobbing up and down. When he says yes, he's not looking at her but at me. I'm the one he winks at.

OVER THE YEARS, Dad and I disagreed about a number of things. He hated it when my hair got long and was mortified that I briefly sported a beard. Though he hardly ever attended church, he was bothered that we didn't make our daughters go, and when he found out that a kid from Indianola got Trish drunk one night her junior year and left her on a turnrow ten miles out of town, he said that if he were her father he would've shot the boy. "Of course," he said, "I guess that'd be difficult for you, since you don't have no gun."

Gun ownership was one subject we rarely ventured near. On my eighteenth birthday, he'd walked into my bedroom and handed me, butt first, his Colt Python, a double-action .357 Magnum that for many years had been concealed between his mattress and box spring. It wasn't the only weapon he had— there was even another handgun, a nine-millimeter Smith and Wesson—but I knew it was his favorite. "This is yours now," he said. "I hope you don't ever have to use it. But you better be ready, if the time ever comes."

Of the things I wanted for my birthday, the Python wouldn't have made the list. Nevertheless, I accepted it with the solemn demeanor that the occasion seemed to demand, and when I left for Ole Miss the gun went with me. For a while I kept it under my mattress, just like he had. But when Jennifer and I decided to live together, she said she didn't want a gun on the premises. So without thinking twice, I went to the pawnshop out on East University and sold it for fifty dollars.

He didn't find out that I no longer had it until after we got married and moved to Loring. One night, when my mother was in Jackson visiting her sister, he asked over dinner if I was keeping it oiled and shooting it from time to time, and I didn't want to embarrass myself in front of my wife. "I don't have it anymore," I said.

Like a baby who's been bumped on the head, he failed to react for such a long time that I almost thought this might not have registered. But I should've known better than that. I did know *him* better than that.

He laid his fork down and, a few seconds later, his knife. "What do you mean, you don't have it? Did you let somebody steal the damn thing?"

"No, I sold it."

"For what?"

"Fifty bucks."

"That's not it. I mean why."

I'd gone through college with little or no help from him and I had a job, was married and one day expected to start my own family. I remember puffing my chest out before announcing, "I believe in gun control."

"You're a fucking idiot." Then he turned to Jennifer: "I'm sorry I used that word in your presence. I should've taken him outside and told him there."

"You can't take me anywhere," I said. "I'm twenty-three years old. And the fact is, I *do* believe in gun control. There ought to be a mandatory one-week waiting period before anybody can buy a handgun, so the feds have time to make sure the purchaser isn't a criminal. Most folks that go out looking for a weapon when they're pissed off will change their minds if you give 'em a few days to cool down."

"Let me tell you something," he said. "If people want to do wrong bad enough, they'll do it. And if then they decide not to, it won't be because somebody made 'em wait. It'll be because a little voice inside them said, *Don't*. And that voice don't need a week to say something." He laid his napkin on the table, got up and left. He didn't talk to me again for at least a month, just tipping his hat and walking right by when we met on the street downtown, more or less how he did towards Ellis.

Maggie didn't come to school the day after we had drinks at her house or the next day either, so I risked asking Ramsey if he knew why she was absent.

We were finishing lunch, and a couple of other teachers had just gotten up and left the table. He wadded up his trash and stuck half a bag of potato chips back into that ridiculous mailbox, then told me she'd called in sick.

"Got a cold?" I asked, trying not to sound too interested.

"Could be. Or maybe she's allergic to defoliant, like me. Every year when they start spraying that shit, my head hurts twenty-four hours a day. It's like I've got fever, even though I don't."

"You ought to be immune by now."

"She should too. You know she lived here when she was a little girl?"

"Yeah. I even knew her back then."

"That right? Then you probably know what happened to her momma."

I was surprised she'd told him about that, and I said so.

"Yeah, I guess I would've been surprised, too, but she didn't tell me. Selina remembered it."

His wife grew up on various farms in and around Loring. "What'd she say about it?" I asked.

Ramsey shrugged. "Just said Maggie's daddy killed her momma for sleeping with another man."

I have a mild form of tachycardia that never manifests itself in the classroom, though I sometimes feel it if I have to get up and speak at an assembly with the whole student body and all the other teachers present. When it kicked in that afternoon, it felt like Mike Tyson was inside my chest and trying to punch his way out. "I heard it was self-defense."

"That's white folks' history. Black folks would say he was defending his terrain."

"Did Selina ever hear who the other guy was?"

"If she did, she doesn't remember it. You know how things were back then, man. If you were black, you didn't know white folks' names unless you had some business with them, and vice versa. Y'all had your world, we had ours." He got up and tucked the mailbox under his arm. Grinning, he chucked my shoulder. "Y'all's world had running water. But ours had *rhythm*."

Later, after all my students had left, I closed and locked my classroom door, sat down and called her. Her cell rang four or five times, then her voice invited me to leave a message. I said I hoped she was feeling better and offered to bring her food or medicine, if she needed anything, though I also said that Jennifer and I would be visiting our daughters in Oxford that weekend. She never did return the call, and initially I thought maybe she'd packed up and gone back to North Carolina.

ALL THE BEST-KNOWN images of Oxford date from the fall of 1962. James Meredith sits at a desk filling out his enrollment papers while Robert B. Ellis, the university registrar, looks on in shock. Some three hundred U.S. marshals form a ring around the Lyceum, facing a Rebel flag–waving mob, some of whom have commandeered a bulldozer. The Indianhead Division of the Second Infantry marches through the square while several white male teenagers—presumably Ole Miss students—hurl bottles at them in front of Gathright-Reed Drugstore, where William Faulkner, dead for only a few months, used to sit each morning smoking his pipe.

Those images accurately convey what Oxford was like forty-four years ago, though not the town today. The pharmacy has become a bookstore, and the weekly alternative newspaper highlights plenty of blues and hip-hop. The Rebel flag is banned from campus activities, and 80 percent of the football team, if only about 15 percent of the student body, is now African American. A statue of Meredith stands near the Lyceum. All may not be joy and love, but the campus and the town that surrounds it have a lot more in common with Boulder, Colorado, than with the place captured in those old photos.

My own feelings about it are especially warm. The Ole Miss library is the only decent one I ever had access to, and as a student I spent hours roaming through the E185s, where Southern history gets shelved. I met Jennifer there one night. She was taking a literature class taught by Evans Harrington, and he'd assigned Elizabeth Spencer's *The Voice at the Back Door*, a novel in which a group of blacks is massacred in the courthouse of a town he said was based on Carrollton, Mississippi. It so happened that Jennifer had spent her summers there visiting her grandparents, and she was astounded to hear that any such event could've taken place without her ever once hearing about it. She told me that frankly she didn't believe it, that Harrington must not know what he was talking about.

We had this conversation after she saw me hunkered down in an aisle, with about ten books piled up on either side of me. She asked if I was a history major, and when I said yes she wondered if I could help her find a source that would disprove Harrington's allegation.

I knew nothing about this novel but had taken my obligatory American literature survey with Harrington the previous year, and I suspected that if he said the town was based on Carrollton and that a massacre had occurred there, he was right twice. Within a few minutes I'd located Vernon Lane Wharton's *The Negro in Mississippi, 1865–1890*, and in the index was a page reference to the Carrollton Massacre.

We read the account side by side, each of us perched on a stack of books in the poorly lit aisle, Jennifer shaking her head, those frizzy bangs sweeping across her forehead. It wasn't a pretty story—between ten and twenty black people were slaughtered in the courthouse, in 1886, for daring to attend the trial of a white man—but I had a hard time focusing. Instead I was noticing how the girl beside me held her breath when yet another detail disturbed her, a faint flush appearing on her otherwise pale face. Unlike the vast majority of Ole Miss coeds, who began dressing for class two or three hours ahead of time and wore so much Maybelline that you had to guess what they actually looked like, she wore the plainest of clothes—a pair of faded jeans, a powder-blue T-shirt—and no makeup or eye shadow. The scent she gave off was pleasant and fresh.

"Well," she said, closing the book, "I guess Carrollton's not the nice little town I thought it was."

"That was a long time ago. Almost a hundred years."

"Yeah. But once you know something so awful happened, you can't ever feel the same about a place." It was hot up there on the third floor, but she shivered, and I barely stopped myself from putting my arm around those thin shoulders. "I mean, Jesus," she said, "my grandfather used to take me to that court-house all the time. His best friend was some kind of clerk—city clerk, county clerk, I don't know—and they'd always sit there and chew tobacco and spit juice through a hole in the floor near the old guy's desk."

I didn't want her to get up and leave without giving me her name. And it suddenly seemed that my best chance of getting it would be to tell her something else she didn't know. After all, Professor Harrington had nabbed her attention with just that kind of info. "Have you ever heard of Theodore Bilbo?"

She laid the book beside the pile she'd been sitting on, then stood up. "Sure. I've lived in Mississippi all my life."

I got up too. Sweat had broken out on my face and under my arms and was running down my back. "You know what he once said about Huey P. Long? He said, 'Half the folks in Louisiana are trying to figure out how to kill Huey. Well, I got the perfect answer for 'em. Just bring him over here to Mississippi, and the bastard'll kill hisself trying to get out of the state.' " My laughter sounded like the gasps of a terminal emphysemic.

She glanced past me, looking for the stairs. Later, she told me she'd been thinking about a story in the *Daily Mississippian* about some guy who'd been flashing himself at coeds. Sometimes in the stacks, or else he followed them outside and displayed his wares there.

I dredged my memory for another esoteric tidbit. "You know about Ledger Lewis?"

"Who?"

"Herbert 'Ledger' Lewis. He was state treasurer for fifty-three years, retired in 1959. He was eighty-six when he quit and completely senile. When they were cleaning out his office, they found King Edward cigar boxes that contained over thirty thousand bucks, the bills dating back to the Depression."

She stepped by me, headed for the stairs. Though I'd never done anything like this before, I followed her. I didn't know what had come over me. My life until then hadn't been abnormal. I'd had two girlfriends in high school and one at Ole Miss, and she and I had slept together several times, once pooling our resources to rent a room at Johnson's Motel for an entire weekend. After that we were less interested in each other but had managed to remain friends.

The stairwell was narrow, barely wide enough for two people to pass, so I stayed a couple of steps behind. She only began to breathe easier, she said later, when she saw the circulation desk and a line of students waiting to check out books.

Back then, at the very rear of the library, a large reading room was sectioned off into individual carrels. It was called the Reserve Room, because back before computers, professors made certain materials accessible to everyone in a class by putting them on reserve, which meant you could sign them out only for a limited period and had to read them there. Like most serious students, I spent a lot of time in there, and it was almost always crowded, especially at night. I was behaving in a really spooky manner, and she said she didn't want to leave and walk back to her room after dark, so she planned to plop down in one of the carrels and wait until I disappeared. Then she'd call her roommate from the pay phone and ask her to come walk her home.

The entire back wall of the Reserve Room was glass, and she headed for a carrel in the corner, thinking she could see when I left the building. She'd just pulled out a chair and was sitting down when my eye registered motion, something streaking towards me. A second later there was a tremendous impact, followed by the sound of shattering glass. Something large and brown tumbled into the library.

Chairs went over, girls shrieking and guys, too.

The doe probably weighed a hundred pounds or so, though it was hard to tell while she was lying down. There were a couple cuts in her side, but other than that the only thing that appeared to be wrong with her was that she'd been knocked senseless.

She was about halfway between my future wife and me. Jennifer had backed up as far as she could, pressing her shoulders to the wall, her face drained of all the color I'd noticed upstairs. She put her hand over her mouth, as if to keep herself from screaming.

I've never been a hunter, never killed anything other than an ant or a mosquito and even feel bad about that. Still, I know a fair bit about deer and didn't have to guess what would happen as soon as she regained consciousness. She'd wreak havoc, jumping all over the place and damaging herself and anybody who got in her way. A deer's hooves are sharp as razors. I once saw one cut a cottonmouth to shreds.

The deer that did that had been brought home by my dad when I was seven or eight years old. She was just a fawn, and he'd found her tangled up in a barbed-wire fence. He bandaged her cuts and tied her to a stake in the backyard during daytime, locking her in the barn at night to keep her safe from predators. After a while he turned her loose, but she wouldn't leave. She'd hang around in the yard and, for the first couple months, let me pet her. After that, she started getting wild again and finally ran off. He'd brought her home in a cotton sack because, he said, even a little fawn could be trouble if she got scared.

I was thinking about that when I noticed the big quilt hanging on the wall behind Jennifer. Like the others on display, it was mounted on a wooden frame and must have measured about ten feet by twelve. I didn't know how it was attached, or whether I'd be strong enough to pull it down or do anything with it if I did, but I had to try. Over at the desk, a frightened attendant held the phone to her ear, and I figured she'd called the university police. The station was just a block away, and they weren't known for taking the subtle approach.

I stepped around the animal, going behind her body rather than moving past her glassy eyes. When I grabbed the quilt with both hands, Jennifer said, "What are you doing?"

"Help me. I don't want the cops to shoot her. We need to roll her up."

Together we jerked and, stitches ripping, the fabric came loose from the frame.

I looked over my shoulder and saw the deer lift her head. "Quick," I said, and we hurled the quilt over her.

As Jennifer described it later, I fell to my knees and butted the deer backwards, so I could get part of the blanket under her. After that, another guy helped me roll her up in it, though she put up a pretty good struggle, one of her hooves barely missing my left leg. By the time two cops came running down the street with short-barreled shotguns, we'd dragged her out the door.

"It's all right," I hollered.

The other guy and I jumped away from her, and within a couple of seconds she'd freed herself. She looked around wildly, head swiveling, front legs rising into one of those beautiful leaps.

The slug blew her into a metal garbage can—blue, with Ole Miss scripted in red—and it tipped over, spilling out the contents. Amid Coke cups and Wendy's wrappers, the doe lay in a heap, much smaller than she'd been a moment ago. I remembered that when my grandfather died and I saw him in his coffin, he also seemed greatly reduced.

The deer was still breathing. Her eyes were open too but no longer looked glassy. Unfortunately, she was very much aware.

"They come out of them fuckin' woods at the edge of campus," the cop who'd shot her said. "Put me in charge, we'd cut every one of them trees down."

The other cop looked at me, then at the guy who'd helped me drag her out the door, then at the group of students who'd emerged from the library. Jennifer wasn't with them. I could see her standing inside, staring at the doe through the shattered plate glass. She wasn't crying, but her shoulders were starting to shake. "We can't let these deer roam around campus," I heard the cop say. "They're a danger. Y'all were nuts to touch her."

I didn't reply, just walked towards the door. As I passed through the crowd, a male voice observed, "Be a shame to waste good meat."

I don't know what I intended to tell Jennifer. I think maybe I meant to apologize for what the cop had done, or to apologize for masculine behavior in general. I probably hazily understood that she had briefly become my prey, even if all I wanted was to know her name.

But all I ended up telling her was *yes* when she looked up at me and asked, "Would you please walk me home?"

Lots of people have said they get extremely emotional when they see their children for the first time after sending them off to college. It doesn't seem to matter whether the kids go two thousand miles away or, like our daughters, only a hundred and fifty: they just look different. It's as if something has been altered in their DNA. But the question is whether the change is really in them or in you.

In my case, I think, the answer was both. Trish emerged from Stewart Hall—the same dorm I'd walked her mother home to that night twenty-nine years ago—in frayed jeans, a ragged purple T-shirt I'd never seen before and a pair of Wal-Mart flip-flops. In high school she was fashion conscious, spending every cent she had in the Greenville mall or, when we agreed to drive her, in one of the bigger stores up in Memphis. Candace, on the other hand, never seemed to care much about her appearance. Now she was heavily made-up, with lots of blush on her cheeks, wearing a new skirt and a pair of high heels she still didn't know how to walk in, looking like she might tip over at any moment. I suspected she'd gotten interested in a boy, whose height I would've pegged at six-foot-three.

And as for me, something was different, too. For eighteen years, every time I saw them, the word that entered my mind was *daddy*. Their presence defined me. In their absence I'd lost my prevailing sense of self. Simply laying eyes on them again couldn't quite give it back.

Trish had never been as warm as her sister, always a little bit stiff, and that hadn't changed. Rather than hug me, she leaned forward a little bit, guardedly preventing me from achieving much contact. But my nose brushed the top of her head, and her hair smelled of pot. I sniffed once or twice.

She laughed and said, "Relax, Daddy. It's not the big deal it used to be. It's actually kind of retro, like you listening to Chuck Berry."

I glanced over at Jennifer, who was hugging Candace, both of them swaying, close to tears, Candace taller now than her mom because of those stilts. "What's an ounce go for?" I asked.

I was trying to play the cool dad like I always had, but she shook her head as if at a kid who refused to grow up. She exchanged places with her sister and I threw my arms around Candace, noticing that her eye shadow was clumsily applied. "Who's the guy?" I said.

She quickly pulled away. "There's not one."

To my surprise, Jennifer took mercy on me. "Be nice to your dad," she told them. "He's envious." She paused, then added, "Your lives are just starting. His is starting to be over."

I have to say, the day was by no means unpleasant. We decided to go to the square on foot and have lunch at Ajax Diner. While we walked, Trish's mouth ran. She's majoring in history—planning on law school one day—and was enjoying most of her courses, though she voiced strong dislike for the guy teaching her American survey. When I asked what was wrong with him, she said, "First of all, he's from Indiana."

"What's wrong with that?"

"Indiana's the cradle of Main Street conservatism—you're the one who told me that, Daddy—and he's always putting his own spin on things."

If she'd found a conservative history professor, I figured she ought to at least appreciate the oddity. He was probably the only one she'd ever encounter. The last program I'd seen for the OAH's annual meeting featured such session topics as Rewriting the History of Rape and Historical Perspectives on Masculinity and Empire Building. "What kinds of things?"

"Well, for instance, he brings in stuff about the war, which doesn't have anything at all to do with what we're studying, and keeps trying to draw these really tenuous links between figures he thinks we'll admire, like Abraham Lincoln or FDR, and George Bush. He said the other day that when people rag Bush for what's happening at Guantánamo Bay, they forget that Lincoln suspended the writ of habeas corpus."

"Well, that's the truth."

"You can't separate a truth from the context in which it's spoken. And you know who said *that*?"

We were walking east on University Avenue, Jennifer and

Candace in front, their arms around each other as they discussed an intro to lit class. It may sound too neat, but we've got an English major, too.

"Yeah," I admitted. "But I didn't say *a* truth, I said *the* truth. And I never argued that the context made it any less true. I was just pointing out that when you evaluate what purports to be a fact, you have to consider the environment that exists when you hear it. Schools of history come and go, and all of them reflect current biases. Every historian shades meaning to one degree or another."

"Well, I don't like the shades in this guy's palette and hope he doesn't get tenure. He needs to go teach at Bob Jones."

The square was largely deserted, as it always is on a fall Saturday when the football team's on the road. We took a booth at the diner, and I ordered myself a beer, Jennifer a glass of white wine. Hearing the girls talk about their classes, I think we both were pleasantly surprised that college seemed to be having the desired effect, increasing their interest rather than slowly draining it out of them, as it so often does. There at Ajax, I believe we felt—for lack of a better word—successful. Our kids were all right. They'd probably stumble at some point, but as long as they knew where they were headed, it looked like they'd most likely reach their destination.

As we waited for our food, I ordered a second beer and lapsed into an expansive, nostalgic mood. I waved my hand around the room, which was decorated with posters advertising blues performances from forty or fifty years ago, a bunch of old license plates, two or three big bottle-cap thermometers like you used to see hanging on country stores. "You wouldn't believe what this place used to look like," I said.

"Was it Ajax back then?" Candace asked.

"Nope, it was a pizzeria. Over there in the middle, where all the tables are, there was a salad bar."

"It was some of the saltiest pizza you ever tasted," Jennifer said. "When your dad and I came in here, the first thing we asked for was a pitcher of water."

"That we always got refilled two or three times."

"We ordered a large combo, even though your dad used to hate mushrooms. He'd pick them off his half and dump them on mine."

"I'd eat a few from time to time. What I really wanted was the Hawaiian pizza, but the mere thought of it made your mother gag."

Candace said, "What's on that?"

"Ham and pineapple," Jennifer told her, shuddering.

Both girls groaned.

"Did you eat here a lot?" Trish asked.

"Whenever we could afford it."

"How often was that?"

Jennifer laughed. "Not very."

They brought our plates—I got the catfish with sweet potato casserole, corn bread and fried okra—and Jennifer and I each ordered another drink. If I had to guess, I'd say we sat in that booth for pretty close to two hours.

It was what I've come to think of as our throwback day. We were as we'd been for countless thousands of meals—a family of four, parked around a table and making small talk. We were, to take the notion even further, parked around a table in the town where everything had started, where I'd helped a girl about the age of my daughters find details of a massacre, where everyone then stood and watched helplessly while a different kind of massacre occurred. If Evans Harrington hadn't told his class about those murders in Carrollton, their mother and I might never have met. And if that deer hadn't crashed through the glass and gotten shot, she wouldn't have asked me to walk her home. One thing, as I saw it that day, led to another.

The fact that I'd been cautioning students against taking a

purely event-based approach to history, with its easy causal lines, didn't come to me until later. There at Ajax Diner, surrounded by the three people who'd meant the most to me for most of my life, it all made perfect sense.

We spent the night at a local B and B. I happened to know that in the late nineteenth century, this was Oxford's top brothel and owned by a notorious woman reputed to be quite handy with a straight razor. It still sported whorehouse décor: big heavy red drapes, a bidet in the bathroom, an enormous canopied four-poster that could've withstood the most rambunctious activity, if anybody put it to the test, but we didn't. By the time I got out of the shower, Jennifer was fast asleep, a mask over her eyes and orange stopples in her ears.

THE FIRST TIME Maggie and I make love, it's raining. The limbs of the pecan trees in the backyard dip and sway, dropping brown hulls, and thunder shakes the walls and floor. It's quite the storm.

By the time we climb the stairs and peel our clothes off, it's after six on Wednesday and we've had a lot to drink, five or six glasses of wine for her and five or six shots of that awful VO for me. Later, she'll joke that we got to where we were because I was full of Canadian courage.

Where we are is a rickety bed she rented with the rest of her furniture, in an otherwise empty room whose green wallpaper is water stained. There's not even a bedside table. Her alarm clock stands on the floor alongside several stacks of books and magazines. I see a copy of *Les Misérables* down there and a few issues of the *New Republic*.

The bed smells like her, and not just because she's in it. The scent of her perfume lingers in a room long after she's left it, acting as her proxy. You can smell her in the hallways and the teachers' lounge, too. For days I've been feeling like she's worked herself inside me. I was drunk before I ever touched that VO.

For a long time nothing happens except I hold her and she presses her face against me. "You're smooth here," she says, running her hand over my sternum. "Like a boy."

It's true. I don't have much body hair, and it's soft, what little there is. In high school, when it started growing on the other guys' chests, I felt self-conscious, but I haven't thought about it in years. I never go swimming, and Loring's too small for a health club, so there's no occasion to get undressed in front of anybody who's seeing me naked for the first time.

"You're scared, aren't you?" she says.

"Yeah."

"You haven't done this before."

It's a statement, not a question, and that spares me the need to answer. I don't have to ask a question, either, but I do. "Have you?"

"Oh, I'm afraid I've done far too much of it."

The crown of her head is touching my chin. I stroke her hair. "For your own good?"

"No." She stifles what feels like a laugh. "For the good of mankind, obviously."

"So why'd you do it?"

This is one of those times when she takes a while to answer. "Well, I was looking for something."

"What?"

"I don't know. I just know I never found it. Every time I tried, I promised myself it would be the last."

"Hard to find it if you don't know what it is."

"You're absolutely right."

I know I should stop this line of inquiry. That, I feel sure, would be the smart thing to do. But being smart isn't where I am. I've thrown intelligence out the window and it's out there on the ground, getting soaked with the pecans. "Your husband wasn't it?"

Her hand stops moving. "My husband was a wonderful man. I'd even say he was a great man, though I didn't really under-stand that until he died. He influenced a lot of people, some of whom never even met him. A memorial service was held in Duke

Chapel, and you wouldn't believe how many people attended. Former students came from across the country. One young man, some kind of official in the Indian government, flew all the way from New Delhi. And numerous old colleagues from CNN. Ted Turner showed up, with three or four bodyguards."

"What about Jane?"

"No, they'd already divorced." Once more her hand is moving. It slides down my chest, over my stomach, a distance you could measure in inches, so why does this motion last forever? "The young man from New Delhi came over, took my hand and said that if you added up all the hours he'd spent in my husband's office, listening to Anthony talk about how he might influence the lives of poor people back in India, he bet it was several weeks, if not months. He had tears in his eyes when he told me this, and of course he expected me to be moved, and I was. But I couldn't help thinking what all those hours added up to for me. Just a lot of time alone."

"Was that the main problem in your marriage?"

"I think the main problem in my marriage was me. Or at least my expectations."

"They were too high?"

"No, they were stratospheric. I wanted what you could get from being married to a man with that kind of drive and commitment, but I also wanted what you couldn't. So from time to time I looked elsewhere."

"I guess I'm the anti-Anthony then. Because I'm just a guy who gets up in the morning hoping to make it through the day."

She climbs on top of me, locks her hands behind her head and closes her eyes. "Well, it looks like you've made it through this one," she says. "The question is, will either of us survive the evening."

. . .

The next morning, at breakfast, I'm so solicitous that Jennifer acts annoyed. "More oatmeal?" I ask while she's sipping her tea. A book lies open on the table, one of those little thin ones the poetry presses publish, and she's staring at it so intently she can't hear me. So I repeat my question. "Want any more oatmeal?"

She looks up sharply. "What?"

I point at her bowl. "More oatmeal. I'd be happy to make some."

"Why would I want more oatmeal? Have you ever known me to want more?"

The truth is that I've never noticed how much oatmeal she eats at breakfast, because for a long time now I haven't noticed her. She eats, I eat, we rinse our dishes and leave, sometimes without bothering to say goodbye. "Just thought I'd ask," I tell her.

"Well, now you know." She dips her head and goes back to her book.

In the shower I lather up, remembering how Maggie's face looked last night with her eyes wide open, the tight lines showing at the corners of her mouth. She remained completely silent the whole time, speaking only with her body. Towards the end she moved harder than I knew a woman could, as though her own rhythm was all that mattered. She rocked backwards, grabbing a fistful of her own hair in each hand, pulling at it like she meant to tear it out in clumps.

Afterwards, as we lay there listening to the rain, she said, "No one has ever made me feel like that except the man I married. I just thought you should know."

I was reminded, in that instant, of Spiro T. Agnew, who told us, shortly before being indicted: *I try to be credible. I want to be believed.* I couldn't help it. I burst out laughing.

She was lying on her back beside me, her hand holding mine.

She let go and said sharply, "Why are you laughing at me?" Her eyes flashed, warning me that she wasn't playing around. I felt sure I'd seen the same look on her face all those years ago, as I lay breathless on the ground after she sent me flying off that porch. She hadn't been playing then, either.

"I'm not laughing at you," I said. "I'm laughing at myself."

"I didn't see you do anything funny."

"It's just so strange for somebody, after all this time, to praise my lovemaking ability."

"I'm not just *somebody*."

"You know what I mean."

"No, I don't. And I wasn't praising your *ability*. That's not what I said."

I understood right then what made her so different. It wasn't the scent of her perfume, and it wasn't that beautiful black hair, which, considering her age, must come in a bottle now. It wasn't her wealth or worldliness, nor the thrill of a shared distant past. It wasn't even how she made love, though nobody had ever made love like that to me. It was her hunger to have things a certain way. She knew how to want. And at the moment, that didn't scare me. "I'm sorry," I said. "Could we back up?"

"Back up to where? To where we were before you climbed into my bed?"

She wasn't touching me anymore, but even without direct contact I could feel the tension in her body. She'd gone rigid. "No," I said, "just back to where we were when you were telling me how I made you feel. Could you say that again, and let me start over?"

I didn't know whether she'd tell me to get my ass out of her house or punch me in the mouth. The expression on her face never changed, and her body remained stiff. "No one . . . has ever made me feel like that . . . except the man I married. I just thought . . . you should know."

"And I've never made anybody else feel like that," I said. "Not even the woman I married."

"How can you be sure?"

"I just am."

Finally, her face softened. "It *is*," she said, "fairly easy to tell."

I park in the teachers' lot next to the Mercedes, get out and go inside. Driving over, I've convinced myself that what happened last night will not be repeated, that Maggie's curiosity has now been satisfied. After all, she said she'd had similar experiences before. Her comment about how I'd made her feel was probably just out of kindness. Maybe she says it every time.

I tell myself that it really would be okay, that in fact it might be better. Jennifer and I have a history, and it lives in separate rooms in the same dorm at Ole Miss. The thought of getting caught, of having to face my wife and daughters after they've found out, is terrifying. You can't hide an affair for long in a town like Loring. I've never had one, but there are just some things you know.

You know, for instance, that a few years ago, an English teacher got caught having sex with one of her students in a pickup parked down close to the Sunflower River. You know that the kid's father wasted no time calling Ramsey Coleman and promising to kill the teacher if he didn't run her off, and Ramsey was only too happy to oblige. She got a job over in Arkansas, in another little town, and it wasn't a year before she had to leave there, too.

You know about other, similar scandals: Linwood Norris, head salesman at the John Deere dealership, a member of the Chamber of Commerce and the father of three boys between the ages of eight and thirteen, slept with one of the checkers out at

Wal-Mart and then became obsessed, following her home from work, tailing her around town, calling her at all hours of the day and night, even though she was engaged and told him that what happened between them was just a big mistake. Finally, she got a restraining order against him, and Linwood's wife took the boys to her parents' place in Jackson.

You know how these things go. Doesn't everybody?

Still, I decide to stop by her room before the bell rings. That just seems like the decent thing. If she wants to smile, as I believe she will, and tell me that while it was really wonderful, it's not something we'll be able to do again, I'd rather hear it than wait till the end of the day.

She's not there. I hang around near the door until two minutes before eight, nodding at the students as they file past, a couple of them giving me funny looks, wondering what I'm doing here. When I finally give up and head for my own room, at the far end of the west wing, I see her: like me, she's been standing outside the door, this small, trim woman in the same white slacks and purple blouse she wore the first day of school. She looks anxious, her hands working nervously as they hang by her sides. She has no intention of leaving. The bell rings, but she doesn't move.

She watches while I walk towards her. When I'm four or five feet away, she says, "Yes?"

I don't know how I know this, but I do: *yes* with a question mark after it doesn't mean yes and it doesn't mean no. It's not a statement, but neither is it a question. What it is is an opening, a space you can either fill in or choose not to.

I don't look over my shoulder to see if anybody's in the hallway behind me, and I don't glance up to check the angle of the nearest security camera, which allows Ramsey to keep an eye out for drug deals, vandalism and knife fights. What I do is eliminate the distance between us just as fast as I can.

MY FATHER NEVER LIKED THE FALL. A lot of farmers feel the same way, and even though he hadn't been one for many years, to some extent he still behaved as if he were, watching the Weather Channel like a suspense movie, tracking October cold fronts as they swooped down off the Great Plains bringing rain and, sometimes, ruination.

As much as he disliked that particular season, my mother always loved it. She never understood a thing about football but enjoyed going to the games, back when I played in high school, and I'd heard her go on and on about the wonderful aroma of burning leaves mixed with the odor of lint from the cotton gins. She even professed to like the smell of defoliant. And while most people were annoyed if they got caught behind a four-row picker on a narrow country road, creeping along at ten miles an hour, it never bothered her. Fall is the busiest time of year in the Delta, and she loved all the activity.

She hadn't often been outside in the last couple of years and not once since coming home from the rehab center back in July. But their van was equipped with a lift, and though I didn't find out about it for a couple months, sometime around the middle of October Dad began taking her out for a ride every few days.

He kept quiet because he knew if he told Jennifer or me, we'd insist he first check with her doctor, who almost certainly would have forbidden it. Sometimes her head lolled forward, some-times off to the side. If they'd had a wreck, I imagine her body would've behaved about like a rag doll's. But by then that wasn't the worst possibility Dad was facing.

The first time they left the house, it was around ten in the morning. I'd have been at school for two hours, and Jennifer would just have left to drive the twenty-eight miles to Delta State. The van—a twenty-year-old Ford Econoline that he'd repainted fire-engine red a few years ago because my mother loved that color—was the only one of its kind in town. We couldn't have mistaken him for anybody else.

That first day he drove out towards the old place. There would've been a few pickers on the road, a couple of trucks moving the pallet modules that have replaced cotton trailers, a live-haul tanker headed for the Southern Prime processing plant. I doubt that anybody waved, like everybody used to. There weren't that many folks left who even knew him.

All along, he acted as tour guide, slowing from time to time, calling attention to points of significance. Where Parker Sturdi-vant's house used to stand, a mile or so from town—now in the middle of a catfish pond. Another couple of miles down the road, the overgrown landing strip where military planes took off back in the '60s, making the house shudder. The Fairway Baptist Church, a little rundown now but still holding services just as it has every Sunday for going on eighty-five years. Not too far beyond that, the remains of the old Fairway Cross-roads gin.

Finally, inevitably, they reached sixteenth-section land and stopped across the road from the place where I grew up. As I said earlier, the house itself burned down many years ago, so there wasn't much to see besides a couple of concrete blocks standing in the tall grass near the edge of the road, a few pieces of rusty tin siding, several rotten two-by-fours and a good bit of broken glass. Otherwise, nobody driving by would've known that a home ever stood there. But he knew and, in some sense, he believed, so did she.

She lifted her head and was gazing out the window. That high-pitched keening began, and while her doctor had maintained that the tune was mostly in my father's imagination, that it was highly unlikely she could retain so many sounds in melodic succession, he believed otherwise and supplied the lyrics for her, singing along in his husky voice:

> *May I sleep in your barn tonight mister*
> *It is cold lying out on the ground*
> *And the cold north wind it is blowing*
> *And I have no place to lie down.*
>
> *Oh I have no tobacco or matches*
> *And I'm sure that I'll do you no harm.*
> *I will tell you my story kind mister*
> *For it runs through my heart like a thorn.*

Afterwards, he couldn't say how long they'd sat there. But at some point he restarted the motor and pulled off down the road. My mother was dozing, chin against chest, and didn't even wake when the van started to move.

Driving back to town, he passed the house where the Calloways used to live, at the intersection of two country roads. The backyard has never been fenced, so when you're driving by you can see what, if anything, is going on, and turning towards town you can see the north side and then the front. There's nothing very fancy about it, just a ranch-style with a carport and that little pool out back. He didn't know who lived there anymore, and I don't either, but whoever it is must have a kid or two, because there's always a trike lying in the driveway and, in the front yard, a football or basketball. The window trim could use a coat of paint, three or four shingles are missing from the roof, and the concrete's cracked in the driveway.

He recalled that there was a time when he wanted a house like this more than anything in the world. He wanted it not for himself but for Momma and me, and I believe he came to think of it as some kind of ideal, something that was out there waiting somewhere if only you could satisfy a certain set of requirements. The problem was, he could never figure out exactly what the requirements were, let alone how to meet them. I doubt it would be accurate, though, to say he had no clue.

Meeting the requirements, he must've suspected, depended on your ability to forget everything you'd learned during that period when reproving looks, raised voices and razor strops were teaching you what the differences between you and the beasts that once roamed the Delta ought to be. When you needed to relieve yourself, you couldn't squat in the middle of the kitchen and let go, as I once heard him say he had as a toddler. When your belly growled, you didn't pick up a butcher knife, plunge it into your brother's chest, cut his heart out and eat it on the porch. But when a panther's bowels grew heavy, it emptied them on the spot. When it got hungry, it found something small and defenseless, then killed and devoured it. It didn't waste time justifying itself. It drew no distinctions between need and want.

I knew from others—my grandfather, my uncles—that my father'd had a harder time than most learning to draw those distinctions, which was why authority figures like his own father and various teachers used to holler and, from time to time, administer a whipping. He'd gotten into a fair number of fights in the school yard, after somebody who didn't wear hand-me-downs made a snide remark about the length of his pants, or held his nose and said *phew!* at his approach. But eventually those lessons sank in, and back when forgetting them might have won him the keys to the house he sat looking at on that mid-October day, he couldn't.

Because in the end, he didn't want the house, or one like it, badly enough. Because what isn't yours, you don't take. For him it was really that simple.

A few days later he was driving my mother around on the other side of town, out close to Choctaw Creek. There weren't a lot of places nearby left to see, and by then he'd gotten scared to go more than fifteen or twenty miles. He wanted to drive over to the big river, pull her up on the levee and let her see it again, but he feared that was too far. His eyesight was not what it used to be—for one thing—and if something went wrong with the van out there he knew he'd have a real mess on his hands.

He also had it in his mind to show her the pool where he'd taught her to swim. I imagine he laughed when he thought about that because in reality she only knew how to for about two or three minutes. He'd taught her by doing what you'd do to a child: he pushed her in, and she flailed around, calling him words she'd never used before or since, but she managed to stay afloat. While my grandmother and I and fifteen or twenty other relatives laughed and slapped our thighs, she dog-paddled down to the shallow end, climbed out, grabbed a cup of punch and threw it in his face.

He was forty years old then, and that was forty years ago. He behaved like a boy that day. It must have seemed impossible to him now that he could've actually been one, much less acted like that on a hot afternoon, which after all was during Vietnam, when kids were coming home in boxes every day. There was plenty in his recent past that would make his heart heavy, and the future held few promises. I remember hearing him tell my mother he didn't have enough spare money to help rent the swimming pool that day, but he did it anyway, and I doubt he was ever sorry. It must have been worth twice as much to see her bound out of the water, soaking wet, and grab that cup of punch.

The house and the pool were hidden behind tall hedges, but if you stopped right at the edge of the driveway, you could at least see the sliding board, which stands at the deep end. As he eased his foot onto the brake, he glanced over to see if Momma was awake.

She was, after a fashion. Her eyes were open, anyway.

"Remember what happened here?" I can hear him asking. "How fast you got from one end of that pool to the other? Lord, you done something special. That day you could've beat Don Schollander. Hell, I bet you could've even beat old Johnny Weiss-muller."

That October afternoon, she was actually responsive. She lifted her head, he remembered later on, so he raised his hand and, when it looked like she was focused on it, pointed out the window, directing her attention towards the driveway. She might have seen it before he did: my familiar old Ford Taurus standing beside a gleaming Mercedes with a North Carolina plate.

FOR MANY YEARS, the chancery clerk in Loring County was Robert Worthington. Back in the '60s, while a member of the Citizens' Council, he wrote incendiary letters to Ellis Buchanan and the *Weekly Times*, alleging all kinds of devious behavior by black people involved in voter registration drives and those few whites like Ellis who supported them. The person he hated most, it seemed, was Charlie McGlothlan, the attorney who led the boycotts and eventually got crop dusted in front of the courthouse. In one letter, Worthington stopped just short of calling for his lynching.

By the beginning of the next decade, though, he'd experienced a change of heart. In 1972, he supported McGlothlan for the state legislature, and even though Charlie lost and never ran again, that was the first of many political campaigns on which they collaborated. When I moved back to Loring to start teaching, Worthington was one of a handful of whites who still voted Democrat beyond the local level. A delegate to the 1984 National Convention, he pledged to Walter Mondale.

Around then, Jennifer and I took a trip to the East Coast to visit battlefields and monuments and art museums, take in a few poetry readings and browse used bookstores. In Philadelphia one day, I picked up a copy of the *Inquirer*, and whose face should appear on the front page, with the Loring County Courthouse in the background, but Robert Worthington's? The article detailed how he'd gone from being an ardent foe of civil rights to a devoted champion.

There on the street, just a block or so from Constitution Hall, I got tears in my eyes. I'd never met Mr. Worthington, but that didn't matter. I knew where he was from and understood just how far he'd come, so I bought several more copies of the *Inquirer*, folded them neatly and put them in my suitcase. A couple of weeks later, when we got back home, I looked up his number and called him.

This was in the days before the Internet, so while he'd known the article was coming he hadn't seen it yet. Since I was the first person he'd heard from who'd read it, he asked me to come right over.

When I got there, he'd just made a pot of coffee and offered me a cup, which I drank at his kitchen table while he read the piece. He was about sixty then, still serving as chancery clerk, married to his high school sweetheart, a woman, he said in the article, he'd loved for forty-five years. She wasn't at home that day. As I recall, she'd gone shopping.

He was an old man who possessed no unusual gifts, as far as I could see, but he'd started his life in one world and adapted to another, and it occurred to me, sitting there watching him read, that he was the most curious kind of immigrant, one who lived right where he'd been born. When he finished and laid the paper down, I told him how I'd felt there on the street in Philadelphia. It was the first time, I said, that I'd ever been proud to come from Loring, Mississippi.

That remark seemed to take him by surprise. "Why?" he asked. "Why would this article"—he tapped the paper with a stubby finger—"make anybody proud?"

"Because you knew you were wrong," I said, "and you were man enough to change. That's a rare thing."

"Oh, son, every day somebody quits doing something he knew was wrong, for the same reason I did, and there's nothing special or heroic about it." It must have been obvious that I hadn't followed his reasoning, so he went on to explain. "I didn't tell this to that Philadelphia reporter, because I knew he couldn't understand. But I imagine you will. The truth is, I don't like black folks. Never have, never will. Now, that's a weakness of mine, and I know it. But trying to convince yourself you're right when you know you're not—well, it gets to be too goddamn much trouble, son. It's just a whole lot easier to give it up." For a minute, I thought he'd leave it at that, and I wanted him to, so I could excuse myself and escape this disappointment. Instead, he added: "If my experience's any gauge, though, I have to admit that doing right's a lot less satisfying."

Spending time with Maggie was the most satisfying thing I'd ever done, so I tried to convince myself it wasn't wrong. Jennifer, I told myself, didn't really care that much about sex anymore—the last few years offered perfect proof—but what she did care about, and what any woman would, was being treated with kindness by her husband.

Therefore, I reasoned, my involvement with another woman, at least while it lasted, might actually make our marriage happier. I started making breakfast for Jennifer, getting up before she did and brewing her tea and fixing her oatmeal. The first couple of times it happened, she was thrown into confusion. "Have you switched from coffee to tea?" she asked me, standing there in her rose-colored bathrobe with yet another thin book tucked under her arm.

"No, the tea's for you."

"Are you eating oatmeal?"

"No, that's for you, too."

I saw her glance at the wall calendar, wondering if she'd forgotten some special date, but the nineteenth of October was just another day. "All right," she said. "Thanks."

I poured a cup of coffee and sat down across the table from her, leaving the *Commercial Appeal* in its wrapper. She glanced at the book of poems—the title was a real eyepopper, *The Beauty of the Husband*—but I guess she thought it wouldn't be quite right to pick it up and start reading. "I had a pretty good class last night," she said. "There's a bunch of older people in it and they all did their assignments, which was really quite amazing. Normally, in that night class you get the dregs who put off registration until nothing else is left."

The previous afternoon I'd gone over to Maggie's for the fifth Wednesday in a row. We'd sat on her couch for a while, drinking and talking, and before long she disappeared into the hallway and returned with two photo albums. We looked at pictures of her and her husband in Japan, Argentina and Saudi Arabia. They'd even been to the Himalayas—a few shots taken in a Sherpa village, both of them soused on *rakshi*, which she said was a potato brew similar to vodka. Her husband had gray hair and a square chin, and it only dawned on me later how much he resembled Arlan Calloway.

I couldn't imagine how looking at those pictures made her feel, knowing that the man she'd spent a quarter century with was now gone, and I said so. "When he was dying," she said, "the worst part was sitting by the bed in the hospital and facing his optimism."

"He was probably better off, remaining optimistic."

"Probably. But until then he'd always been such a realist, and that's what I loved most about him. The first time he found out I'd been sleeping with another man, I cried and promised I'd never do it again, if only he'd take me back, and do you know what he said? He said, 'This is a measure of what you mean to me: I'll take you back knowing full well I will go through this again and again.' And he was right."

"And now you feel terribly guilty about it?"

"I *am* guilty. And I would be whether I felt it or not."

"Do you wish you hadn't done it?"

She shook her head. "I could say yes, but what would that be worth? I did it. It's a fact. And now I'm doing it again."

I pointed out that there was one crucial difference: she was no longer married.

"Yes," she said, "but you are. And I imagine that for whoever keeps tabs on this, it's the same thing."

"We could stop," I said, though I didn't mean it. Maybe she could, but by that point, I knew I couldn't—or wouldn't, anyway, of my own accord.

"I don't think so," she said. "Not anytime soon. We'll have to get caught and be humiliated."

After that sobering exchange, neither of us said anything for a while, and then I asked a question that had been on my mind ever since she came back with those photo albums. "You don't have any pictures of your mom, do you?"

She closed the one that was lying in her lap. Several seconds passed before she made a sound, and when she did it was just to heave a deep sigh.

"What?" I said.

"I knew when I went to get the albums that you were going to ask. But then you didn't, and I'd just about decided you wouldn't after all."

"Look, if you don't want to go there, it's all right. Forget it."

"Oh, but I already am there. Or I guess I should say I'm already *here*."

"Please," I said, as she got up off the couch and gathered up the albums, "really, just let it go."

She went off down the hallway, leaving me sitting there feeling like a member of the paparazzi or, worse yet, a plain old voyeur. A few moments later she returned with a frayed manila folder, sat down beside me and opened it, and there stood Nadine Calloway, in black and white, eye to eye with an enormous dark-colored horse whose nose had a lighter streak down the middle. Her left hand was reaching out to pet it, and her mouth was open as if she were talking to it. Her dress had padded shoulders and a cinch around the waist.

My throat felt constricted. I was afraid that when I spoke, my voice would come out as a croak.

Maggie saved me the trouble. "As you can see," she said, "I don't look anything like her. If I thought I did, we wouldn't be where we are. I don't want to be a substitute for someone else. Not even my mother."

My voice was actually more like a squeak. *"What?"*

"You always had such a crush on her," she said. "It was worse than most little-boy crushes, and I sometimes wondered how it made your mother feel. I guess it didn't bother her, though, because she adored my mom. Everybody did."

"You aren't a substitute for anybody," I said, "and nobody could take your place." I spoke without thinking, saying what I believed the moment called for, and it wasn't until later that I realized I'd inadvertently told the truth. She'd created a desire nobody else would ever satisfy. When she went back to North Carolina—and I reminded myself every day that she eventually would—she wouldn't leave behind a hole. She'd leave a bloody wound.

She pulled off the top snapshot and quickly showed me the two underneath. In the first, her mother had stepped away from the horse but was still looking at it, her head cocked slightly to the side, her right hand shading her eyes. In the second, they'd turned away from each other, the horse's left foreleg a foot or so off the ground, beginning to bend, and her mother's right hand was raised, thumb in the air, seemingly gesturing backwards at the horse. It looked as if she was speaking to the photographer, since she was staring right at the camera and her lips had formed a word. Whoever was taking the pictures had stepped farther back before snapping the last one. You could see a wooden post and a couple strands of wire between the lens and Nadine.

"That's an electric fence," I said. "See this little white thing there?" I pointed with my fingertip. "That's a porcelain insulator."

"A little electricity never scared her. I remember that she crawled under it, dress and all."

"What was the occasion?"

"She wanted my father to buy that horse."

"I don't recall your having one."

"We didn't. He said no. Then he laughed and offered to get her a riding mower instead."

"Whose horse was it?"

"Just one she saw beside the road. Somewhere nearby. I've thought several times in the last few weeks that I recognized the spot. But lots of things look different now with all these fish ponds where the cotton used to be."

She put the snapshots back in the same order, then closed the folder. When she looked at me, there was no missing the moisture in her eyes. "Satisfied?"

"Sure. Thanks for letting me see them. I guess I overstepped a boundary by asking."

"Well, we're stepping over every boundary we can find. What's the harm in one more?"

She carried the file back down the hallway, and left it wherever she kept such things, and when she came back we grilled a couple of steaks and ate dinner in her kitchen, drinking a bottle of the best French wine I'd ever tasted. I asked her where she'd gotten it, and she said she'd gone to Memphis on Saturday and bought it at Wild Oats. When we finished, we dumped the dishes in the sink and then she said, "Would you like to go upstairs?"

While I made love with a woman who'd driven one hundred seventy-five miles in search of better wine than she could find in Loring, my wife was feeling happy because she finally had a few students who'd read the essays she'd assigned and turned their work in on time.

The next morning, when I thought about that I was so moved that I reached across the breakfast table and laid my hand on Jennifer's. She flinched. "What?"

"I love you."

"Oh," she said, "is that right?"

"Yes," I said, "that's right."

"Okay." She gave my hand a little squeeze.

She finished her oatmeal, and while I showered she went into the study and was sitting at the computer, staring hard at the screen, when I left the house. I don't think she even heard me say goodbye.

THAT AFTERNOON, I went over to stay with Momma so Dad could go see the doctor, who thought they might need to change the dosage on his blood pressure medication. Before leaving, he told me that when election day rolled around he was going to cast his ballot for Bennie Thompson, our seven-term congressman, who happens to be black. He added that he still loathed the Democrats for wanting to take his guns and thinking higher taxes would solve every problem, but he couldn't forgive the Republicans for the big mess in Iraq.

Momma was asleep, so I sat there in the recliner thinking about a book I'd read several years ago that had been on my mind, *An American Insurrection: James Meredith and the Battle of Oxford, Mississippi, 1962*. At the time, I was struck by the fine job William Doyle does of conveying the hysteria that prevailed in the state in the days before Meredith finally flew into Oxford aboard a government plane and was escorted onto campus by Deputy Attorney General Nicholas Katzenbach and a team of U.S. marshals.

About halfway through the book there's an account of a speech delivered by JFK on the evening of Sunday, September 30. Preempting regular network programming, he issued an appeal for calm, telling the people of Mississippi that "the eyes of the nation and of the world are upon you and upon all of us, and the honor of your university and the state are in the balance."

The first response an oral historian usually gets from any-body being interviewed is "I can't remember much of anything about that." But if you start providing the subject with details about the times or events that interest you—even the most trivial information, like, say, the absence of sugar in Coca-Cola in 1943, when it was being reserved for troops, or the flimsiness of the paper Sears, Roebuck printed its catalogs on that same year—it's amazing what else starts to emerge. The brain stores information in a peculiar fashion, and sometimes a momentous recollection is tangled up in the seemingly mundane.

When I read Doyle's account of that speech, I remembered something I hadn't thought about in years: being hustled off to bed after the president spoke, my mother bending over me and telling me not to worry, though she sounded worried herself. A few moments earlier, right after JFK went off and Ed Sullivan came on, my dad had left the house with the Colt Python tucked under his belt.

What happened that night at Ole Miss would almost cer-tainly never have occurred but for the groups of armed men, most lacking any connection whatsoever to the university, who drove into Oxford to try to keep the federal government from enrolling a black student. Somewhere, in the part of the mind that most of us learn to shut down, I'd always wondered if my father was among their number. But I never asked him about it. There are plenty of white guys like me in Mississippi who don't know what their fathers did during the civil rights era, because they don't want to know. They'll ask about World War II and feel themselves aggrandized when they hear how their dads stormed Omaha Beach with the First Infantry Division or treaded water for twelve hours in the Leyte Gulf, waiting for Bull Halsey's flagship to pick them up. Having a father from the Greatest Generation is one thing. Knowing he was a member of the Citizens' Council is quite another.

And it's something else altogether to wonder why he left the house with a gun on the night that a neighbor—who'd been his friend since childhood, though he'd recently announced plans to take his land—killed his own wife.

When Dad came home from the doctor, he hung his hat on the coatrack in the hallway and walked into the kitchen to get a drink of water. He must have heard me enter the room behind him, but he didn't turn around.

"How'd it go?" I asked.

"He says I'm doing all right for an old coot."

"Great," I said. "By the way, Dad, I read a book a few years ago about James Meredith and Ole Miss, which got me thinking back on what I remember. And I've been going over it again in the last few days."

He turned the glass up and drained it. It clinked when he set it down.

"I remember hearing JFK speak, and having to go to bed, and it seems to me that right before Momma tucked me in, you left the house. Is that right? Or did I make it up?"

He placed both hands flat against the countertop on either side of the sink. He was wearing a light blue long-sleeved shirt with the sleeves rolled up, the back dark from sweat, even though the day was cool. "I was out looking after your interests," he said.

"*My* interests? What would those be?"

He turned around then, and for once he didn't stoop, just stood straight and tall, towering over me as he had when I was a boy. "You wouldn't have understood it then," he said, "and you won't understand it now, so I don't intend to waste my time trying to explain. But I'll tell you this: the answer won't never be found in no book."

Local History

ELLIS BUCHANAN had a drink in his hand. He was standing in front of our CD rack, scanning titles, every now and then pulling out a disc. Most of them failed to win his approval. "Now this gentleman," he said, tapping a jewel case, "has an unusual name. *Kaukonen*. Rhymes with *Salonen*." He peered at me over his wire rims. "And there, I imagine, all resemblance ceases."

I didn't know anybody named Salonen but guessed he was some classical composer. "Jorma Kaukonen founded Hot Tuna and also played with the Jefferson Airplane," I said. "He was one of my heroes when I was a boy."

He put the CD back on the shelf. "You're just a boy now. Otherwise your taste would be more refined. A man ages like wine."

"Wine doesn't age well if it's made from poor grapes."

"You come from good grapes. At the moment you're still too sweet, but you'll sour in due time."

It was Saturday night and we'd asked him over for dinner, along with Ramsey and Selina Coleman and, at the last minute, Maggie.

Inviting her was my idea. These days, I can't even begin to imagine what was going through my mind when I told Jennifer I wanted to include the new French teacher. And an act of the imagination would be required, because the man who made that decision, whatever went into it, no longer exists. You could write a biography about him, but the facts would take you only so far.

By the time she rang the doorbell, the rest of us were sitting in the living room, sipping wine, listening to Louis Armstrong and chatting about the upcoming congressional elections, all of us agreeing that Bennie Thompson was a shoo-in and the Democrats had a shot at controlling both houses. Jennifer got up to let her in and for a moment they stood framed in the doorway, my wife in brown slacks and a beige blouse, a red-and-blue apron cinched at her waist with OLE MISS MOM scrolled across the front, and Maggie in black jeans, a black sweater and high heels, a purple scarf draped around her shoulders.

"You must be Maggie."

"And you're Jennifer."

"Can I take your handbag?"

"Sure. And this scarf, too, if you don't mind."

I took my time getting up. "Maggie," I said, "I don't think you've met Selina."

"No. I haven't had the pleasure."

Selina used to be beautiful, but she's put on a good bit of weight in the last few years, and the cushions sighed when she rose off the couch. "A pleasure's just what it is," she said, taking Maggie's hand. "I've got a cousin who teaches at Duke, in early childhood education. Endesha Reedy. I don't suppose you know her?"

"I'm afraid not. Most of the people I know there are either in the Sanford Institute or the Department of Romance Studies."

When Ellis meets a woman for the first time, he rises so fast you can hear his bones pop. They sure popped that night. "This is Ellis Buchanan," I told her. "He edited our local newspaper for about thirty years and stirred up lots of trouble. These days he mostly stirs his drink."

"As lies go," Ellis said, "that one's in the bald-faced category. I don't drink anything that has to be stirred."

He offered her his hand, and she took it and held on to it. "Not even coffee?" she asked.

"Most certainly not coffee. Dear, do you know what caffeine does to a person's metabolism?"

"Speeds it up?"

"No, though that's a popular misconception. Research shows that it actually causes it to slow."

"Whose research?"

"Mine."

He was looking down at her, and she was looking up at him, right into his eyes, each of them apparently so focused on the other that for a moment it was as if the rest of us had left the room. I was used to seeing Jennifer look at him that way, and back when I was his intern the two high school girls who helped deliver papers gave him the same rapt attention, though he was almost fifty.

"I'll bet Luke would pour you a glass of wine if you asked him," he finally said.

"I'll pour you several glasses. As many as you want."

She let go of his hand. "One will do," she said. "I'd hate to show my greed the first time at a new place."

The main course was lamb rubbed with mint and basil. Jennifer chose to roast it, rather than trust me to grill it, given how many dinners I'd burned in the past. My lack of zeal for cooking was one of the things that had come between us. She had little tolerance for bad food, and before Candace and Trish became adept in the kitchen, she'd often come home from a long day at work to find frozen French fries stinking up the place while I read in the backyard with weenies burning on the grill.

Late that afternoon, after popping the lamb in the oven, she'd gone to the mailbox and plopped a wad of stuff, mostly junk mail, on the kitchen counter. A few minutes later, while making myself a cup of coffee, I glanced down and noticed she'd gotten a letter from *Tin House*, one of the journals she subscribed to, and the envelope had been opened. Her name and address had been typed, so it didn't look like a renewal notice.

She was sitting there at the table, drinking a cup of tea and reading the *Commercial Appeal*, and her cheeks had more color in them than I'd seen for a long time. They were glowing.

"Did you get a poem accepted?"

She raised the cup and took a sip, then swallowed and set it back down, her eyes not once leaving the paper. "Actually, they took three."

"And you didn't tell me?"

"I didn't know you'd be that interested."

"Are you serious? Three poems at once?"

"Well, it happens like that sometimes. Until now, it just never happened for me."

I walked over and put my arm around her and was amazed, once again, at how small and brittle her bones were. She felt breakable. "That's a great outfit, too, isn't it?"

"Yes," she said, "I'm afraid so."

Now, sitting opposite her at one end of our dining room table, with Maggie and Ellis on one side and Ramsey and Selina on the other, I considered her response. She'd just experienced her greatest success. What was there to be afraid of? The only answer I could come up with was that she probably feared she'd never succeed again.

I'd recently noticed how poorly I understood her. Having convinced myself that I knew what Maggie wanted—passion and excitement—I still couldn't fathom what Jennifer's hopes were, beyond the urge to see her poems in print and get her daughters through college so she could quit that onerous job at Delta State. She was as much a puzzle to me as the poems she wrote, which often were impenetrable.

The meal she'd prepared was her second great success of the day, drawing compliments from everybody and a request from Selina for the recipe. Jennifer promised to e-mail it, and Maggie asked if she could send it to her as well. While I watched, she wrote her address on the back of a business card Jennifer handed her, then said they should go out for coffee one of these days. Rather than get sick at that prospect, I actually felt the warm glow of pride.

We'd finished the lamb and started on our salads when Ramsey thought of something he said he'd meant to ask earlier: "That institute you mentioned up at Duke, Maggie? Was it named for Terry Sanford?"

She nodded. "The full title is the Terry Sanford Institute for Public Policy."

"He was one fine man," Ramsey said. "Ask me, he was about as good a person as you could find in the South at that time. I bet you'd agree with that assessment, wouldn't you, Ellis?"

I was sure Ellis admired Sanford. He admired all the great Southern liberals—folks like Hugo Black, Lister Hill and Maury Maverick—so it surprised me when he frowned and said, "Not entirely."

It surprised Ramsey, too. "No?"

"He could afford the positions he took on race, Ramsey," Ellis said, "because he knew the tobacco industry would do everything in its power to keep him in office—and in North Carolina, if you had Philip Morris and R. J. Reynolds behind you, that was about all that really mattered. My wife died of lung cancer, and Sanford moved heaven and earth to keep the surgeon general's warning off cigarette packs. The line of his I'll always remember is, 'We don't label automobiles dangerous, though they're one of the greatest killers.' I wouldn't be too quick to grant him sainthood."

Maggie speared a shred of lettuce. "Who *would* you grant sainthood?"

"Well," I interrupted, "I'd nominate Ellis himself."

"Oh, I'm far from saintly," he said.

I laughed. "Bullshit. Saints are associated with miracles, and it's miraculous you managed to survive the Sixties. Any number of people in this town would've liked to kill you." I assumed everybody could tell I was joking.

And everybody could, except him. "I never *performed* any miracles," he said.

"Tell us something you did," Maggie said, "that wasn't saintly. What was your Philip Morris moment?"

Ellis has never been at a loss for words. He'd fired fusillades of them at Ross Barnett, Byron de la Beckwith, Clinton Finley and the Citizens' Council, even though it was not unreasonable to fear they might fire back with something more than rhetoric. But that night he just sat there stiffly, staring at a spot somewhere to the left of Selina's head.

To fill the uncomfortable silence, I said, "Speaking of unique moments, here's one. This afternoon, Jennifer had not one but three poems accepted by *Tin House*, one of the best magazines in the country."

That lifted Ellis out of whatever dark mood he'd lapsed into. "My God, child," he said. "And you managed to keep quiet about this all evening?"

"I was going to give you a copy when it comes out. They said I'll be in the spring issue, right around your birthday."

He lifted his wineglass and proposed a toast, and after we'd all had a sip he said, "You need to bear in mind that I'm nearly eighty. When spring comes, you might well be composing my epitaph. So why don't you go get those poems and read them for us right now?"

Her cheeks were about the color of the Cabernet we'd been drinking, and she shook her head, but by then a chorus was demanding that she read to us before dessert. Finally, she got up, went into the study and came back with a single sheet of paper. "All right," she said, "here's one of them." She sat down, took another swallow of wine, then began reading.

> *The sea of sleep has cast me out again*
> *With a stone around my neck*
> *The pale dawn seeps through the blinds*
> *Raindrops slice at the window panes*
>
> *Light hurts, sound hurts, silence hurts*
> *I have wrapped myself in pain*
> *Each day an open wound*
> *Words won't disentangle from my brain*
> *My scream stays stuck in my throat*
>
> *I must wean myself from this body*
> *Let it turn to stone, let it drown*
> *I'll be weightless, echoless*
> *Thin smoke drifting over sand*

For a moment, nobody said anything. I, for one, didn't know what to say, but then I've never felt comfortable commenting on her work. And this poem seemed so relentlessly dark I was stunned.

"Goddamn, Jennifer," Ramsey said. "You got a lot of pain packed into that thing. Must've used the word *hurt* at least three or four times."

Selina just sat there looking embarrassed.

Ellis said it seemed fragmented to him, like a lot of contemporary poetry, but he liked the imagery and thought the poem as a whole was very well executed.

As for Maggie, she reached across the table, touched Jennifer on the wrist and said, "I've felt like that myself. Though I could never express it so beautifully."

"Well, it's a persona poem," Jennifer said, as if to preempt the suggestion that those emotions were actually hers.

"I know it is," Maggie said, still touching her wrist. "And there have been a great many days when that persona was mine."

"Mine, too," Ramsey said. "Last summer, when my French teacher drifted off like gin smoke over tall cotton—man, I felt like I had a stone around my *own* neck. And then here comes Maggie to save my worried ass."

Everybody laughed, and before long we were toasting Jennifer once more, then raising our glasses to *Tin House*, Ole Miss, Duke University, Walt Whitman, Bennie Thompson, Thurgood Marshall and Maury Maverick.

It's fitting, isn't it, that this particular evening should end on an image?

We all said our goodbyes, exchanging drunken embraces, the one Maggie gave me punctuated by her fingernails digging into the small of my back. I told Jennifer I'd handle the dishes, and she said okay, she was whipped anyway, and went off to bed. I toted plates and glasses, cups, saucers and silverware into the kitchen, then gave everything a good rinse and stacked it all in the dishwasher. You lose track of time when you're drunk—I do, anyway—but I'm sure a good fifteen or twenty minutes passed before I punched the button to start the wash and turned out the kitchen light.

The last thing I do every night is check the front door. I've been doing it as long as I can remember, all the way back to childhood, even though I knew my dad had already locked up. This night I checked the dead bolt and lock chain and then, for no reason I can name, pressed my eye to the peephole.

The Mercedes was parked on the opposite side of the street, the lights off, with no sound of an idling engine, no exhaust visible from the tailpipe. Gradually my eyes adjusted to the dark and I could make out her silhouette. While I watched, she brought her hands to her face. A flame flickered and disappeared. There was just a single pinpoint of light, the orange glow of a cigarette between the lips of a woman who doesn't smoke.

"SOMETIMES THINGS JUST HAPPEN."

My father said that with perfect equanimity, without the slightest trace of anger or exertion, though when he spoke those words he was holding me a couple feet off the ground while I beat the air with my fists and tried to kick him, his right arm wrapped around my chest like a piece of steel.

The muley-headed Jersey my grandfather called Mollie stood some distance away, in front of the pump house, where he'd kept the grain he fed her and the other cows. He'd owned three, and except during the winter, when he drove them into the barn at night, they were always in the pasture behind the house.

This was around the time the USDA declared fresh milk unsanitary and I began drinking it from cartons that my mother bought in town. Grandpa never made the transition, and it wasn't purely a question of economics. When I asked him why he went to so much trouble—getting up early to milk them, toting the bucket inside, straining the liquid through cloth cut from an old flour sack—he smiled and said, "Fresh cow milk'll put lead in your pencil." I couldn't see the connection between milk and lead pencils, but he just laughed and said that one day I would.

My father had grabbed me because a few moments earlier, he'd returned from the funeral home and caught me shooting Mollie with my BB gun. The first time I hit her, she just stepped to the side, as if she'd barely felt it, and this enraged me. I got a little closer and tried to shoot her in the face but missed three or four times in a row, then went back to shooting her in the flank, where I'd have a broader target. After five or six BBs pinged her, she began to snort and toss her head.

I didn't hear my dad drive up, didn't hear the truck door slam, didn't know why suddenly the BB gun lay on the ground where I'd been standing. "Easy," he said. "Shooting that poor animal won't bring your grandpa back."

"I don't care," I hollered. "Somebody's got to pay."

"She's not a somebody. She's a something. And making her pay won't do a bit of good."

A few days earlier, my grandfather had gone out to feed the cows and discovered that Mollie had somehow nosed open the latch on the pump house, dragged a burlap sack out and eaten every last bit of grain. Then, for good measure, she relieved herself on it.

This was undoubtedly what made him mad enough to haul off and kick her. The problem was that she moved and he missed, and the next thing he knew he was lying on his back, all the wind gone from his lungs, his leg turning purple and growing hot. Though he didn't know it at the time and managed to make it home under his own power and return to the field the following day, he'd dislodged a blood clot that had formed in his leg. It was headed straight for his heart.

When I finally got tired and quit thrashing, my dad let me down but kept pressing my body against his. "Sometimes things just happen," he said again, as if they'd happened to him over and over. "It may be like the song says—that we'll understand it all in the sweet bye and bye—but right now there ain't no point in wondering why. Your grandpa's dead, and poor old Mollie here's alive."

. . . .

Sometimes things just happen.

It's an unexceptional statement but one that a child has diffi-
culty processing, because it contradicts almost everything else
he's been told by those whose wisdom he depends on. I parroted
it back once myself, when I was about twelve years old and had
brought home a report card showing that I'd made a D in math.
My dad demanded to know how this could possibly have
occurred, since until then I'd never made less than an A. The
truth was that I'd become fixated on a girl, Audrey, who sat
directly in front of me, and I spent most class periods passing her notes. But you can't tell your dad about anything that
foolish, so I said, "Sometimes things just happen." And he, perhaps recalling that moment near the pump house, said, "Yeah,
they do. But it's my job to make sure they don't happen to
you." Then he picked up the phone, called my teacher, learned of
my distraction, and the next day I was moved to a different
desk.

It might be my imagination, but it seems to me now that
when Dad first made that observation, I'd already heard it once
before, on the morning I learned Nadine Calloway had been
killed. But he hadn't said it then—if, in fact, anyone had.

Certainly somebody said something. Somebody would've had
to. And it's reasonable to think it was my mother. Because, after
all, it was the first of October, which in 1962 fell on a Monday. In
other words, I had to attend school. And there was cotton in the
field—not a lot, never enough—so my dad would've been out
there with my grandfather, who was still alive at the time.

News would have traveled the way it always did. Somebody
driving into town would've passed the Calloways' house and
seen three cars from the Loring County Sheriff's Department
parked in the yard. These days she'd speed right by, because we
now behave like people in most other parts of the country. Misery is all around us, and we're sophisticated enough to ignore it.
But in 1962 curiosity runs unchecked. What's happening at the

neighbors' house is your business, too. So she parks on the side of the road and walks over to the deputy who's standing by the mailbox smoking a cigarette and asks him straight up what's wrong. He glances towards the house, then drops his voice. "Don't tell nobody I told you. But last night Arlan Calloway shot his wife."

"Did he kill her?"

"He sure did. He sure by God did."

She can't even remember, this neighbor, why she wanted to go to town in the first place. It's too early anyway, all the stores are still closed, so she turns around and drives home and pounces on the phone. She calls somebody who then calls somebody else. While the rest of the country is discussing Ole Miss, where two people lie dead and the air stinks of teargas, the phone lines in Loring are singing a tragedy of a strictly local nature.

At this point in my life you have to drag me out of bed. So that morning Mother draws the covers off me, grabs my feet and swings them off the mattress, wraps her arms around my shoulders and pulls me upright. She's still holding me as I sleepwalk to the bathroom, where I sit down on the side of the tub while she fills the sink with warm, soapy water. She soaks a bathcloth in it, then starts washing my face and hands, and that's when the telephone rings.

"Stay here," she says. Her footsteps recede down the hall, and I lean towards the pedestal and rest my forehead against the cool porcelain. I'm still in that position when she returns.

"Honey," she says, "something terrible's happened, and there's no point in keeping it from you because you'll hear about it anyway."

I assume it's got to do with the trouble up in Oxford, with the speech the president gave last night, and I don't care one bit. Whatever happened there has nothing to do with me. It's one hundred fifty miles away and might as well be the moon.

"Arlan shot Nadine," she says, wiping her eyes with the back of her hand. "And honey, I'm afraid she's dead."

Death is something I know about in theory. Dogs and cats die—you see them all the time on the side of the road, stiff limbs splayed away from their bodies—and all the great Civil War heroes are dead, people like Robert E. Lee and James Longstreet. Two of my grandparents are dead, but that's all right because I never even knew them. The folks out at Loring Memorial Gardens are dead, too. But Nadine has been teaching me to dribble and is going to take me to the gym and show me how to shoot a free throw. And she can't be dead because you can't shoot free throws like that.

For a moment I think I'll cry because she's way too nice for that to happen to her. But that moment's soon submerged in a sea of excitement: I know a dead person. She's dead, and when I get to school I can be the one to tell about it. Because surely Eugene and Maggie won't be there today. They'll have to stay at home, so the story belongs to me.

Mother's little man takes a stand before the sink, wide awake now. "Why did Mr. Calloway shoot her?"

"What?" Wiping her eyes didn't accomplish much. They're red and her face is wet.

"I said why did Mr. Calloway shoot her?"

"Oh, honey, I don't know."

"When will we find out?"

"We might not. Sometimes things just happen and you never get to know why."

This is the most preposterous thing I've ever heard. What do we study in school if not *why*? There's a reason why one and one make two, and why the rain falls, and why we call this color green and that one blue. Sometimes things just happen? That just won't do.

"He had to have a reason," the six-year-old sage replies, with what he hopes is a tone of derision. "You don't shoot a person just for fun."

Sometimes things just happen.

Sometimes you step out the front door, as you have countless times before, but for some reason the world looks different. And because of that, you see everything in a new light and notice what might otherwise have escaped your attention.

For instance: directly across the street from your house, in the very spot where the previous evening a red Mercedes was parked for God knows how long, you see a single cigarette butt. For all you know, cigarette butts might've been lying there every morning for the past month. There's a drain nearby, so when it rains anything on the pavement's going to be washed away, just like this butt will in a day or so, when the next big cold front blows through.

Wondering what she saw when she sat there, you assume she was looking at your house, waiting for the lights to go out, and you try to fathom what her feelings would've been when the last window went dark. That's what's on your mind when you bend over in your driveway, as you do every Sunday morning, to pick up the *Commercial Appeal*.

And that's when you think, once again, about the man who used to deliver that paper in the middle of the night before going in to Parker Sturdivant's barbershop to cut hair. He might get drunk on Saturday evening and bring the Sunday paper late, but the last thing he'd want on Sunday night was a drink, and the Monday paper was always there long before the first farmer got up to eat breakfast.

LIKE ALL THE OTHER public schools in Mississippi, Loring High designates two dates—one in the fall, one in the spring—for staff training in behavior management techniques. We call these staff-development days, or SDDs. Students get to stay home while we have to listen to a lecture from a police officer about what to do if somebody opens fire in the classroom. "Should that come to pass, y'all need to duck." After that we watch a video collage gleaned from Ramsey's surveillance cameras, with cuts and additions from one semester to the next, showing various drug transactions, a couple of slow-motion knife fights and—the concluding scene now for more than five years—a kid called Bobby Street, nicknamed Main, unzipping and shooting a stream of urine into a rival gang member's locker. This event led to a full-scale lockdown and the arrest of more than fifteen students, and as the episode plays out on-screen Ramsey always intones, "Some actions are best performed in the restroom." Then everybody can go home.

It's a colossal waste of time, of course, but you can get on Ramsey's bad side by calling in sick on an SDD. Nevertheless, the Monday after we'd celebrated Jennifer's success over dinner, I left the house while she was still in the study and phoned the school as I drove down our street and told the secretary I had a bad cold. A few minutes after eight, by which time I knew Maggie would be at the police lecture, I left her a voice-mail saying the same thing and that I'd gone to the drugstore and picked up some NyQuil and was going back to bed.

The previous afternoon, while sitting in the car outside Wal-Mart, I'd placed a call to a number over in Arkansas. The man who answered had one of those raspy voices that only a lifetime of smoking and drinking earns you. I told him who I was and waited to see if my name meant anything to him, but it didn't seem to. So I asked if he was the same Andy Owens who used to cut hair at Sturdivant's Barbershop in Loring, Mississippi, back in the early '60s. And when he said he was, I served up my lie.

Andrew Owens, no middle initial, aged seventy-seven, lived about five miles south of Pine Bluff, some distance west of U.S. 65. He'd told me on the phone there were several other mobile homes on his road and that few of the mailboxes had numbers on them. But I'd be at the right place, he said, when I saw a trailer with a rusty garbage barrel near the front steps.

I finally found it, got out and rapped on the door.

Within seconds it swung open. "Come on in," that raspy voice said.

He was bald and bent, with a hugely wrinkled face and a bulbous nose, and he wore a pair of glasses with black plastic frames and thick lenses. The front of his shirt was soiled, most likely by tobacco spit. "Say I used to cut your hair?" he asked, squinting at me.

He looked only vaguely like the man I remembered. That Andy, even if you saw him slumped over the wheel of his truck after spending the night with Jim Beam, had a thick growth of hair and always wore a clean, fresh-smelling shirt. He was well built, too, with prominent shoulders that suggested he once might have been a good football player. "Yes sir," I said. "You sure did."

"I do a good job?"

"The best."

"Looks like you might could use a trim right now."

"Yes sir, I guess that's a fair assessment."

"Parker never could cut hair worth a shit. He only did it so's he'd have somebody to run his mouth to. Said your name's Mark?"

"Luke."

"Knew it was one of the disciples. Woke up thinkin' if it wasn't Mark, it might've been John. Knew it wasn't Philip nor Andrew, neither, me being an Andrew myself. Didn't reckon it could've been Judas. Folks generally don't name their kids that." He gestured at the counter separating the living room from the kitchen. It was covered by whiskey bottles—Evan Williams, Ancient Age, Black Velvet. All of them were the 1.75 liter size, and most looked empty. "Like a drink?"

At ten a.m.? "I better decline," I said, "since I've got to drive back."

"Don't reckon you'd mind if I was to have one."

"No sir. Go ahead and help yourself."

"You can sit over yonder," he said, nodding at a lumpy sofa, above which a framed newspaper article hung askew. "Get yourself comfortable, if you can."

I walked over to the couch and scanned the article. In 1967, the Pine Bluff Chamber of Commerce had named the best service providers in various categories, listing Andrew Owens as "Top Barber." The article said he owned the Lake Side Barbershop. As I sat down, I heard him splash whiskey into a cup. It was what bartenders call a long pour.

He dragged a chair away from the kitchen table that had plastic decals plastered all over the top of the backrest. I noticed that they were everywhere: on his walls, on the kitchen cabinets, even on the coffee table. SUNOCO RACE FUELS, BASS PRO SHOPS, PERMA-COOL, RED LINE. "Like my decals?" he asked.

"Impressive," I said. "Looks like you've got a few hundred."

"That's my hobby. There's folks tells me you can buy 'em by the pack on the computer, but I never fooled with nothin' like that. I come by mine honest. I see one I like, I buy it. I don't want nobody else choosin' for me. Understand, my sister'll send me one from time to time. But she's got a handle on my taste." He took a big swig, then wiped his mouth on his forearm. "I drink too much," he said. "Always have. If I cut your hair back at Parker's, I don't reckon that'll surprise you."

"Actually," I said, "the main thing I remember is that us kids fell all over ourselves trying to jump in your chair and stay out of Mr. Sturdivant's. That's what made me think of you. This project of mine that I mentioned, it'll be looking at how businesses developed in the Delta, roughly from the end of World War Two until the beginning of the twenty-first century. And if I'm right about it, you had two jobs, so I thought you could tell me a little bit about both. You used to deliver the *Commercial Appeal*, didn't you?"

The look that came over his face was one I'd seen a lot of back when I was doing interviews for my Depression-era oral history project. It would appear on the faces of people who'd accepted their own insignificance as a given and were startled to learn that anybody else thought otherwise. "I sure enough *did*," he said. "Started deliverin' it just before Christmas of Fifty-eight and kept at it till I moved over here."

"And when exactly was that?"

"December of Sixty-two."

I pulled out a pen and the small notebook I'd bought at a convenience store in Dumas. "December of Sixty-two?"

"Yessiree."

I wrote the date in my pad. "What made you leave Loring, if you don't mind my asking?"

"Don't mind at all. I finally got my hands on a little bit of money and decided to go into business for myself. They had a shop over here for sale. I done real good for a long time." He pointed at the article on the wall above my head. "I noticed you taking a look at that," he said.

"Top barber in Pine Bluff. That doesn't surprise me one bit."

"To be a good barber, the main thing you got to do is *listen.* You got to hear a man out when he tells you how he wants his hair cut, then you got to figure out how to make it look just a tad better than he imagined. That's why Parker never was no good. Only person he ever listened to was hisself." He took another slug. "Way things worked out over here, though, I finally run into debt and had to sell the place. Wasn't because I didn't do a good job. Even drunk I cut hair just fine, didn't nick nobody's ear or nothin' like that, but there's some folks that don't care for the smell of whiskey. I spent the next twenty-five years workin' in a chemical plant. Around there, it stunk so bad nobody could smell the fumes comin' off me."

I used to love how he smelled and suddenly felt like I needed to say so, and did.

He laughed. "That was talcum powder you smelled on me," he said. "See, I'd rub a little bit of it into my hands after I washed 'em—and maybe you didn't notice, but I always washed my hands after each and every haircut. That's just standard practice, but you'd be surprised how many folks get in a hurry and quit doin' it. You remember what it was like on Saturday morning at Sturdivant's?"

"Yes sir," I said. "Sometimes it seemed like half the town was in there."

"Absolutely. And old Parker'd come in with fertilizer on his hands, grab them clippers and set to work on folks' heads. If you'd dropped a few cotton seeds on their scalps, they'd of took root."

I posed several questions about Sturdivant's, asking how many haircuts he'd give in an average week, whether or not the price changed dramatically during the time he worked there, how often he had to renew his license and what that cost, how frequently his clippers had to be replaced. I hadn't come to get answers to any of them, yet they were interesting in and of themselves, and I noted each one in my pad. Then I said, "Now could I get you to talk a little bit about the paper route?"

"You sure enough could. Let me just get another little drink." He got up, poured himself another one and sat back down. "What you want to know?"

"Well, to begin with, do you remember how many subscribers you had?"

"Seems like by the time I moved away, I must've had close to three hundred. Where you say you lived?"

"Out near Fairway Crossroads. James May's my father."

"Tall, skinny fellow that liked a crew cut?"

"Yes sir. That was him."

"His hair, unless I misremember it, was naturally oily. Some fellows, you put your hands in their hair and it's like dippin' 'em in Crisco. Nothin' they can do about it, that's just how it goes, and washin' it all the time just makes it worse. Anyhow, when it come to the paper route, Fairway wasn't but a small part of the picture for me. See, I had all the folks that subscribed on Route Two, but I had them that lived on Route One as well. My territory stretched from south of Choctaw Creek all the way up to the county line. Now, you may not know it but there was a little bit of a war goin' on in them years between the *Commercial Appeal* and that rag down in Jackson."

"The *Clarion-Ledger*?"

"Yes indeed. And when I started, the guy delivered that Jackson paper had the edge."

"Do you remember who that was?"

"Fellow name of Buzz Dirken. *Buzz* was short for *Buzzard*, and they called him that because he looked like one. Now, he didn't have my main liability, because he never took a drink in his life, but he couldn't throw worth a damn. See, folks don't want their paper wet and they don't want it muddy and they sure as God don't want it hittin' the front door like a goddamn brick at two or three in the mornin'. He pitched 'em in the ditch, under folks's trucks, even throwed one right through somebody's window one night. Time I quit, I had old Buzzard beat to shit."

"If I recall right," I said, "the barbershop opened pretty early every day, didn't it?"

"Nine a.m. And I never unlocked the door late one time. Not one damn time."

"Yet you delivered those papers in the middle of the night. So what was a typical day like for you back then? Did you ever sleep?"

"Well, I closed up every day at five, so I'd head on home, usually have a drink or two—never more than three or four, except come Saturday—and then I'd lay down about seven or seven-thirty and sleep till twelve-thirty or one. Get up, have a little coffee and eat me somethin', and I'd be waiting at the bus station when that Greyhound dropped 'em off. Sometimes the bus was a little early, sometimes a little late, but I'd usually throw the first paper around two or two-fifteen. Most days I'd pull back into my own yard by five o'clock. Jump out, run in and lay down on the couch, grab two or three hours and start all over."

I couldn't help but express amazement that he'd borne up under that kind of schedule. "How'd you survive doing that for five years?" I asked. "A week would plumb kill me."

Is there anything more beautiful than a smile on a time-ravaged face? "Them was the best years of my life," he said. "I couldn't wait to start my day. I loved cuttin' hair and I loved bein' by myself late at night throwin' papers. My drinkin' hadn't got out of control yet, my wife hadn't left me, and I still had my dream. See, I'd always wanted to own my own shop. I had a goal, you know what I'm sayin'?"

I did—even though it'd been a long time since I had any specific personal ambition myself. If you'd asked me to identify the exact moment I lost it, I wouldn't have been able to. I figure most folks just wake up one morning and understand that it's gone. My goal now, if I had one at all, was to keep sleeping with Maggie as long as I could without getting caught. I tried not to think about next month or next year. I only looked forward to the next Wednesday.

"Speaking of owning your own shop," I said, "you mentioned coming into some money that made it possible. Would I be prying too much if I asked if you earned it by working two jobs? I'm especially interested in entrepreneurial activity, and it sounds like you busted your butt and made your dream a reality."

He laughed and took another swallow. "I busted my butt all right," he said, "but I would've had to bust it a good bit longer to *make* the money to open my own shop. Naw, I got lucky for once in my life and found me an investor."

"Someone here in Pine Bluff?"

"Naw, actually it was somebody over in Loring."

"Mind if I ask who?"

He fell silent and shifted in his chair, looking down into his cup as if maybe it held the solution to this particularly vexing problem. I knew he was trying to decide whether to lie or tell the truth. Finally, he lifted his head and said, "If I tell you, you ain't gone put the answer in no book, are you?"

Since there would be no book, it was easy enough to say, "No sir. I give you my word."

After he told me, I knew I'd been right to wonder if Ellis Buchanan possibly could've forgotten Andy Owens.

Half an hour later, after promising to send him a copy of my book if it ever got published, I rose to leave. As if he were a shy boy about to ask the prettiest girl in town for a date, he ducked his head and wondered wouldn't I like a little trim, free of charge. So I told him yes, and he went off down the hall and returned a moment later with his clippers and a pair of scissors and a yellow bedsheet.

I straddled the chair he'd been sitting in, and he draped that sheet over my lap and chest and gave me the best haircut I've had since 1962.

THE PUBLIC RECORD, in the form of a marriage certificate on file at the Mississippi Department of Vital Records, can tell you that Nadine Annalou Bevil married Arlan Baker Calloway before the justice of the peace in the Gulf Coast town of Willis on December 15, 1950. Her parents' names—Annalou Patrick Bevil (deceased) and Hardy Bevil, of Hard Cash—are duly noted on the certificate, as are those of his parents, Norma Kay Calloway and John Bell Calloway, of Loring. The document is illegibly signed by the justice of the peace, whose name is typed below: A. E. Reno. The witness was one Josephine Melton.

From the Loring County Register of Deeds, you can learn that Ellis Buchanan officially assumed ownership of the *Weekly Times* on August 25, 1960. If, like me, you enjoy looking through old newspapers, you can quickly determine that the first issue with Ellis's name at the top of the masthead was published on September 7, 1960, and that in his first editorial he introduced himself to his new audience, telling them that he had previously owned and edited the *Clearwater Gazette*, over in east Mississippi, that he was the husband of Olivia Buchanan, *née* Wadsworth, originally of Winona, and the father of a three-year-old son, Wilbur Cash (Will), and a two-year-old daughter, Alexandra Olivia (Allie). You can learn, from this same editorial, that Ellis intended to stake out a progressive position on "the most important issue facing the Delta, not to mention the state and the nation: civil rights."

The public record won't tell you a single thing, though, about how Ellis Buchanan bumped into Nadine Calloway in an aisle at the Loring Piggly Wiggly in the fall of 1961.

Around 2:00 p.m. on the day I went to see Andy Owens, I got back home, made a peanut butter sandwich and washed it down with a glass of beer. Then I went back outside and walked down the street.

Ellis came to the door in his bathrobe. I'd never seen him like that before. His hair hadn't been combed, and he had what looked like a fever blister on his upper lip.

"Hey," I said. "I hope I didn't get you out of bed."

"No, not really. Though I was taking a nap."

"So I'll drop by another day." I started to turn away.

He reached out and grabbed my arm just below the elbow. He didn't do it gently either. "You might as well stay," he said. "I'd just as soon answer your question now rather than tomorrow or the day after."

His fingers stayed locked around my forearm. His hand was big and, given his age, surprisingly strong. I remembered him telling me once that he could palm a basketball. "What question?" I said.

He let go, pulled a handkerchief from the pocket of his robe and blew his nose. "The one you convinced yourself you didn't come here to ask."

"I'm sorry?"

"You thought we'd talk around the subject, I guess, and you'd gradually steer the conversation in a certain direction, like Perry Mason, I suppose, and then you'd say, 'Oh, and by the way, I drove over to Arkansas today and interviewed Andy

Owens for a book I'll never write.' Is that how you imagined this would go?"

Of all the people I knew, he was the only one who'd never once spoken to me in anger. For more than thirty years he'd maintained the same ironic stance, suggesting with every word and glance that if I wanted to live a long and happy life, I needed to regard myself and all my actions with a measure of skepticism and a heavy dose of humor. Now he was dead serious, and mad.

"I'm sorry," I said. "He called you, I guess."

"Yes. He may be a drunk but he's loyal, and the two of us reached a bargain that you got him to violate today." Finally, his face displayed a trace of the old familiar smile. "You see, he was dying to give somebody a haircut, and along you came." He turned towards the kitchen. "I'm drinking bourbon. What about you?"

"I was already persona non grata when I met her," he told me, balancing a glass of whiskey on his knee. The bottle—Knob Creek—stood on the coffee table. I'd taken one sip, and it had burned worse going down than anything I'd ever swallowed. "One of the first things I'd done at the paper was to editorialize against Mayor Finley for holding a Citizens' Council meeting at City Hall. I said it was his business if he wanted to host meetings of such a shameful outfit at his own home, but that if he held any meetings on public property, they ought to be the business of all our citizens, the majority of whom, he might not have noticed, happened to be black. That caused a big ruckus. Then, after Ross Barnett spent three hundred thousand dollars in state funds installing gold-plated faucet handles on all the bathtubs at the governor's mansion, I wrote that the stink of his racist policies would still cling to him. That kind of thing. They all thought my behavior was thoroughly outrageous, and began to cross the street when they saw me coming down the sidewalk."

In a short time, he told me, he made quite a name for himself. One day a *Time* reporter who was writing an article about Tut Patterson, a Citizens' Council founder, showed up at his office, and a week or so later, when the piece ran, Ellis got quoted: "Tut's aptly named. He's a kind of pharaoh lording it over the most reactionary elements of Southern society. And I personally look forward to seeing him entombed."

That line resonated. Dead animals began appearing in his driveway—a skunk here, a possum there, the occasional exotic creature like a porcupine or an armadillo. He made mean sport of the perpetrators. "Thanks to some of our friends and neighbors," he wrote, "I've been sending a lot of business to a certain taxidermist over in Greenville. Before long I'll be putting the results on display in an exhibition that I plan to title 'Pets of the Citizens' Council.' An art critic at the *New York Times* has announced his intention to attend the grand opening."

That's what was going on in his life when he turned around one afternoon in the Piggly Wiggly and saw an absurdly tall woman with frizzy auburn hair staring at him. He'd noticed her around town before—always from a distance—but didn't bother to ask anybody her name. She wasn't news. Why should he care?

He had his kids with him. They'd come in search of ketchup, mustard and mayonnaise, for a cookout later on that day.

"You look," she said, without introducing herself or saying hello, "like you could still ring one in from thirty feet."

It had been years since anybody said anything to him about his exploits on the basketball court. The only sport that matters much in Mississippi is football. "Believe me," he told her, "I never hit from thirty feet in my life."

"I'd love to trust you," she said, "but in this instance I don't. I used to listen to your games. I heard you hit from thirty a bunch of times."

"You heard Stan Tinsley telling lies. You know what we used to call him?"

"Mouth of the South?"

He nodded. "Did you go to Ole Miss?"

"No, but I played basketball."

"Where?"

"Hard Cash High. They don't have a team anymore. The town chose not to exist."

"It's a pity more towns don't make that choice, isn't it?"

"This one, for instance?"

Rather than answer, he told me, he snapped his fingers. "Hey, wait a minute. You didn't play on that state championship team, did you? Back in Forty-nine? Wasn't that Hard Cash High? Beat Jackson Murrah by two in overtime?"

This time, she was the one who didn't answer. Because before she could reply, his son grabbed his hand and jerked it. "Daddy! Come *on*."

No single emotion, she'd tell him later, would account for the look that flitted across his face. Annoyance was certainly part of it, she said, but she detected traces of guilt, confusion and resignation, too. All sensations with which she'd forged an intimate acquaintance.

"We probably ought to head home," he told her. "Their mom likes to eat at six sharp."

She stepped closer, as if to measure his height and let him measure hers. Six feet, he guessed. Maybe even six-one.

"Want to shoot a few sometime?" she asked.

"A few what?"

She almost died laughing. "Baskets," she said. "What'd you think I meant? Kids?"

"South of the tracks," Ellis said, "there used to be a basketball court. Really, it was just a patch of mud packed hard by all the bare feet that had played on it. Near the end of Church Street, behind what used to be called the Negro Masonic Building. We went down there because both of us knew that while a few eyes might be watching us through parted curtains, what they saw would never make it across the tracks. White people could meddle in black people's business all they wanted, but we took it for granted they'd never meddle in ours."

The hoop, he said, had been welded to a rusted deck plate that looked like it was lifted from a cotton gin, and the deck plate was bolted to a telephone pole. Which was odd, when you thought about it, because in that part of town, at that time, few people had phones.

Dribbling idly with his right hand, he used his left to point at the goal. "If I drive and dunk on you," he said, "at least we won't have to worry about the backboard falling on us. That thing's really up there."

"What makes you think you can drive and dunk on me?"

He didn't really think he could. He'd never dunked in his life, though he'd once had the bad luck to play against the Oklahoma A&M center Bob Kurland, who'd park himself beneath the basket and stuff them in all day. Threatening to dunk on her just gave him something to say. His legs didn't feel springy, they felt shaky. He felt shaky all over.

He'd felt no different the day before when he called her house. He'd jogged back to his office and dialed the number after seeing her husband walk into the Western Auto. When she heard his voice, she laughed and said she'd been wondering when he'd call. A real ballplayer, she told him, couldn't resist a challenge.

"I might drive and dunk on you," he said, continuing his dribble. "You're a girl. I'm a boy."

It was cool out, but she wore yellow shorts along with a pair of red Keds and a black worsted pullover. He had on an ancient pair of sweats, the same ones he'd worn years earlier at Ole Miss.

"I'm a girl," she said, "that plays like a boy."

"Twenty-one?"

"Yeah, but no free throws."

He tossed her the ball. "Ladies first."

She tossed it right back. "Do you see any ladies? I sure don't."

"Okay. Have it your way." He backed up a few feet, then dribbled into the area where the lane would have been if there was one. Pulling up, he shot right over her. Too late, she put her hand in his face.

The ball whooshed through the remains of the net, his first basket in years. He didn't go to games anymore or listen to them on the radio. He'd never even seen one on TV.

"See?" he said. "The fact is, I've got a natural height advantage, and more often than not that's what this game comes down to."

"There's such a thing as court intelligence, too. And I have a feeling that I'm probably smarter than you."

The next time he hit from twenty feet. "You may be smarter, though I seriously doubt it, and in any case it doesn't make much difference. Your body is a prison."

"Yeah, and I have a feeling yours is, too." She grabbed the ball and zipped it to him. He realized only later, he told me, that it was an unusually crisp pass. Passing, when he played, was his weak point, but the offense was set up for him to be the ball hog.

He drove the lane again. This time she jumped in front of him, sticking her face right in his chest, and he bowled her over. Rather than pull up and shoot, he reached down and offered her his hand, letting the ball skip into the ditch.

She slapped him on the wrist. "That was a charging foul," she said. "My ball now."

"Au contraire, ma'am. That was a blocking foul. Your left foot was about six inches off the ground. I'm not even sure the right one was down."

"Bullshit. But if you need to cheat to stay ahead, take the ball. And by the way? Fuck you."

It was the first time in his life, he said, he'd heard a woman use that expression, and he knew the shock showed on his face. But she'd provoked another reaction, too. They were playing a game and, when they started, the object was merely to score the most points. The end result was a foregone conclusion. Now the object of the game, as far as he was concerned, was to lower her self-esteem. Why should she have so much of it anyway? She might be a tall, good-looking woman, but she'd never gone to college and was married to a terminal redneck.

He lifted the ball out of the ditch, wiped off the slime, then walked to the end of the court, turned and drove on her. This time she got set, determined to hold her ground. He gave her a little head fake, which threw her off balance, and breezed right past her for a layup.

He walked the ball back up the court, bouncing it chest high. "You should have accepted my offer"—*bounce!*—"to let you go first. At this rate"—*bounce!*—"you'll never get to take a shot. If you'd gone first"—*bounce!*—"you could've taken exactly one."

The next time down the court, he switched the ball to his left hand and shot over her right shoulder. He hit from fifteen, from twenty. She was breathing hard, her face bright red, her sides starting to heave. "I can't believe," he said, after hooking one in down low, "that it's in a school district's best interests to spend money on girls' basketball. Maybe that's why your town went broke. Hard Cash? What a joke."

He told me he finally decided that in order to complete her reduction, he really ought to let her shoot one. So on his next possession, he drove the baseline, lifted his right foot as high as he could and shot between his legs. "Damn," he said, when it caromed off the makeshift backboard. "Missed one."

She grabbed the ball and shoved it at him. "Look, I don't

need your charity, okay? We can just quit if you don't want to play."

"I don't really want to quit yet. I actually expected to make that shot. Why wouldn't I? I've made everything I put up all day. Maybe you don't want to play? Scared you'll get stuffed?"

She wasn't fooling anymore, he said, and hadn't been for the last few minutes. Her sweater was damp, dark spots spreading under her arms. He found himself wishing he could see her glistening flesh.

"I'm not scared I'll get 'stuffed,' as you put it." She still had the ball in her outstretched hands.

He wasn't about to take it. "You know you can't make a shot on me," he said, smiling as if to show he bore her no ill will for that "Fuck you," though he did and he could tell she knew it. "Are we agreed about that?"

"No, we're not agreed about that."

She walked the ball to the other end of the court. He bent his legs, crouching. She turned and dribbled towards him, keeping the ball close to her body, dribbling with the pads of her fingers. When she drove close enough, he committed and went for the steal, but she had a nice spin move. He recovered in time to slap at the ball, but he knew perfectly well that he'd hit the back of her hand. "Foul on me," he said.

"Foul on you."

She brought it in again. This time he took nothing for granted, moving with her towards the corner, then back to the top of the key, keeping his left foot forward, left hand extended, palm up, to swipe at the ball. She was a lot better on offense, he told me, than defense.

When she tried her spin move this time, he was ready. She leaned into him as she put up her shot, and he got nothing but ball. He shoved it right in her face.

She wheeled away, holding her nose.

"Hey, look, I didn't intend to do it so hard," he said, which wasn't exactly true. He laid his hand on her shoulder.

He told me he never saw it coming. One minute she was bending over with her back to him, and the next thing he knew she'd punched him in the mouth. It hurt. She hit like a man.

He put his hand to his mouth, then lowered it and looked at his bloody fingers. "You know what?" he said.

Her nose was still red. "What?"

"Fuck you, too."

He said it, and God knows he meant it, but when she stepped closer he couldn't make his feet move. Her face grew big, then even bigger. Her mouth opened, her tongue flicked out and she licked that blood from his lips.

Listening to him talk about the day they shot baskets, I wondered if I'd ever run into him when my mother took me into town on her shopping trips. I didn't know him then, so he would've looked like just another man who was obviously better off than my father, who wore a tie and wasn't a farmer. If I had seen him around this time, I wouldn't have known that he'd lately been split down the middle, that over the next several months two versions of Ellis would inhabit the same space, each trying to outlast the other.

"We never played basketball again," he said. "We took to meeting wherever we could, often around noon, usually in a town nearby. Our favorite was Belzoni. I didn't know anybody there, and neither did she. There was a café on the highway back then that served the best chili burgers either of us had ever eaten. She had this way of hiding her mouth behind her palm if I made her laugh while she was chewing. The gesture would've seemed precious and dainty if a smaller woman like my wife had made it, but when she did it there was an offhandedness about it that I found entrancing.

"I loved drinking with her in the middle of the day. She always had alcohol. Sometimes it was regular bonded whiskey, in a bottle with a printed label. Sometimes it was clear stuff in a Mason jar and she wouldn't say where she got it, just laughed, turned it up, took a swig and smacked her lips. She'd say things like 'Who would've thought corn and chicken shit could taste *this* good?' "

He told me it thrilled him when she said "shit" or "fuck" or even mild swearwords like "damn" and "hell." Those words were exciting not because they sounded dirty in her mouth but because they didn't.

Most of all, he loved how she behaved when removing her clothes in a motel room, talking about inconsequential things, mostly, as if nobody was watching her disrobe. "Ever heard the term *bill-dropping*?" she once asked, unbuttoning her blouse on a blustery day in January. They were in a motel across the highway from the café in Belzoni. The radiator was on—you could hear water gurgling through the pipes—but so far it hadn't accomplished much.

"*Hill-dropping*? I don't think so."

She tossed the blouse onto the foot of the bed and reached around behind her back to undo her bra straps. "That's how they plant cotton now. They've got these four-row planters that drop four or five seeds in little hills about eighteen inches apart. It used to be that the planter would just drop a steady stream of seeds down the middle of the row, but not anymore."

"And it's an improvement?"

"Yeah, because they don't have to put hoe hands in the field to thin the cotton out." She dropped the bra on top of her blouse. "Remember when they first started calling those things bras instead of brassieres?"

"That was just after the war."

She unbuttoned her jeans and pulled them down over her thighs. "My momma had a thick accent like they do back in the woods in Sharkey County, and she never learned to say 'bra.' She called them 'briars.' "

He said she didn't make love like he'd expected. Given her aggressiveness on the basketball court, the forthrightness with which she stripped and her occasionally profane tongue, he was prepared for a certain degree of crassness, but instead she always lay down beside him and rested her head on his chest and said, "Hold me for a while before you get after me." And so he always did. He held her and stroked her hair, and she put her palm on his stomach and let it lie there.

She talked sometimes about her husband. From the outset she'd made it clear that she had no plans to leave him, and not just because they had kids. There were things about Arlan to admire, she said, even if he couldn't see them.

"Well, I'm afraid I can't. Not much point in trying to conceal that." He knew he should change the subject, or at least fall silent, but that wasn't in his nature. He asked if she knew what went on at those Citizens' Council meetings.

"I can guess."

He told her about the one at City Hall, how her husband and my father and the other men spoke openly about putting black people who'd registered to vote out of their houses and making sure they couldn't find work.

"So far," she said, "they've been pretty successful at it."

"They won't succeed forever. They'll start failing soon, and I wouldn't like to be them when that day comes." He heard himself drone on: "That fellow your husband hangs around with, the one who looks like a beanpole?"

"James May?"

"He follows your husband around town like a pet. He's got 'loyal dog' scrawled on his forehead."

"He and Arlan knew each other growing up."

"He always has such a hungry look in his eyes."

"Maybe he's never had enough to eat."

Ellis told me that Nadine said my father wasn't a bad man and neither was Arlan, that they both grew up poor, went off and fought in the war and, after they came back, had never known a day when they didn't have to work hard. The thing was, she said, if you didn't own at least a thousand acres, in the Delta you were a nobody. And if you wanted to be a somebody, according to Arlan, you had to join the Council. He talked all the time about securing their children's future.

When she said things like that, what Ellis found himself thinking of was a future with her. For him, that meant stolen moments, and he failed to see why they couldn't steal them forever, but she said when they started they were already in overtime. "You're at the free throw line," she liked to tease. "Better sink another one if you can before the buzzer."

Her tone, when she made those kinds of statements, was far too breezy for his taste. She'd started it all, making the initial approach, stalking him at the grocery store when he had his kids in tow. She was the one who got emotional when they met to shoot baskets. He did tell me he conveniently managed to overlook the fact that he'd gone to the trouble of finding out what he could about her husband, then flipped through the phone book and called her when he knew Arlan wasn't at home. But even so, if he saw her downtown with *her* kids, she wouldn't even glance at him.

He in turn couldn't stand the sight of her children, especially the girl. He saw them all one day on Front Street, right there in front of the Piggly Wiggly, a week or two before Christmas, a life-size Santa rotating above them in the window, Nadine talking to my mother, a sack of groceries tucked under her arm. He knew better than to speak. All he did was try to make eye contact as he passed, but the girl caught it and her dark eyes flashed.

"Do you ever wonder," he asked, lying beside Nadine in bed in the motel down in Belzoni, "what it would be like to see each other at night?"

"Oh, hon, what difference would *that* make?" Once again: easy and breezy.

"What difference does *any* of this make, then?" he asked. "I go to the store to buy ketchup. I'm not thinking of you, I don't even know you exist. I'm mentally composing the first paragraph of an editorial when you pop up out of nowhere and start that shit about me ringing one in from thirty feet. You're lucky I don't wring your neck."

"You won't wring my neck," she said, "but Arlan would if he ever found out what we're doing."

He laughed. "That little man? He couldn't get his hands *around* your neck. You're too damn tall."

"He could if I was lying down."

He told me he hated to think of her lying down with Arlan Calloway. A journalist was supposed to be married to the truth, and for much of his life he had been, but after they got involved he lied to himself all the time. He told himself his main problem with her husband was political, when deep down he knew perfectly well that if Arlan would just walk out his front door, taking the kids with him and leaving his wife alone for the taking, he'd forgive him for every racist notion he ever subscribed to. The Meredith case was winding its way through the courts by that time, and Arlan could have stood on the corner of Front Street and Loring Avenue with a big sign saying LYNCH JAMES MEREDITH, and Ellis never would've mentioned it in the paper, so great would his gratitude have been.

He wanted to be with her every few days—in this motel room or another, it didn't really matter much where. He wanted something permanent in a transient environment, something he could leave behind today and go back to on Thursday and find it just as strong because he'd left it alone for the last forty-eight hours. That, he told himself, was what he wanted.

"Don't you ever get scared?" she asked him there in the motel.

"Scared of what?"

"Your wife finding out."

He couldn't imagine how she could. They had one car, and he drove it. She was busy taking care of their kids. She stayed home all day, and hardly anybody around Loring knew her. Anyway, nobody knew about Nadine and him. They'd been careful about that. "No," he said, "I guess I don't."

"I do. I wouldn't want to do that to another woman."

Even when somebody's lying motionless beside you, you can feel when she starts to pull away. He'd never known it until that day but could detect it then, some faint lessening of the pressure exerted by her hand on his chest. They'd been seeing each other for three months. Though the end was hardly imminent, he could feel it coming, and this made him want to do something rash. It never occurred to him, he told me, that what he was doing right then, at that moment, *was*.

"I've never seen the inside of your house," he said.

"Well, I've never seen the inside of yours, either."

"I don't know what the floor looks like in your kitchen."

"You don't need to."

"What we're doing is not about need," he said. "It's all about want."

"How do you turn the word *profound*," she asked, "into a noun?"

"Profundity."

"Then, hon, I think you've just uttered one. What we're doing is all about want."

It certainly was, and he wanted her, so he turned towards her and pulled her into his arms, thrilled by her size, though until now he'd always been drawn to smaller women. "I hate it when you talk so flippantly about this coming to an end," he said. "Just plain hate it."

"I want you to," she whispered, her nose nestling against his neck. "Remember how you felt when you played your last game?

That's how I want you to feel when this ends, only ten times worse. And I want you think about that every time you're with me."

"My last game ended in a loss."

"So will this one," she said.

They kept it up, Ellis told me, through the spring of '62, meeting for lunch and sex whenever they could. Her daughter was in school, her son in kindergarten with me, Arlan in the field, so it was easy enough to slip away every few days. "Then when summer rolled around," he said, "she fobbed the kids off on your mother a couple of times a week."

"I remember that," I said, and for a moment it was as if I were watching a movie, in which a little dark-haired girl with skinned knees begged her mother to take her along to wherever she was going.

While they conducted their affair, the rest of the people in the state—and a good many folks in other parts of the country, too—became intensely focused on the Meredith case. It was clear, Ellis said, that a showdown was coming. In late June, in New Orleans, the U.S. Fifth Circuit Court of Appeals ordered Ole Miss to admit Meredith for the fall semester. But one member of the court began issuing stays, the first three of which the full court of appeals invalidated. When the maverick judge issued a fourth stay, Meredith's lawyers, joined by the Justice Department, appealed to the U.S. Supreme Court.

People were starting to go crazy, and Ellis registered their madness, which at another time in his life would have absorbed all his attention. But the editorials he wrote that summer, as the state became a powder keg, were tame. He weighed in on the issue a couple of times, duly noting there was no point in trying to put off the inevitable, that the longer they drew things out, the worse the consequences would be, but his words lacked the passion that was being spent in cheap motels from one end of the Delta to the other.

In early September, Supreme Court Justice Hugo Black announced that after polling the other members of the court and finding all in agreement, he was voiding the stay and ordering Ole Miss to enroll Meredith immediately. "People couldn't even focus on football," Ellis said. "That tells you just how bad it was. All kinds of crazy things happened. Meredith would try to register and be turned away by the governor or the lieutenant governor, and the Justice Department would issue another threat, and that would lead Barnett to make another insane speech. At one point some group out in Orange County— I believe they called themselves something like the First California Volunteers—sent a telegram urging him to hold fast and pray because they were en route."

One day, when he and Nadine were having lunch at an Italian restaurant over in Leland, she asked what he thought was going to happen.

All around them, farmers on their lunch break were discussing the same topic, making sweeping gestures with their knives and forks, their palms pounding the tables. They inveighed against the Catholic in the White House, though apparently it didn't bother them that the owners of the restaurant were Catholics, too.

"Nothing much," he said. "Barnett will rattle his saber some before falling on it in front of the Lyceum."

"You don't think folks'll turn out in force?"

"Folks? What folks?" He waved his hand around the room. "The plantation aristocracy? Not a chance."

She wound several strands of pasta around the tines of her fork. "There's been some talk," she said.

"There's always talk. What kind are you referring to?"

"People in the Council. Some of them are saying maybe it's time to take up arms, that what's worked before may not work now."

"You mean your husband intends to load his six-shooter, march off to Oxford and take potshots at, say, the National Guard or the federal marshals?" He shook his head. "If you want to make me laugh, you'll need to tell a better joke."

She laid down her fork still wrapped in spaghetti. "Look, I'm not telling jokes here. If something happened, it wouldn't be funny. He doesn't want to go to Oxford, but he doesn't want to let his friends down, either. I think he's scared of getting embarrassed."

He knew and she did too that the organization had been embarrassing from the outset. But insulting her husband wouldn't wash, and he could tell from the way she sat there— both elbows on the table, legs spread apart as if she was about to push herself up—that she was an inch from walking out. It was amazing, he thought, how the balance of power could shift. Ten months ago, James Meredith had been just another black man Ole Miss could dismiss, and now he had the federal government doing his bidding. Ten months ago, she was trying to attract his attention in a grocery store and he was stuffing a basketball in her face. "It won't come to that," he mumbled, picking up his own fork. "Nobody's going to Oxford, except Mr. Meredith."

That seemed to satisfy her. Her shoulders relaxed, and she went back to eating, and before long, Ellis said, it was all forgotten—up until late in the evening on Sunday, September 30, when the phone rang at his office and he picked up the receiver and she told him he was wrong.

Ellis had been there since the afternoon, listening to the radio and talking on the phone with a friend of his in Oxford, a retired professor who'd taught him at Ole Miss. He'd been calling his ex-students around the Mid-South, people who ran little papers like the *Weekly Times*, pleading with them to do whatever they could to keep their readers calm. "Tell them," he urged Ellis, "not to come. Please." He said he'd seen pickups with license plates from all over the state, from Alabama, Tennessee and Georgia, too, even a few from Texas. The U.S. marshals had arrived by plane earlier in the day and when transported into town were pelted with bricks and bottles. Now a National Guard unit was heading onto campus. He'd just seen the trucks through the window, light from streetlamps reflecting off the Guardsmen's bayonets. Nobody knew Meredith's exact location, but rumor had it he was inside the Lyceum, hidden in the registrar's office. Folks were forming up in the Grove, cars were set on fire, the air smelled odd.

Ellis told me that when Nadine called, he was considering a special edition that he'd print himself, a few hundred copies he could distribute around town under cover of darkness so people would see them first thing in the morning. If it kept even one person from jumping in his truck with a shotgun and heading for Oxford tomorrow, at least he would've made that small difference. So he was less than eager to pause and have a chat. He didn't stop to wonder why she was free to call on a Sunday evening. "Listen," he began, but she cut him off.

"Still want to see my kitchen floor?"

"What?" He could hear her breathing. Normally, she wasn't a heavy breather. He'd talked to her on the phone countless times and taken naps beside her, but not once could he recall ever having been aware of her breathing. Which seemed odd, if you think about it.

"Arlan's gone," she said. "I begged him not to go, but he did it anyway, and now I'm here unguarded."

He was having a hard time, he told me, processing both the

information and the invitation, if that's what it was. It occurred to him that maybe she'd been drinking. This wasn't a bad night to be drunk. "Whose idea was this?" he asked.

"Going to Oxford was James May's idea. He called and said they ought to do it, and Arlan was so worried about losing stature in his buddy's eyes that he agreed. So he loaded his shotgun and went to pick him up. Now they've ridden off to defend states' rights. Probably both of them'll get shot."

After Ellis relayed that conversation, I became aware of my own breathing—or, more truthfully, my failure to breathe. I sat there motionless, feeling as if my face had turned to plastic. For a moment I couldn't speak. "My dad called Arlan Calloway?" I finally said. "Going to Oxford was his idea?"

Ellis lifted his glass of whiskey and sloshed it around a little, as if it contained ice cubes and he wanted them to melt. "You came here to find out what happened, didn't you?"

"I came here to find out why you bought Andy Owens a barbershop."

"I bought him a barbershop," Ellis said, "in part because your father made that phone call. If you look at it in a certain light, James and I were coinvestors."

When he realized Nadine's husband was gone, he dismissed his plans for a special edition. The thought of being with her at night, in her own house, possessed a strange allure. "What about your kids?" he asked.

"Sound asleep. Tomorrow's a school day. Reading, writing and arithmetic."

He wasn't worried about his wife. It went without saying that his job required him to visit odd places, at odd hours. Tonight, of all nights, he needed no excuse.

Crazy, yes, and dangerous, too. But doable.

"I'll be there in half an hour," he told her. When she started to give him directions, he said, "I know where you live." What he didn't tell her was how many nights he'd driven by there, looking at the lights along the front of the house and trying to figure out which room was hers.

"Park down the road a little ways," she said, and he told her not to worry, he had no intention of leaving his car in her driveway where every redneck headed for Oxford could see it.

"Actually getting there took me a lot longer," Ellis said. "I discovered that hiding a car in the Delta's no simple matter. I finally drove into somebody's cotton field and parked on the turnrow, figuring that as long as I got back before the pickers showed up I ought to be okay. And I fully intended to return before then, because I had no guarantee that Arlan and your father would go all the way to Oxford or, if they did, that they'd stay any length of time. Of course, as she said, there was always a chance they'd both get shot.

"I remember that while I was slinking up the road to her place, I couldn't help wondering what would happen if they really *did* get shot. I imagined Nadine remaining my mistress, living several miles out of town where most of the people who saw me visiting her would be field hands. Her kids didn't even figure into my calculations."

Gravel crunched when he stepped into her driveway. The house was dark—so dark that for a moment, Ellis said, he wondered if she'd changed her mind, if she'd turned everything off and gone to bed. Just then, the porch light popped on.

She opened the door. She was wearing a bathrobe, a pink one that looked surprisingly threadbare, with ragged strands dangling from both cuffs. It was too short, having been made for a much smaller woman. "You look scared," she said.

It bothered him that she spoke in a normal voice, and what she said bothered him, too. He *was* scared, all of a sudden, but it seemed wrong for her to point it out. Who wouldn't be scared going to the home of another man's wife? Especially if he knew that when the other man left, he had a loaded shotgun? "Well," he said, "then maybe I am. Aren't you?"

"Do I look scared?"

"Not especially."

"Well, then, that's a good indication I'm not. With me, what you see's what you get. You ought to know that by now."

She turned and walked off down a dimly lit hallway, and he couldn't think of anything to do but step inside. Once past the threshold, he closed the door and then groped around until he found a dead bolt and threw it. This made him feel secure until he realized that, since there was also a back door, if he needed to leave through the front in a hurry that dead bolt might be his undoing.

"Take a look," he heard her say from somewhere down the hall. "Here's my kitchen floor."

He followed the sound of her voice. The floor, when he saw it, was just black-and-white linoleum that held the scent of Lysol. There was a Frigidaire in one corner, a gas range in the other, in the middle a table with four chairs arranged around it, on top of the table a bowl of wax fruit and, above that, dangling from the ceiling, a lamp with a white bell shade. The journalist in him logged details, looking for one that stood out from all the others and, if aptly placed in an article, would make the reader sit up and take note, but he couldn't spot it. The scene was unbrokenly familiar.

"So what do you want to do?" she asked, her hands hidden in the pink robe's pockets. "Complete a little home-inspection tour? Want to check my pipes and make sure they're not obstructed?"

He suddenly wanted to be anywhere else. He'd never in his

life changed his mind so fast before. Usually there was a kind of bridge between one mind-set and another, when you knew you were taking corrective steps, going from over here to over there, though on that night it was instantaneous. He wanted not only to get out of her house but also to get away from her and stay away. He thought of his wife sleeping at home alone and wondered if he'd been lying to himself about her, that maybe she did know or—even worse—*suspect* that what used to be hers had been spread around from town to town, in one rented bed after another. The Delta wasn't that big a place. God only knew who might've seen them together. How, he asked himself, could he possibly have been so foolish?

While he stood there trying to compose the speech he intended to deliver, he heard a noise come from down the hall, and it sounded like a footfall, like somebody's bare heel hitting the floor. "What the hell was that?" he said.

Later, he'd wonder how much it cost her to say what she said next, or even if you could ever put a price on the kind of courage it must have taken. He'd become convinced she always knew exactly what he was thinking, which meant she must have known what his answer would ultimately be.

"I'd leave with you," she said, "if you asked me to. I thought I wouldn't, but now I know I would."

He'd never felt so stupid in his entire life. How could he have failed to see this coming? It was there that day in the grocery store. He should've seen it on her face, in her eyes. She wanted more from life, and who wouldn't? "That noise," he said. "Did you hear it?"

She studied him as if she were breaking him down into his various components with an eye towards reassembling them into a more coherent whole. "What noise?"

"A moment ago."

She laughed. "You're trying to buy time," she said. Her hands came out of her pockets, her arms crossed over her chest.

As if performing in a Christmas cantata, she broke into song. "Angels we have heard on high, sweetly singing o'er the plains."

"Jesus," he hissed. "Are you out of your mind?"

"And the mountains in reply echoing their joyous strains."

He stepped over, grabbed her and gave her a good shake. Her breath smelled like whiskey.

"Gloria, in excelsis Deo!"

"Stop it!"

"Gloria, in excelsis Deo!"

After that she subsided, insofar as a woman her size could be said to. Another minute or two passed while they stood face-to-face, his hands still gripping her forearms. Eventually she said, "I'm sorry."

He let go of her. "You don't need to be. I'm the one that's in the wrong."

"You give yourself far too much credit. In case you didn't notice, you had a partner in all of this."

"I noticed," he said, "and I was grateful."

Just like that, Ellis told me, they had consigned it to the past. And just as she had in so many motel rooms and lunchrooms, she began to speak of things that didn't matter—or of things that might matter a lot to others and even to both of them if they hadn't been where they were right then. "What do you reckon's happening up at Ole Miss?"

"I imagine all the actors are putting on quite a show."

"Think Meredith's still alive?"

"Oh, I'm sure he's very much alive. By now he might have been named chancellor."

"Speaking of now," she said, glancing over his shoulder at something on the wall behind him, "I think maybe you better be going."

He turned around to see what she saw, and there it was, the detail he would've seized upon if he'd been writing a story about what had taken place in that room, in these last few minutes: a burnt-orange wall clock designed to look like a basket-ball, with black script across the top that read 1949 MISSISSIPPI STATE GIRLS CHAMPIONS.

The hands told him it was 2:05 a.m.

Did he kiss her before leaving? He told me he liked to think he had, but that in truth he couldn't remember. They might have shaken hands. Or simply nodded at each other and said good night. He did know, though, that the moment he stepped out of the house his heart was full of promises—that he would never again cheat on his wife, that she'd always know where he was and when he was coming home, that he'd take a greater interest in their children, that he'd moderate his tone when stating opinions while continuing to stand up for the ideals he believed in. He would work hard to make friends of his enemies.

These were the things he was telling himself as he walked down her driveway. And because he was so thoroughly focused on those thoughts, he didn't notice the sound of the engine until he was halfway between her house and the road. Too far to turn back. Not a bush within thirty feet, not a tree within forty.

He assumed it was Arlan returning, that he'd realized it was fruitless to take up arms for a cause that was lost nearly a hundred years ago, that the more he considered it, the less he relished facing off against professionally trained soldiers armed with the best modern weaponry. He could've come to all those realizations, though, and still blow several holes in a man walking away from his house in the middle of the night. Nobody would have blamed him if he did, not even Ellis.

But the truck that braked at the foot of the driveway was old, and Arlan Calloway's was new.

The driver rolled down his window, grabbed something white and pitched it towards the driveway. Like any good deliveryman, he followed its arc, to make sure it didn't land to one side or the other, where the morning dew might render the news-print blurry.

It hit just a foot or two away. In the few seconds it took the driver's gaze to meet his own, a memorandum of understanding was drafted. On the other side of the Mississippi River, in Pine Bluff, Arkansas, stood a small brick building with a FOR SALE sign in front. It wouldn't remain empty much longer.

"Hey, Mr. Buchanan," Andy Owens said. "What you doing way off out here?"

Ellis leaned over and poured himself another shot of Knob Creek. "So that's what I can tell you," he said. "That and noth-ing more. I got the news the next morning along with the rest of the town. Heard it from Elnora Napier when I walked into the office. You can probably imagine the emotional cocktail I drank that day—grief, shock, shame, fear, big slugs of self-disgust. I told myself that morning that I'd never get over it—that I couldn't and shouldn't allow myself to—and I can see that on some level I was right. Everything comes back at you one day. But since I don't ever want to discuss this again, in however much time I have left, I'm going to ask you a question now, if that's all right."

There wasn't much I could do except nod. I thought his ques-tion would be about Maggie and me, and I didn't know how I would answer it. But I was wrong. Because all he asked was "Is there anything at all, Luke, that you'd like to tell me?"

I picked up my glass and drank down the last of that burning whiskey, then set the glass on the table. "Yes," I said. "I'd like to tell you how sorry I am that I came here today."

Sunset

ONCE OR TWICE A YEAR throughout my childhood, we went to visit my cousin—the same one I'd tripped off that country store's porch into the mudhole.

His family was much worse off than mine. They lived in south Jackson, in a depressing little house on a potholed street. He had few toys and often left them lying out on the ragged lawn all night, where they were damaged by the elements or stolen by the neighbors. When I went to visit, I always brought a few things for us to play with—a football, say, or a bat, ball and glove.

My cousin, however, had one thing I didn't, and it was a source of pride for him, perhaps because it held so much interest for me. A deep drainage ditch—really, it was more like a canal—separated his house from the one behind it, and at certain times that waterway turned into a veritable river, with a swift current upon which a cheap plastic boat could do amazing things. We'd throw one in and then race each other through his backyard and his neighbor's and out onto the little bridge that spanned the canal at the next street, usually just in time to grab the boat before it disappeared beneath our feet.

The visit I'm thinking of now must have roughly coincided with two things—a big Mississippi rain and the 1964 Tokyo Olympics—because the canal was a raging torrent and both my

cousin and I had recently become infatuated with a British athlete named Lynn "the Leap" Davies, who'd won the long jump
by springing almost twenty-six and a half feet.

Out there hopping around in the soggy yard, each of us made
increasingly ridiculous claims about our own jumping prowess,
my cousin boasting that the previous spring he'd jumped so far
that the coach at Wingfield High School asked his grade-school
principal if he could borrow him for his own team, but the principal said no, it was against the rules. I, in turn, replied that I'd
once jumped over the "main road" that ran near our house—
adding, for good measure, that halfway across I noticed a truck
coming towards me, so I gave a little extra kick and soared right
over the hood.

At this moment, my cousin got a mean gleam in his eye.
"How wide you reckon that main road is?"

I modestly said twenty-five feet, careful not to upstage our
new hero Lynn the Leap.

He grinned and pointed at the drainage ditch, where a rusty tin
can was just bobbing by, headed for the Pearl River and the Gulf
of Mexico. "That ditch there," he said, "ain't but twenty feet
across, so I don't imagine you'd have much trouble clearing it."

At this age, I was not unresourceful. I'd even say I was a good
bit more resourceful than I am now. I gestured dismissively.
"That thing's not worth jumping," I said.

"You can't do it, so you're scared to. It's ten feet deep and
there's snakes in it. Big 'uns."

While he sneered at me, I studied the ditch. It didn't look
twenty feet across, and I didn't believe it had snakes in it, either,
because I'd never seen any. Furthermore, I knew perfectly well it
wasn't that deep, because it had been empty the last time I was
here, and we'd climbed down and poked around in the refuse
that littered the bottom, and I felt sure that my head rose several inches above the bank.

The courage possessed by certain children is a curious thing.

Fearful one moment and foolhardy the next, they lack the ability to logically assess risks. I backed up all the way to the wall of my cousin's house. Then, while he watched with a fascination he couldn't quite disguise, I took off towards the canal.

Once his feet left the ground, Lynn Davies practiced the hitch-kick technique, making it look as if he were running in the air, so I did the same thing. I was still hitching and kicking when I splashed into the water.

My head went under, and I got a noseful of filth. My ears filled up, too, and I heard chugging sounds and felt something cold and slimy against the back of my neck. Furiously, I flailed to the surface, then stroked towards the opposite bank. The current dragged at my legs, threatening to pull me back in, but I managed to get a handhold and then a toehold. While my cousin laughed his ass off and hollered, "Luke the Leap! Luke the Leap!" I climbed out into the neighbors' backyard.

Later that day, after I'd been hauled into the house, whipped and bathed and wrapped in blankets and warned not to even think of going outside, I heard my cousin rapping at the windowsill. I walked over and stuck my head out.

"Hey," he said, "watch this." He backed up against the house, just as I had, took a running start and, when he launched himself into the air, gave a rebel yell.

That he didn't even make it as far as I had gave me enormous satisfaction. He dropped like a rock into the middle of the canal and, because he couldn't swim at all, was carried swiftly towards the bridge, flapping and howling. The only thing that saved him from being either decapitated or drowned was an older boy who happened to be crossing the bridge just then. He reached down and grabbed my cousin's arm and held on until a couple adults heard their screams and ran over to fish him out.

I remember thinking that a person would have to be really stupid to make such a catastrophic mistake, right after watching somebody else do it.

. . .

Each fall, on a weekend in early November, there's an event called the Mid-South Festival of Poetry and Poetics. My impression is that it's not that big a deal—it's staged by third- or fourth-tier schools like Delta State, Arkansas–Pine Bluff and UT-Martin—and the writers who speak and judge the student competitions are rarely people I've ever heard of. But Jennifer always goes, along with a couple other teachers and three or four students whose poems and essays have been selected as finalists.

This year it was being held in Clarksville, Tennessee, and she left before dawn on Friday morning, picking up a colleague en route. I'd alerted Maggie ahead of time, and we agreed that we'd have dinner that night at Mann's over in Greenville. My intention—assuming that a half-formed impulse qualifies—was to buy her a really great meal with plenty to drink and then, on the drive back to Loring, gently tell her that we needed to break things off. Where I'd find the words to say what only the most frightened part of me really wanted to say anyway—well, I told myself I'd deal with that later.

Mann's Eatin' Place, if you've never heard of it, is something of an institution. In the shadow of the levee, in a clapboard shack with a sagging front porch, it serves the best steaks you can get anywhere. Bill Clinton frequently dined there when he was governor of Arkansas, driving one hundred fifty miles for the pleasure, and it's not uncommon to see famous actors or musicians, either, though they're usually ushered into the back room, where not even the reeking john can spoil the taste of that meat.

Jennifer and I didn't go there very often for one simple reason: you can't get a steak there for less than fifty dollars, and our budget could seldom stand the stress.

Greenville used to be the nicest town in the Delta, but in the last twenty years it's gone to seed, the older members of the moneyed class dying off, their kids leaving for Atlanta, Nashville, Raleigh or the Redneck Riviera. Most of the stores that once lined Washington Avenue are now closed, and when you turn off onto the side streets, you'll find yourself in a place where life is coming apart at the seams, people sitting on over-turned washtubs around fires made of scavenged packing crates, a profoundly aimless look in their eyes.

"Jesus," Maggie said as we parked across the street in a dingy lot filled with pickups and cars, including two Lincolns and a Caddy, "I don't remember the area looking anything like this."

"You've been here before? You didn't tell me that."

"My dad brought us here on my eighth birthday."

"How can you be sure it was Mann's? That was what— forty-five years ago?"

"I've seen photographic evidence. My brother's got a picture of me staring at my steak, and on the back of it my father wrote *Mann's Eatin' Place, Greenville, Mississippi, May 2nd, 1961*. That's all the proof I need."

Crossing the street she clasped my forearm, which worried me a little since it *was* Friday night and by no means impossible that somebody from Loring might be there. When the elderly black watchman who's always sitting on the porch hopped up to open the door, I managed to extricate myself by pulling out my wallet and handing him a couple bucks.

Inside, the place was packed. The front room contains an enormous oven, before which the current proprietor—Short Mann, as they call him, is easily six feet tall, though a good six inches shorter than his father—stood with a pair of tongs, every now and then pulling out a sizzling slab of beef and throwing it on a platter. A couple of women, both black, labored over a sil-ver bowl that must have been three feet wide, mixing up the watery salad nobody likes but everybody tolerates, and three or four waitresses hustled in and out of the hallways that lead out of the main room. Fortunately, I didn't see anybody I knew. Walking across the street, I'd started feeling spooked.

"Somebody'll be with y'all in just a minute," Short Mann assured us.

Maggie leaned against me, squeezing my hand, her hair brushing my shoulder. "This reminds me of a place in Durham. But there it's not steaks. It's that tangy, vinegar-based barbecue."

A waitress finally led us down the hallway to the right, into the room where celebrities sometimes sit. It looked like a family reunion was in progress back there, four long tables lined up together to accommodate five or six guys and their wives and ten or twelve kids with the pug-nosed features of a pit bull. We took a small table in the corner, underneath a photo of George Jones, standing on the front porch with his arm around Short Mann. He'd signed the photo with a Sharpie and beneath his name scrawled *Dam fine steak.*

After we were seated, our waitress, a washed-out blonde who'd been working there as long as I could remember, remained standing by our table with a pad in her hand. They don't have menus, since if you know enough to go there, you know what they serve. "The thirty-two-ounce T-bone," I said.

Maggie looked at me as if I'd lost my mind. "Are you crazy?"

I laughed. "It's the smallest one they have."

"We got carryout boxes," the waitress said.

"I'm afraid we'll need one," Maggie told her. "Unless, of course, his appetite's a lot bigger than mine."

Secreted away in the back room with an extended family that had *hill country* written all over them, I recovered my nerves. I was out on the town with my girl—for the last time, I reminded myself—so we might as well have fun. "My appetite," I said, "will not let us down. We'll take a couple of those liquid salads, the home fries and two Heinekens."

"How y'all want your steak?"

"Medium-rare okay?" I asked Maggie.

"Medium-rare's perfect."

"The beers'll be right up," our waitress said. Her gaze lingered on me a little too long, and I realized that like a lot of people who serve others and hope like hell for a decent tip, she probably had a good eye for faces. "Steak'll take a while," she said, "but looks like y'all's in good company." She stuck the pencil behind her ear and hurried off towards the kitchen.

Maggie leaned closer and said, "She knows."

"Knows what?"

"What I'm not."

"How can you be so sure?"

"Previous experience. But I intend to hold my spot."

I knew that Jennifer had left her a message after the dinner at our place, suggesting they get together, but Maggie had neither replied nor written back to thank her for the recipe. When Jennifer mentioned it, I told her that Maggie, who after all had never taught school before, was probably just overwhelmed by all the changes in her life. A couple of times I'd started to raise the issue with Maggie, though I was reluctant to bring up anything that had to do with that particular evening. The image of her sitting there in her car with a cigarette clamped between her teeth still disturbed me, so for the most part I tried not to think about it.

The waitress reappeared with two sweaty bottles of Heineken. "You look to me like you'd probably appreciate a glass, wouldn't you?" she asked Maggie. Without waiting for a reply, she set down two plastic cups and took off again for the kitchen.

Maggie eyed them. "That's a glass?"

"It's what passes for one here."

"Well, I don't care. I like where I am." Again she squeezed my hand. "And I love who I'm here with."

I used to say "I love you" all the time. For the first few years of our marriage, I said it to Jennifer so often that she claimed I'd divested it of all meaning, like the Pledge of Allegiance. I said it to our daughters, too, and while Candace would always say it back, Trish had only done so once as far as I could recall, and that was the night the kid from Indianola got her shitfaced and left her in the cotton field. I told her I loved her when I found her out there on the turnrow, sobbing and smelling of vomit, and she said she loved me, too—though the next morning, when I reminded her of it, she shook her head. "Remember one thing, Daddy. I was *really* drunk."

That night at Mann's I said, "I love being here with you, too." Which isn't really the same thing.

We finished our beers fast, so I caught our waitress's eye and signaled for two more. These she stood alongside the others. At Mann's they don't remove your empties, just leave them on the table as if to provide you with proof, should you need it, that you're having a great time. I poured Maggie's cup full, then took a swig from my bottle.

"I wonder if this is the room we ate in back then," she said, glancing around at the photos hanging on the wall. "In that picture my brother has, you can't see much besides me and my steak."

"It easily could've been. I doubt this place has changed much since the day it opened."

"Did you come here often when you were a kid?"

"I didn't eat here until I was a senior in high school."

"Really?"

"My family couldn't afford it," I said. "That first time, Ellis and his wife brought me here to celebrate after Ole Miss gave me a scholarship."

"You're really close to him, aren't you?"

"A lot closer than I've ever been to my own father. Back when it mattered, Ellis was on the right side, and my dad wasn't. That led to a fair amount of unhappiness between us."

"Because of the racial issue?"

After what Ellis had told me about that evening back in 1962, I'd had a hard time facing my dad, because it was difficult to avoid the obvious conclusion: he'd talked Arlan Calloway into going to Oxford to keep a black student from enrolling at Ole Miss—looking out for my interests, as he'd put it—and then Arlan went back home, discovered something had happened in his absence that he didn't like and killed his wife. Whether my father saw it like this, I didn't know—only that when I'd said the name *Calloway* a couple months ago, he looked as if it was the last thing in the world he wanted to hear. "Yeah," I told Maggie, "because of the racial issue."

She took a sip of beer. "It sometimes seems that's all anyone here really cares about."

"In Mississippi, especially the Delta, it's how you tell the good folks from the bad ones."

"So you consider your father a bad man?"

I didn't want to pursue that line of discussion because, for one thing, I had no idea if she knew her dad had gone to Oxford with my father that night—and I certainly wasn't going to ask. "No," I said, "but when the chips were down, he played the wrong hand."

"Aren't the stakes a lot higher now, with your mother's illness? How many men would do what you tell me he's doing? Most people these days would just throw up their hands and cart her off to . . . well, whatever you want to call one of those places. Isn't that what you'd do? If it were your wife?"

The dunce cap, so long an object of ridicule, was originally designed by the thirteenth-century logician John Duns Scotus, who believed its conical shape would funnel wisdom into the gray matter of anybody who wore it. I must've had it on that night, even though the folks having their reunion looked over a few times and never cracked up laughing. I just sat there pondering what I'd do if Jennifer ever ended up like my mother. "I guess it would depend on factors beyond my control," I finally said, "like whether I could still move around and handle taking care of somebody. But honestly, what's the point in what-iffing? I'm not in that situation. If I ever find myself in it, then we'll see what I'd do."

"I guess so," she said. "Well, let's hope that day never comes." She raised her plastic cup. "To Jennifer's health," she proposed, turning it up and taking a swallow.

Our steak spilled off both sides of the platter and had to be at least two inches thick. Short Mann had made surgical incisions at various points, making it easier to tear the meat away from the bone.

After ordering more beer, I pulled loose a chunk of porterhouse that could've been a meal in itself and served it on Maggie's plate along with a mound of home fries. Then I took a piece for myself, still leaving more than half of the steak on that big white platter.

We didn't talk much while eating, just savored the meat. Sometimes it's good to be reminded just how wonderful life's finest moments can be, and whenever I consider the best times I've known, I always go back to that night at Mann's with Maggie. I was eating a meal I couldn't afford with a woman I couldn't afford, either, with all her attention focused on me, and nothing ever seemed better. My notion to tell her our affair was over had dissipated, like a squall line that blows itself out. I would do it, I promised myself. Just not now.

The party next to us broke up about the time we finished eating. As they were leaving, I asked the waitress to bring us a carryout box, and we stuffed a huge chunk of steak inside. "I'll let you have this," Maggie said, "since you're on your own for a while." I started to protest—I couldn't risk Jennifer finding that box in the trash can with MANN'S EATIN' PLACE written on the lid in bright red letters—but she insisted, so I tucked it under my arm.

In the car, I gestured at the dashboard clock. "It's not even nine yet. Any ideas?" I assumed we'd go over to her place and crawl into bed, as we had so many times in the last couple of months.

Instead, she said, "Let's get a bottle of champagne and ride around."

So I drove back to the highway and, at a liquor store on the outskirts of town, bought not one but two bottles of Freixenet and asked the clerk for a couple paper cups. I popped the first cork in the parking lot, stood the cups on the hood and poured them full.

"What do they do to you in Mississippi," she said as I pulled back onto the highway, "if they catch you with an open container?"

"Confiscate it and drink it themselves." This reminded me of a story I hadn't yet told her. "An uncle of mine was sheriff up in Lee County," I said, "back in the Fifties when the whole state was still dry. And he had a deal with the local bootleggers. He'd raid them once a month, take half of whatever they had on hand, then he and his deputies'd have a big party out behind the jail. Well, one year he decides to take my aunt and cousins to the Smokies on vacation, and because he'd miss his regular raiding day he hits all the bootleggers a couple days early.

"He heads off down into a holler where there's this one old guy he's been dealing with for a good fifteen years, and when the bootlegger sees him he whips out a shotgun and fills my uncle's chest full of buckshot. Once he's out of danger, my dad goes to visit him in the hospital and asks what happened. And he shakes his head and says, 'Aw, hell, James, it was my fault. I should've just waited till we got back off vacation.' "

I tell the story often. It's almost always good for a laugh, especially if I'm giving it to an outsider who likes seeing Southern stereotypes confirmed. All I got from Maggie, though, was a faint smile, and that froze me in my seat. "I'm sorry," I said. "I just realized how insensitive it was, that particular story."

"*I'm* sorry. You wanted me to laugh, but I've got my mind on something else."

"I know, thinking about what happened to your mom."

We were coming into Leland, just passing Barsotti's, for sixty years a good place for a cheap plate of pasta, when she let me have the laugh I'd been trolling for. She laughed so hard, and so long, that most of the champagne sloshed out of her cup. Some of it even got on me. I felt a damp spot near my right knee.

"You think that's what I'm thinking about?" she said. "Tonight?"

I pulled up to the stoplight at the intersection of 82 and old Highway 61. "Okay," I said. "So you're not thinking about your mom, then why don't you tell me what's so funny?"

"The evening I came to your house for dinner?"

"Yeah?"

"You remember I left the table and went to the bathroom?"

I did remember because for one brief moment I'd thought about following her, under the guise of showing her where it was, hoping to take her in my arms and kiss her there in my own house. But for once sanity prevailed and I stayed in my chair. "Vaguely," I said. "I'd had a lot to drink."

"Well, I'm laughing because on my way back I decided to open the door to your bedroom. I couldn't stop myself—I just wanted to see inside. But do you know what?"

The chill I felt had nothing to do with the champagne she'd dumped on my knee. "What?"

"It was locked," she said. "Now, don't you think that's funny?"

SHE'D CHOSEN MY SIDE of the bed, which is where I found her when I stepped out of the bathroom. Her clothes lay neatly folded on the wicker chair, her flashy turquoise boots standing side by side on the floor in front of our closet. Her eyes were shut. At first I thought she was teasing me, pretending to be asleep, but then realized I was wrong. She barely stirred when I crawled in beside her.

I reached over and switched off the light, but I couldn't sleep. I lay there listening and, every time a car went by, had to fight off a surge of panic. Jennifer hadn't called or left a message, and that seemed odd since she always had before. When she'd gone to the conference in the past, of course, the girls were still home, and she couldn't let an evening pass without speaking to them.

Earlier, while we sat on the living room couch and drained both bottles of Freixenet, still using those paper cups, I'd tried to stall the conversation, in hopes that before long she would say she wanted me to take her home. I might even have talked about the weather, which was unseasonably warm. The truth is I don't remember what I said. *This is not a game*, is what I remember thinking, *this is her life*.

Lying there in bed I considered, for the first time in many weeks, just how difficult it is to keep a love affair secret in a place as small as Loring. People know before you know they know, in the way we all know things without having any information. There's a feeling in the air around two people who are focused on each other. Even if they don't touch, even if they studiously ignore each other in public, folks pick up on it.

Our house was built in 1927. It's one of those old Delta houses where there's a skeleton key that fits all the interior doors. We used to use it to lock our bedroom door from the inside, but quit doing that after the girls got older because, as Jennifer noted, you can hear the lock turning from a mile away. I hadn't even seen the key for years. So either Maggie was lying about the door being locked that night, or Jennifer had gone to considerable trouble in order to do so. If I'd had to wager, I would've bet Maggie was telling the truth.

All the stuff I'd just put down my throat—steak, fries, beer, champagne—threatened to come back up, and my stomach acid was churning. Every time I thought about Jennifer coming home unannounced—pulling into the driveway, slowly walking across the yard, climbing the steps and unlocking the front door—I wished that my existence could somehow be erased. That scenario, of course, didn't account for Maggie at all, and for the first time I felt a great pity for her. I saw how much had been taken away from her, and knew that I'd soon become yet another mark in the loss column of her life. Anyway, I hoped that was all I'd be, that she'd go back to her big house in North Carolina, find someone else and forget about me.

In other words, I wanted to emerge from our entanglement guilt free. Doesn't everybody? People want it up until the very moment their wish is granted, and then they really hate it that they meant so little to the other person, that he or she actually managed to get over the pain rather than die of disappointment. Illicit lovers are like ravenous nations, eager to retain the ground they gained at somebody else's expense.

I lay there listening, determined to stay awake until the sun came up, at which point I planned to get out of bed, go into the living room and hold a loud, fake conversation on the phone with one of the girls, then tell Maggie that they'd been involved in an accident in Oxford and I needed to run up there and check on them. I'd offer to drop her off at her place on my way out of town. Fortunately, I'd parked the car in the garage, so none of the neighbors would see me walking out the front door first thing in the morning with a woman most people in town would probably recognize by now.

I never experienced that misty moment when you know you're about to fall asleep. If I had, I would've popped out of bed and gone out back to do calisthenics, whatever it took. I must have dropped off around 4:00, though, because I remember looking at the bedside clock at 3:47.

That's what I thought when I woke up—that somehow I'd dozed off for a moment, that it was now maybe 4:00 a.m. But then why was it light outside? Why were birds singing? And whose voices were those that sounded like they were coming from the living room? I'd made damn certain to chain the front door.

My feet hit the floor like two sacks of concrete. Wildly, I looked around the room for my clothes, then realized I'd left them in the bathroom. I grabbed my robe off a hanger in the closet and pulled it on. Jennifer must have washed it recently, because the belt was missing, so I drew both halves of it together with one hand and swiped the other at Maggie's foot, protruding from the covers.

Eyes still closed, she stretched luxuriously, her palms reaching up as if to touch the ceiling. In that instant, I think, I must have hated her. "Goddamn it. Wake up."

She opened her eyes then, and whereas I still didn't know exactly what was happening and why some young guy was saying, "Hey, this is a cool-looking house y'all got," she sized up the predicament immediately. "It's your daughters," she said quietly, sitting up in bed, then swinging her legs over the side and placing her feet silently on the floor. "Get out there and talk to them. And Luke? Try not to look like you just robbed a bank."

"What about you?"

"I did rob the bank," she said. "Just get out there and talk. Act happy to see them."

In the hallway I tripped on a throw rug that had been in the same place for about twenty years. When I walked into the living room, the front door was open and Trish was there along with not one, not two, but three guys. One of them was about six-three and must have weighed damn near three hundred pounds. He had on faded jeans and an Ole Miss football jersey—number 92. The other two guys were carbon copies, standard-issue Ole Miss frat boys: khaki slacks, knit pullovers, scuffed loafers.

"Hi, Daddy," Trish said. She'd arrayed herself on the couch in what Jennifer called her Jean Harlow pose: one long leg on the cushions, the other off, her chin propped up on an elbow. "Looks like you had some fun here last night," she observed, eyeing the Freixenet bottles and empty cups on the coffee table.

"Mr. Buchanan came by," I said. It amazed me how easily the lie rolled off my lips, especially since I had no idea I was going to say that. "He and I started talking about Hodding Carter and the *Delta Democrat*, and I opened a bottle."

"This is what our dad does when he wants to be wild," Trish told the guys. "He kicks back and talks about dead people."

The guy in the jersey laughed. The other two just grinned like they were embarrassed, though it was unclear whether it was about me or themselves.

Candace strolled through the front door carrying one of those thirty-two-ounce sodas they sell at 7-Eleven. "Forgot this," she said. The moment the big kid saw her, I knew what she meant to him. His whole face changed, and he looked astonished, though she couldn't have been out of his sight for more than a minute or two. His right hand rose, then fluttered help-lessly in the air. You could tell he wanted to reach out and touch her, but not with her father in the room.

"Daddy," she said, "this is Rick Bailey."

"Pleased to meet you, Mr. May." He offered that dangling hand and I was happy to take it, just to give him something to do with it. Such a big hand, and so helpless and sweaty.

"Rick's on the team," Candace said, "but he's injured."

"Just got my feelings hurt a little bit," he told me. "But I'll be playing again next season."

"We decided to drive to Fayetteville," Candace said, "for the game tonight."

"We're playing the Razorbacks. *Sooey*, pig!" Trish squealed. Her eyes, I noticed now, were red rimmed. She'd definitely been toking.

"And this," Candace said, nodding at the other two guys, "is our friend Billy Kershaw and his brother Bobby."

Still holding my robe closed, I shook hands with each of them.

"We just took a notion to do this about three or four this morning," Rick said. "I feel bad about waking you up, Mr. May, but Trish said you never slept past seven."

"What time is it, anyway?"

"A quarter past eight," Trish said.

"How'd you get in?"

"When we saw the front door was still chained, Rick lifted the garage door high enough for me to crawl inside, so I came through the laundry room."

"Well, I'm glad to see you guys," I lied, "but isn't this a little bit of a detour?"

"Rick's from Arcola," Candace said. "We'll stop at his place and pick up his sister."

"To kind of balance things out," Trish said.

And then, I figured, everybody would go one on one. I wondered which of the Kershaw twins would get down in the trenches with her.

"People say it gets cold over in Arkansas," Candace told me, "so we decided to pick up our down jackets." She turned and started down the hall.

"Get mine too, okay?" Trish called.

At that moment it occurred to me to wonder whether I'd shut the bedroom door when I'd bounded through it. Surely to God I had, hadn't I? I took off down the hall after her, but I was too late. The door was wide open, and my daughter had paused to look inside. I stood there shaking, an icy sweat flowing out of every pore. I could feel it trickling down my back and legs.

The bed was partially made, the covers thrown back at an angle on my side, exposing a triangular stretch of fitted sheet. The closet yawned open, as did the bathroom. Maggie was nowhere in sight.

"Want me to make you guys some coffee?" I asked, trying to keep the tremor out of my voice. I hoped that when I went into the kitchen, I'd see the chain dangling from the back door, and in the end I found just that, proving she'd mapped her exit strategy before getting into bed.

"Sure," Candace said, "some coffee would be nice."

But for some reason, she continued to stand there rather than move on down the hall.

When I was a boy, my grandfather had an annoying little dog named Johnson. He could have been named for LBJ, though that seems unlikely, or—more plausibly—for Paul B. Johnson, Jr., who succeeded Ross Barnett as governor. I don't remember and am not sure I ever knew.

Johnson, who I guess was a rat terrier, stayed busy from morning till night, causing as much trouble as he could, gnawing on people's shoes while they tried to eat, chewing the Memphis paper to bits if you didn't get it first thing in the morning, before Grandpa turned him loose. He'd pick up virtually any small object with his mean little teeth and carry it off to places none of us ever discovered. And unlike most Delta dogs, he was nonracial. Usually, dogs belonging to black people would only bark at whites, or vice versa, but Johnson barked at every living creature who entered his sphere of existence.

As far as anyone could tell, he was completely useless—up until you put him in a boat and paddled out on a lake, at which point he finally fell silent. Then, when you passed over a bream bed where the bluegills were spawning, he'd stick his nose into the air and sniff, letting you know it was time to drop your hook.

Standing there in the hallway, Candace did the same thing. She sniffed once, then twice. And though she never said a word, just trudged at last down the hall to get those down jackets so they wouldn't freeze to death up in Fayetteville, I knew exactly what she was thinking: That's not Momma's fragrance.

BEING SOMEONE'S CHILD, it seems to me now, is a maddening state of affairs. You can always sense when something's wrong in your parents' lives, but you generally don't know what it is, and they aren't about to tell you, even if you're already an adult yourself. They have—or believe they do—a vested interest in preserving your ignorance. There are questions they don't want you to ask, and if by some accident you happen to pose them, they'll either refuse to answer or just lie.

From an early age I understood that my father was a man of few words. In Parker Sturdivant's barbershop he seldom spoke. In the rare instances when he did, it was usually to say something about the weather or to comment on how the fish were biting or not in Lake Lee. He never complained about his wife like the other men did, nor did he join in when they talked about football. His father hadn't let him go out for the team when he was in school, since practice would've interfered with his cotton picking. Never having played—in a society where tall, athletic-looking boys were duty-bound to uphold their town's honor on Friday nights by catching passes, leveling runners or scoring touchdowns—was something I don't think he ever lived down. It just gave him one more reason to hate the fall—which, as I once heard him say, was the season when his fortunes always fell.

Oddly enough, given his membership in an organization

openly dedicated to preventing the advancement of blacks, he spoke far more freely in their presence than around the men in the barbershop. One day I heard him tell a black man named Tea Burns, as they crawled around in the dirt beneath our old Allis-Chalmers, that there were times when he wished the Sunflower River bridge would collapse while his mother-in-law was driving across it, then went on to say that he also sometimes hoped she'd contract a deadly disease, though he never explained why. I heard him tell another black man, whose name I don't remember, how much he hated having to go and beg Herman Horton for money every March, that he'd rather drop his drawers in the middle of Front Street and take a crap while the whole town watched. Nodding sympathetically, that man, whoever he was, said, "Yes sir, I know just what you mean. There's days when I'd like to shit downtown myself."

While I couldn't imagine why my father wanted bad things to happen to my grandmother, what he said about turning Front Street into a bathroom made me giggle. But later on, when I imagined having to face Eugene and my other friends if he ever did anything like that, I became deeply unsettled. Something was wrong in my dad's life, I could see that, though I didn't know what it was or how I could help fix it. I just figured it wasn't anything he and I would ever discuss, and that assumption, I'm sorry to say, was correct.

On that September day in 1962, when Arlan Calloway made his remarks about the land we lived on being "public" and then clapped my father on the back, it was unusually quiet in the pickup going home. Normally, Dad would gaze out at whatever cotton field we were passing and offer some bit of information he thought would prove useful when I started farming myself, and it was a given that I would. "Time's coming," he might say, "when most folks'll be growing those high spindling stalks like's in that field out there. That stuff slides into a mechanical picker nice and easy. But those old breeds with lots of heavy branches down low, that's where the real yield is. Pick by hand just as long as you can." Or "Been me, I would've rotated soybeans or peanuts into that patch this year. That land's tired, and soybeans and peanuts are a source of free nitrogen." That day he didn't say a thing. He didn't even look out the window, just trained his eyes on the ridge of gravel in the middle of the road, gripping the steering wheel so tightly that his knuckles turned white.

I wondered how our land, and the house we lived in, could be "public." The school I went to was public, and it said so on the side of the bus I rode: LORING PUBLIC SCHOOL SYSTEM. That meant anybody could go to school there, as long as they were white. In that sense, all of us owned it. But if our land was public, and our house, too, that must mean that they belonged to everybody, not just us. This made me wonder if everything else I'd thought was ours was public property as well. Did my father own the pickup we were riding in? What about our tractors, our cotton trailers, our combine? And all the stuff in our house? Did Eugene have as much claim to my clothes and toys as I did?

Up ahead, on the left, the Calloways' place came into view. Mr. Calloway's truck wasn't there—he'd driven away from the barbershop in the opposite direction, as if headed downtown—but Nadine's sky-blue Tempest was parked in the driveway. I'd gotten to know that car fairly well, having ridden to town in it on numerous occasions with her and Eugene and Maggie. She always let me sit up front beside her, making her own kids ride in the back. "Luke's company," she said if either of them complained, "though he's also family." She'd reach across the seat after saying that, giving my hand a little squeeze and following it up with a wink.

I waited to see if my father would slow down and look across the yard, as it was common to do when you passed a neighbor's house. Whoever was inside might glance out the window when they heard you driving by, and it would be offensive not to wave. You even waved at people you didn't know, if you passed them on the road, or at least you raised your hand, unless, of course, they happened to be black. If they were, waving seemed to be optional, but my father always did it, so I did, too.

Not only did he fail to slow down that day, he actually sped up, as if he wanted to put the Calloways behind us just as fast as he could. He continued to stare straight ahead.

I looked over the gun rack in the rear window, thinking maybe Nadine had stepped outside when she heard us, but I couldn't see through the cloud of dust. "Daddy?" I said.

He acted as if he hadn't heard me. Though he was known to be the slowest driver in the county—something the men in the barbershop joked about sometimes, claiming they'd fallen asleep at the wheel while creeping along behind him—he pressed the accelerator to the floor.

Cotton fields dissolved into a white blur. The wind whipping in through the window took my breath away, and I had to turn in his direction to fill my lungs. What I saw scared me. His jaw was locked tight, his bottom lip quivered, and his right cheek looked damp, though it wasn't hot out.

When we got to our house, he wheeled into the yard so fast that for a moment I thought he intended to drive right into the living room and knock all the walls down, since apparently they weren't ours anyway. As I braced myself against the dashboard he finally slammed his foot on the brake, throwing up dirt and gravel. Later that afternoon, while he was out in the field, I inspected the deep grooves in the driveway.

I expected him to jump out of the truck, slam the door and storm inside, but he didn't. My mother was home, and my grandmother was there, too, and I doubt he was in a hurry to give them any news. On the other hand, he must've been afraid that I wanted to ask him about the conversation in the parking lot. It's nice to think that if I had known of his apprehension I would have kept my mouth shut, but that gives the child I was then too much credit. I was interested in only one thing: how all that talk about our land being public would affect me.

"Daddy?"

He didn't answer right away. What he did was turn loose of the steering wheel, resting his left hand on his thigh. He turned his right hand over and studied it for a moment, as if he'd never noticed it before. Then he reached across the seat and patted my knee. "Yeah, son?"

The whine I heard in my own voice only scared me further, but taming it was beyond my control: "Was Mr. Calloway saying he might take our house? Is that what all that stuff about things being 'public' was about?"

"Arlan ain't nothing but a blowhard," he said. "You know what a blowhard is?"

"No sir, I don't."

He puffed his cheeks out until it looked as if they'd explode, then blew all the air out at me, and it smelled like coffee and cigarettes. He lifted his hand off my knee and mussed my hair. "That was just a waste of breath, wasn't it?"

"Yes sir. I guess so."

"Well, sometimes that's what Mr. Calloway likes to do. Wasting a little breath's just his way of staying amused. Didn't do that, he'd bore himself to death. He's not going to take our house, don't you worry."

Just like that, he put it out of my mind, which I believe he would've said is what a father's for, had we ever discussed that topic in later years, after I became a father myself. "Well, good," I said. "He doesn't need another house anyhow. He's already got one of his own."

"Yeah, and he probably ought to spend a little more time worrying about what goes on there. But that's for him to decide, not me." He glanced at his watch. "Come on," he said, "and let's eat us some Viennas and saltines. I believe I saw a big bottle of RC in the refrigerator. That still your favorite soda water?"

"Yes sir, that and Dr Pepper."

So we got out of the truck and walked towards our house. And if he sagged any beneath the weight I'd deposited squarely on his shoulders, it was never apparent to me.

THE DAY MY DAUGHTERS almost caught me in bed with Maggie, I waited until I saw their friend's car turn the corner at the end of our block. Then I ran through the kitchen and out the back door onto the porch.

Our backyard isn't fenced—few in this part of the world are. I could see our picnic table and the little shed where I kept the lawn mower and the few hand tools I knew how to use. Ten or twelve years ago, somebody, probably one of the neighbor kids, got in there and stole a set of screwdrivers and a power drill, so I put a padlock on the door. In the dew, still heavy that early in the morning, I could see a trail of footsteps leading right up to it, then they veered off into the yard next door.

I went back inside and dialed Maggie's number on my cell phone. I got her voice-mail, and rather than leave her a message I threw my clothes on, jumped in the car and started down the street, trying to imagine what route she'd take if she'd decided to walk home.

I didn't get far before my phone rang. When I answered, she said, "You looked terrified when you heard those kids in the living room. I felt so sorry for you."

I was just passing Ellis's house, so I drove a little farther before pulling to the curb. "Yeah," I said, "it scared the hell out of me. Not much point in trying to conceal that."

"No, there certainly isn't."

"Where are you?"

"At my place."

The only way she could have gotten there so fast would've been to sprint the whole distance, and even that was pushing it. "How'd you get there?"

"Caught a ride."

"A *ride*? With who?"

"Does it matter?"

"It might."

"Your friend Ellis. He just left here a couple minutes ago. I invited him in for coffee, but he said he had to go run some errands."

"Ellis Buchanan? Jesus, where did he see you?"

"He was pulling out of his driveway when I walked by."

"What did you tell him you were doing over here?"

"I told him I woke up at five-thirty, couldn't go back to sleep and decided to take a long, long walk."

"You think he believed you?"

"Of course not, but he's too polite to show it."

"What did he say?"

"He just said that it was a nice morning for a walk and that if he were a little younger, he might've taken one, too."

It occurred to me then that before the day got much older, I probably ought to do something smart and quit sitting in the car in front of somebody else's house, talking on the cell phone. So I told her I was going home to take a shower and I'd call back once I'd had some coffee. She said that was fine and hung up.

I pulled around the block and went back to my house, where indeed I took a shower and put on a pot of coffee. Waiting for it to brew, I phoned my wife.

When she answered, there was noise in the background that sounded like a marching band. "Hey," she said, "what have *you* been up to?"

At a moment like that, what do you think of? A thin-shouldered girl sitting on a stack of books in the aisle of a library. What a doe's eyes look like when she's dying. The amazement you heard in the voice of your young wife when she told you she was pregnant, and how you felt as you sat beside her in the operating room, holding her hand while a doctor and several nurses hovered over her performing a C-section. The sweat that ran down your back when your daughter stood in the hallway sniffing a strange odor. It's a wonder I got any words out. "Nothing much. What's that I hear in the background?"

"We're at a café. They're having some kind of parade outside on the street. I think maybe there's a home game today."

"How's the conference going?"

"Just fine. I read last night, at an open-mike thing." Until now, she'd always been harsh about stuff like that and poetry slams. If your work's any good, she claimed, a stranger sitting alone in a room with six hundred poems on his or her desk should be able to recognize it. And if no one did, maybe you should quit writing and go grade some more papers. You could never accuse her of getting too romantic about her poems, though she always acted as if she thought I was about to.

"It's great you got up there and read," I said. "Did they like it?"

"It seems so."

"Hey, that's fabulous. I'm proud of you." She didn't say anything, so I kept talking: "The girls dropped in on me this morning."

"I know. Candace just called me."

"She did?"

Until then she'd sounded cheerful, though now I thought I heard that querulous note creeping in. "I just said she did."

"She had a gigantic guy with her, and unless I'm dreaming he's her new boyfriend."

"I think you might be right. Look, I should probably go—

there's another session in fifteen minutes. We'll talk tomorrow, when I get home." And just like that, she was gone.

I poured myself a cup of coffee, then went into the living room and sat down on the couch. But I didn't want to look at those champagne bottles and cups right then, so I carried my coffee into the study, where I called Candace and got her voice-mail and told her to travel safely and let me know when they were back in Oxford. Then I called Trish, with the same results. And then, because I wasn't ready to call Maggie yet and couldn't think of anything else to do, I dialed my dad.

I hadn't been over there since Wednesday and hadn't even talked to him since Thursday morning. I'd promised to come by on Friday afternoon, but in my excitement about having an evening alone with Maggie, I'd forgotten.

The phone rang six times before he lifted the receiver. "Yeah?"

"Hey, it's me. How're you doing?"

The answer was a long time coming. "How *could* I be doing?"

"I'm sorry I didn't make it by yesterday. There was an issue at work, then I came home to grade some papers and damn if I didn't fall asleep. By the time I woke up, it was too late to call."

"Too late for you, maybe. Over here we didn't sleep."

"What's wrong?"

"Well, to start with, your momma took another fall."

That got me up off the couch. "What kind of fall?"

"Is there more than one kind?"

"I mean, how did it happen?"

"It happened just like it did," he said.

"When?"

"Whenever it happened. Son, you think we time everything? Over here it's always sunset."

"Listen," I said, "I'll be there in five minutes."

"Suit yourself," he said. "Five minutes or five hours, it won't make much difference."

.   .   .

I unlocked the front door, but it was still chained, so I rang
the bell and hollered, "It's me." When he finally let me in, I
saw what shape he was in and knew I needed to get him to the
doctor. It looked as if he hadn't shaved in days. He was bare-
footed, he'd buttoned his shirt unevenly, and the odor coming
off him made me gasp. Most disturbingly, his right eye was full
of blood.

"This is how things get towards the end," he said. "If it's any
comfort to you, it ain't half as bad as I was scared it might be."

"What happened to your eye?"

"Blood vessel busted, I imagine."

"When'd you first notice it?"

He actually laughed. Then he shook his head. "Lord God,"
he said.

I didn't see what was funny about my question, and said so.
All that did was make him chuckle again. "Let me tell you about
something I read one time," he said. "I can't remember the name
of the book, but it belonged to an old boy I bunked with in the
navy. Took place during the French Revolution. There's a scene
I never will forget, just because of my reaction to it. See, they're
about to use the guillotine to execute this fellow for being an
aristocrat or something, and two of 'em grab him by the arms
and throw him down face-first on the board he'll be layin' on
when the blade falls. And when I read it, I thought, Now ain't
that awful, making him hit his nose so hard?" He stuck his hands
in his pockets. "You think I'm worried about having a red eye?
Lord, boy, you got some learnin' left to do."

There wasn't much point in asking him again how my mother
had fallen. He wasn't going to tell me, and I could figure it out
anyway. He'd gone into a stupor, probably because of his diabetes medication, which was a diuretic that often left him
drained. And at the end of her bed, there was a small space

between the foot and side rails that she was thin enough to slide right through.

The question was, how badly was she hurt? "You think she broke anything this time?" I asked, as casually as I could.

"I don't believe so. I remember how her hip looked last time, and I'm not seeing anything like that now."

"Of course, you're not a doctor."

"No, and neither are you."

He hadn't moved since I came in. As old and stooped as he was, he still filled the hallway. To get to my mom's room I'd have to get past him, and he didn't seem inclined to yield any ground.

"Okay if I go in there and see her?" I asked.

"She's your momma," he said, then stepped aside and let me by.

She was lying on her right side, facing the wall. Her right hand stuck out behind her body, in a position no one with any control over her muscles would have tolerated for more than a few seconds. I won't try to reproduce the noise she was making. The best I can do is to say that it reminded me of how a scratched record sounds when it starts skipping.

I walked around the foot of the bed so I could see her face. She had a purple bruise on her forehead and a small gash on her bottom lip.

"Momma?" I said.

She never looked at me, just kept staring at the wall and making that sound. I pulled the covers back and scanned her legs and ankles to see if they were bruised or if there was any obvious sign of a break, but nothing caught my eye. I knew I ought to lift her gown and look at her hips and her rib cage but couldn't bring myself to do it. I knew, too, that her diaper was full and needed changing. I couldn't make myself do that either, not even by thinking of how often she'd changed mine.

My father was standing in the doorway. "If you got something to say," he said, "go on and say it now."

"You know what I'm going to say."

"Yeah. You're about as easy to read as Zane Grey."

I stepped back around the bed. "Dad," I said, "the first thing is, both of you need to see the doctor."

"I've seen him. He's a two-hundred-and-forty-pound package of conventional wisdom. Ain't nothing he can tell me I don't already know."

"Look, it's getting to the point where you can't handle it."

"No, it's gettin' to the point where *you* can't. I'm handling my part just fine. That's what I said I'd do when I got married. I said I'd care for her, and later on I said I'd care for you, as long as you needed me to. Looks like maybe you still do."

"What's that supposed to mean?"

He crossed his arms over his chest. "You really want me to answer that question?"

I knew from how he'd put it that I didn't. There was no chance he could answer it without spelling out some qualitative differences between the two of us. And what could I say in return? That unlike him, I'd never called another human being a "nigger" or voted for candidates who, if allowed to, would've rolled back every single civil rights initiative since the 1950s? That I hadn't supported failed wars or sent twenty dollars a month to the NRA so it could maintain its choke hold on our political system? Those things were true, and they were not insignificant, but they dealt with public affairs. And what we'd end up discussing, I suddenly felt sure, was a private misdemeanor. "I guess maybe not," I said.

My father stepped over and put his arm around my shoulders. "It ain't all perfume, son," he said. "We sign on for the smelly parts too."

I went out and did some shopping for him and bought him a couple newspapers, and by the time I got back he'd changed my mother's diaper and she'd finally fallen asleep. I kept an eye on her long enough for him to take a shower, then made him a ham and cheese sandwich and sat with him in the kitchen while he ate it. Momma was still asleep when he finished, so he told me to take off and let him get some rest. He'd call me if he needed me, he said, and if he didn't I should assume things were all right. I promised to drop by again the next day.

It was midafternoon when I got home. I stripped off the bed-clothes, put them in the washer, opened all the windows and turned on the attic fan. Then I found some brandy in the kitchen and poured myself a big slug that I downed in three or four gulps and finally sat on the couch to call Maggie.

I knew exactly what I was going to have to tell her, and I think she must've known, too. I would say all the most pre-dictable things: that I really did love her and, in a perfect world, would gladly have spent the rest of my life with her, enjoying her company and all the excitement she offered. That I'd never met anyone else like her. That I wished she could somehow for-give me if I'd caused her pain, and that I wanted to remain her friend. All of this, except the last, was true. I knew, as surely as I knew my name and date of birth, that we couldn't possibly be friends, and what I really wanted was for her to leave and spare me and my family the misery that was sure to come if she stayed in Mississippi.

I got her voice-mail but didn't record a message. I called her off and on until almost eleven, each time with no luck. I could have climbed into my car and driven over to her place and knocked on the door, but I didn't. Instead, cell phone in one hand and remote in the other, I sat there on the couch watching Ole Miss and Arkansas on ESPN, hoping for a glimpse of my daughters.

OVERNIGHT, a cold front blew through, and when I woke up the next morning, our recent spate of warm weather was over. I turned up the heat, then flicked on my cell phone. It immediately began beeping, informing me of three text-messages and a voice-mail.

The first text was from Trish: *fooey pig boo hoo they beat us how r u?* The second was from Candace: *We're at a Waffle House in Little Rock and it's three a.m. I miss you, Daddy. I hope you're all right. I'll send another message when we get back to Oxford.* Her last text said, *We're here, Daddy. I love you. I hope you're okay. Maybe you could call me tonight?*

Jennifer had left the voice-mail. "Luke," she said, "I wanted you to know we got up early and are leaving a lot sooner than we'd originally planned. I should be home before lunch. So if you've made a mess there—well, you still have time to clean it up." In the background, I heard a woman laugh.

I put on a pot of coffee, then took a look around the house to make sure no evidence remained from the other night. I didn't see anything that didn't belong there, so I went outside for the Memphis paper and read it while drinking my coffee.

The previous evening, I'd decided to call Maggie first thing this morning and get it out of the way, so whatever her reaction was going to be, I could put it behind me. But now that didn't seem very smart, or even right. I'd see her at school the next day, and we could make arrangements to talk after work. She at least deserved a chance to tell me whatever she wanted to in person, though that wasn't an encounter I was looking forward to.

Jennifer pulled up in the driveway at a quarter till twelve. One look at her, and I knew the conference must have gone well. She hopped out of the car, slinging her hair and smiling, and I hugged her, grabbed her overnight bag and carried it inside. In the kitchen, while I made us sandwiches, she told me that the poetry editor of the *Missouri Review* had heard her open-mike reading, walked up to her afterwards and said he'd like to publish her work, and that when she thanked him and explained that three of the poems had already been accepted by *Tin House*, his response was "What about the other two?"

"And what did you say?"

"I told him they hadn't been taken—that in fact his journal had rejected them last spring. And he said, 'Well, everybody makes mistakes. They've been taken now,' and then he smiled and put out his hand. So I gave him the poems, and he'll send me a contract next week."

"Jesus. You could have a book soon."

"You know, I never even dared to think about that. But now it doesn't seem so far-fetched. Those are two of the best lit magazines in the country. Maybe I'm not as bad as I always assumed."

In that moment I understood what bound us together, beyond simply a shared history. We both thought we lacked some essential quality that might've made us consequential in ways that we weren't, but the main difference was that she'd never quit trying to find it in herself. Whereas I always had tried to find it in someone else, some historical figure or local exemplar, hoping to parlay those lessons into making myself special.

I put the plates down on the table. "I never thought your poetry was bad," I said. "It's just that I never really understood it, though I tried to. That's a comment on me, not you. You want something to drink?"

"Now that," she said, "is a comment on you."

"What is?"

"Asking me if I want something to drink before I've had a chance to respond."

She was smiling, so I said, "I'm sorry. By all means—please respond."

"First I want something to drink."

"Like what?"

She was standing behind her usual chair, where she'd sat for years when all four of us were gathered around the kitchen table. There was her place, and my place, and Candace's and Trish's. We never moved around. If I'd ever walked in and found her or one of the girls in my chair, I wouldn't have known how to react. That's what marriage and family do to you—or what they'd done to us, anyway—and right then it seemed utterly correct. Who doesn't want to know where he or she belongs? Who wants to have to look for a place?

"How about some champagne?" she said. "Got any Freixenet?"

I'd always suspected I would make a poor criminal, that I'd either fail to lie when that was called for, or that I'd just lie badly. Now I knew my suspicions were sound. "Freixenet?" I said.

"Uh-huh. Like you drank the other night with Ellis. Except that, as you and I both know, Ellis Buchanan hates champagne. He won't even drink it on New Year's Eve."

We faced off across the table. Oddly enough, she was still smiling. It struck me then, as it does every time I remember the moment, that Jennifer can't act. She is what she is, and everybody knows it. And that day she was anything but displeased.

"Well?" she said.

"I guess one of the girls mentioned it."

"I guess so. Candace called first and never said a word about it. I could tell something was bothering her, though. But Trish wanted to tell me how hilarious it was that you and Ellis had spent an evening sitting there sipping bubbly and discussing the dead."

"Didn't you check with him?" I asked.

"No, because I know he'd lie. He'd lie so convincingly, and with so much charm, that I might be tempted to believe him."

If I'd been an abject canine, this is the point at which I would've rolled over and exposed my belly, begging for mercy and then requesting to be finished off. "What do you want me to do?" I said. "Or say?"

"I don't want you to say anything. I really don't. What I want you to *do* is sit down and listen while *I* say a few things. But before that," she said, "I want you to go over there to the pantry. Down low, in the right-hand corner of the bottom shelf, there should be a bottle of Cook's that I want you to take out and put in the freezer."

What she wanted to talk about, after my shaking hands jammed in that bottle of champagne beside our Thanksgiving turkey, was poetry. Specifically, the writing of it. She wanted to tell me what she'd heard a poet say at the conference. She said he wasn't exactly major, so I wouldn't know his name—not that I would've if he *had* been.

This minor poet, whoever he was, participated in a panel discussion about workshops, and almost nothing he said made any sense. "For instance, he told us that on the first day of class, he hands out a sonnet—always Shakespeare's 'My love is as a fever'—and tells them to memorize it. They think they'll be tested on it, or they'll have to get up and recite it in front of their peers, and that makes a good many of them drop the class. Which he said is a nice by-product of this particular assignment."

She shook her head. "Anyway, the next time the class meets, he tells them they have forty-five minutes to write a sonnet of their own, then gives them the topic. Since he lives near Pamlico Sound in North Carolina, his favorite theme lately has been the pollution of the Noose River. Can you imagine having to write a sonnet on that in forty-five minutes? Or even forty-five days? Or ever? Nearly everything he said was just about that crazy.

"But then he said something that really got my attention. That he hates it when he hears other poets advising their students to write what they know, because they almost always take that to mean 'write what you yourself have experienced.' In his opinion, that's too limiting. *He* always tells his students there are different modes of knowing, and that you should be free to write about whatever you can imagine.

"And that got me thinking about what we know and how we know it. I thought about it all the way home. It was pretty clear to me from talking to Candace that absent any verifiable facts about how you spent your Friday night, she still knew something—even if she couldn't, or wouldn't, say what it was. And it was clear to me that I knew it, too, and had for a while. And it really has nothing to do with facts and, in some sense, experience.

"The facts, as I know them, are that Saturday morning there were two empty champagne bottles on the coffee table and that Ellis didn't help drink them. For all I *know*, you drank both of them yourself. That's a possibility I wouldn't be able to exclude, based on the information I've got at this moment. Everything else belongs in the category of what I can imagine. And that's just as real to me, maybe even *more* real—though I don't know, and can't imagine, whether you can understand what I'm saying.

"The other thing I know is my own reaction to all of this. I'm not surprised—not even particularly disturbed. But there was a time, Luke, when I would've been both, and it wasn't as long ago as you might think."

I believe I must have put my head in my hands by that point. I don't know for sure, but it seems like that's what all this would demand. I do recall trying to figure out what to say when she saved me the trouble.

"If you want me to know things differently from how I know them now," she said, "you can give me the facts. If you don't want me to, just keep them to yourself. You've always valued them more than I do anyway, so as far as I'm concerned they're all yours. Use them however you choose. To me, they're worth nothing at all."

She waited to see if I would speak, and when I didn't she got up and walked to the freezer, took out the bottle of champagne, stripped off the tinfoil and popped the cork.

I PULLED INTO THE DRIVEWAY over at Maggie's at a quarter past five. Her car was gone. I'd called her as soon as I left my house—or what had been my house until today—but she hadn't answered.

I climbed out and walked towards the back door. I wasn't wearing a coat, only a threadbare pair of Levi's and an Ole Miss sweatshirt, and it had gotten really cold. Leaves crunched beneath my tennis shoes. She hadn't raked the yard the whole time she'd lived there.

I looked in the kitchen window. All the lights were off, and darkness was falling, so I couldn't see much: just a newspaper lying on the counter, a coffee cup beside it and next to that a yogurt container. Thinking maybe she'd gone shopping, I sat down on the steps to wait, hugging myself and calling her every few minutes.

Earlier, after Jennifer and I drank that bottle of champagne, she'd reached across the table and taken my hands in hers. "Luke," she said, "I want us to go to bed and make love. Then I'll ask you to get up, walk out of this house and drive away. Where you go's up to you, though I'm sure your dad could use some company. And I want you to tell the girls—whatever version of the truth you like. One story's about as good as another."

So we went off to bed, and neither one of us said a word the whole time. She kept her eyes open, which was unusual for her, and at one point, I remember, she reached up and ran her fingers through my hair. Then she watched while I got dressed, and when I looked at her and started to tell her I loved her, she shook her head and turned towards the wall. I used my key to lock the front door.

I sat on the steps at Maggie's until I was almost frozen. Then I went back to the car, started the engine, turned on the heater and sat there a little while longer, calling her a couple more times, with no answer still. Finally, I put the car in gear and drove out to the big new Wal-Mart on the highway but didn't see her car in the lot. It wasn't parked at Sunflower Food Store or at Piggly Wiggly. There was no Mercedes at the school, either, just an old VW that belonged to one of our janitors and the football coach's pickup.

I ran by her house again, but the driveway was still empty. I thought about going to see Ellis, but it occurred to me that Jennifer might've hit on the same idea and I wouldn't know it until he opened the door. Unless I called first, and I didn't have that in me.

It was after six o'clock, and then I remembered promising my father that I'd drop by. I dreaded the conversation we'd need to have, though I already understood it would come as no surprise. For all I knew, the whole town was already talking, and while it was hard to imagine anybody calling to say his son was screwing around, he'd certainly found out somehow.

I backed out of Maggie's driveway and headed for town. At Loring Avenue I almost took a left, to go to my house and beg Jennifer to forgive me and let me try to start over. But that argument, if I was going to make it, wasn't likely to succeed tonight. And my sense of things was that the time to start over had come in August, when our daughters left home. Instead of doing it with her, I'd done it with someone else.

All the lights at my parents' place were off. It seemed unlikely they'd gone to bed this early, so I called and the phone rang ten times before I gave up. So I got out of the car, walked over to the house and rang the bell. When nothing happened, I pounded on the door for a minute or two, again with no result. By that point I was concerned. Absurdly, I whipped out my cell phone and started to call Jennifer, to ask what she thought I should do, though I managed to press the red button and stop the call before the phone rang on her end. I know it didn't go through because she told me so the next morning.

I fumbled with my key ring until I found the one for their front door and unlocked it, only to discover that the chain was still on. So I backed up about three feet and threw my shoulder against it, which accomplished nothing except giving me a stinger. When the pain eased off a little, I reared up again and this time performed my best approximation of a karate kick, and the door splintered and smashed into the Sheetrock.

"Dad?" I hollered. "Hey, Dad?"

But he never answered, and down the dark hallway I heard my mother groan.

THERE WAS A GUY who used to hang around the history department when I was at Ole Miss, a tall, slope-shouldered man with thin silver hair who always wore a maroon Harvard Windbreaker, no matter what the weather. You'd see him sitting on a couch near the elevators in Bishop Hall, his legs crossed above a few inches of hairy ankles, since he never seemed to wear socks. He'd be reading something rarefied like the *New York Review of Books* or the *Times Literary Supplement*, often reaching down to break a piece off the gigantic Hershey bar invariably lying in his lap.

At first we thought he must be a latter-day grad student, a guy who'd retired from his job and come back to pursue some degree he'd probably never use. But then a professor told one of my friends the real story.

This gentleman didn't need a graduate degree because he already had one, a Ph.D. from the University of Chicago in Eastern European history, and he'd written two books I soon found in the library. The first dealt with an event called the "Miracle on the Vistula," when the Polish army, commanded by Field Marshal Pilsudski, repulsed the Russians in the Polish-Soviet War of 1919–1920, and the second examined the liquidation of a Czech village after the assassination of Reinhard Heydrich. One day in 1972 he'd been summoned from his classroom and informed that his son had been murdered after exiting a subway station in Queens. A couple months later, his wife, an economist, told him she'd fallen in love with a woman and was going to leave him. His response was to drink a bottle of Scotch and try to hack off his arm with a butcher knife. He'd been in and out of institutions ever since, and was at Ole Miss only because his best friend, the chairman of our department, had actually given him a room in his house.

I couldn't understand why he'd done any of this. After all, it wasn't as if he'd caused his son's death. As for his wife, well, she'd figured out her sexual nature was different from what she'd thought. Sometimes, I reasoned, things just happen, and as long as you're not at fault, why blame yourself? At the age of twenty, I failed to grasp the difference between guilt, which can almost always be atoned for, and grief, which can only be borne.

On the day my father was buried, I stood at the edge of the grave, flanked by my daughters and my wife. Ellis was there, too, as were quite a few of my colleagues and several students from my honors class. Selina and Ramsey came, my boss doing his best to conceal his displeasure. I didn't yet know it, but Maggie had e-mailed him from North Carolina the day before, saying that teaching wasn't for her and she'd decided to go back home. That must've confirmed the rumors he'd been hearing for several weeks, that she and I had become more than friends. He hadn't said anything to me about it, given the circumstances, but earlier, at the memorial service, I'd noticed him studying me and my family, shaking his head as if he couldn't fathom why an otherwise intelligent man would do something so stupid. I didn't understand it myself.

We'd invited a few people over to our house for a lunch catered by our faux French café—leek tarts, duck with cranberry mustard, that sort of stuff—but I couldn't eat a thing. Jennifer had told me that once everybody left, she wanted me to talk to Candace and Trish and let them know, before they went back to school, that I'd be moving out. I had the distinct impression she was eager to get on with her life.

The Colemans were among the last to say goodbye. Ramsey asked if I planned on coming to work the following week, and when I nodded he said, "Well, take your time. But when you do get back in the saddle, come by the office and let's chat, all right?" So then I knew I had at least two conversations to dread, not just one.

The caterers cleared away their trays, and Jennifer announced that she was going to walk Ellis home, leaving the three of us alone. I asked if they'd like a glass of wine. Trish, who hadn't cried at the funeral home or the cemetery, said sure, but Candace shook her head, wiped her eyes again and stood there as if she were in the dock, waiting for her sentence to be pronounced.

I poured Trish a glass and another for myself, then said, "Let's go into the living room and sit down." Though they weren't yet aware of it, my daughters were about to become revisionists who'd come to question every fact they thought they knew about the family they'd grown up in. Even the most innocuous actions—the peck on the cheek I'd given their mother after dinner before going back to school to work on lesson plans until midnight—would be reevaluated in the light of what they were about to hear.

So there we sat, the two girls and me, and I didn't even know where to begin. Should I start with the day school opened, when I saw Maggie for the first time in forty-four years, or should I start on the afternoon I went to her house for the first time? Or should I reach even further back, to when she tripped me off the porch of that store? It's a lot easier to say when something ended rather than when it began. Most of us can recognize the end from a mile away, but the beginning always slips up on us, lulling us into thinking what we're living through is yet another moment, in yet another day.

I knew that afternoon I was living through a moment like no other and wanted it to pass in fewer than sixty seconds. There was time neither for providing causal analysis nor for cloaking my failures as husband and father in a golden flowing narrative, in which I'd done *this* in *that* setting, entertaining x emotion before finally succumbing to y urge as rain pounded down and lightning flashed and wind shook pecans off the trees. There was nothing to do except reduce the truth to its essence, discarding all the surrounding data that would interest them even less than it did me.

No, there was nothing to do except say it, so I did. "Girls," I told them, "I'm in trouble."

LIKE A POLITICIAN who's been hounded from office, I tried to stay out of the public eye, doing my grocery shopping in Greenville and keeping to myself as much as possible when not in the classroom, mostly just sitting around my parents' house watching *The World at War* on the History Channel before falling asleep on the couch. I did drop by the nursing home every afternoon to look in on my mother, and sometimes I could tell Jennifer had been there. There would be a rose in a vase on the bedside table, or her hair would be freshly brushed, or she'd smell faintly of Jennifer's perfume. I finally had my talk with Ramsey, who began by telling me we'd been friends for a long time and that he felt like he could come to me if he ever needed to, so why hadn't I felt like I could come to him? Well, I said, I didn't know I was in trouble until it was way too late for talking about it to do any good. He leaned back, locked his hands behind his head and, instead of issuing me the warning I expected, only said, "I can sure see how it could happen. If you're going to ruin your life over a woman, you want it to be one like Maggie."

As for the woman in question, she hadn't answered any of my e-mails or voice-mails, though I'd left her so many that she could've accused me of being a stalker. A couple of times I went by her house and peeked in the window, and the kitchen looked exactly as it had on the day my father died. Then, around the middle of November, a U-Haul truck was parked in the driveway next to a car with a Tishomingo County license plate. Somebody else was moving in. What they did with her stuff, I have no idea.

I kept calling her, though, leaving messages every few days, and finally, on the Monday before Thanksgiving, she answered. I was so shocked that I couldn't speak.

"If you don't say something, Luke," she said, "I'm going to hang up. And I won't ever answer again."

"I don't know what to say," I told her.

"Then why did you call me?"

"I wanted to hear your voice."

"I'm not a CD. You can't just put me on and hit play."

"I know that."

"So what was it you wanted to say?"

I was standing in the kitchen, where a layer of grime coated everything. A lot of the stuff in the refrigerator was already out-of-date. I couldn't remember if I'd taken a shower today, or even the day before. I'd be spending Thanksgiving with Ellis—at least he'd said I could. The girls would be at their mom's. Candace, I knew, would have her boyfriend with her, the football player who'd gotten hurt, and I suddenly wanted more than anything in the world to be there with all of them. "Why did you leave?" I said, choking on my own words. "You come in here and stir everything up, then take off at the first sign of trouble."

"*I* took off?" she said, her voice rising. "Yes, of course I did—out the back door, like some petty criminal. And you did what? Did you come looking for me? No, you sat there in your house all night. Watching a fucking ball game on TV."

"How do you know that?" I asked.

"How do you think? I drove up and down your street. For

hours. I could see you sitting there. You put me out of your mind, just like some inconvenient fact."

"I tried calling you. Didn't you have your cell?"

"I didn't want to be called. I wanted to be *sought.* You made your choice that day, and I wasn't it."

I sat down, propping my elbow on the kitchen table and resting my jaw against my knuckles. I couldn't quibble with her interpretation. Things were pretty much as she said. I'd made my choice, and it hadn't been her. And like Jennifer she wasn't the kind of woman who'd let you backtrack.

I knew we were speaking for the last time. She wouldn't want to talk to me again, and I no longer had anything to say to her, having already said it with the actions she'd described. There was, however, one last question I needed to ask: "The night your mom got killed," I said, "your dad and mine went to Oxford together. Did you know that?"

I thought at first that she was about to end the call. But finally her voice broke the silence. "Yes," she said. "I'm the one who answered the phone when your father called."

"Can you remember what he said?"

The distance between us could no longer be measured in the miles that stretched out between Mississippi and North Carolina or wherever she happened to be. "Yes," she said, "I do. That and a whole lot more."

While I sat there at my parents' kitchen table, she told me exactly what she recalled about that night, her voice as coldly matter-of-fact as if she were repeating a speech she'd delivered a hundred times before. And when she finished, she said, "See who you got tangled up with? I bet you wouldn't have, if you'd known." She paused—giving me a chance to disagree, I supposed, and when I didn't the connection got broken without her goodbye.

And I thought that, finally, there could be nothing left to find out about October 1, 1962. This was a notion I clung to for just over a month.

On Christmas Eve it snowed, something I'd seen in Loring only once before, the year I was seven. I recalled my father hustling me out of bed the next morning, telling me to hurry up and get dressed, there was something outside he wanted to show me. He wouldn't let me go into the living room, where I knew Santa had left my toys. Instead, he marched me through the kitchen and out the back door. He was carrying the Kodak he'd given my mother a couple of years earlier for her birthday.

When we got outside our house, the bright sunlight glaring off all that white blinded me. My dad told me to shield my eyes with the back of my hand, and that's what I did as I followed him through the yard, our shoes crunching the crust with every step. At the north end of the house, near the chimney, there were two parallel grooves in the white powder on the ground, maybe four feet apart, and in between them a bunch of heart-shaped indentations. These started right at the base of the chimney and ran across the entire yard before evaporating near a pine thicket that separated our house from the field beyond.

"See?" my father said. "He must've landed the sleigh right by the chimney, and after he jumped down off the roof he needed a little bit of runway to take off. Looks to me like they just barely cleared them trees. That would've been a mighty mess, wouldn't it—if he'd crash-landed over there and hadn't nobody but you got their presents?"

While I stood there staring at the ground, reveling in the thought that something so mysterious could also be so demonstrably factual, my father backed up a few steps and took my picture.

I knew that photo had to be around here somewhere, and on Christmas Eve—sitting alone in the house and watching the big wet flakes float down while waiting for Ellis to arrive with the ham he'd baked and the bottle of wine he'd promised to bring— I badly wanted to see it.

Until then, I hadn't gone through my father's things. His desk drawers were full of stuff that at other times in my life had seemed fascinating: old checkbooks, farm ledgers, letters from former shipmates, newspaper clippings announcing that his granddaughters had made the honor roll, expired driver's licenses, medical bills and so on. He'd never been any good with a camera—tending to behead his subjects—and I'd never known him to put photos into albums, but my mother had, up until her illness.

I turned on his desk lamp and went through the three drawers quickly, not turning up much that captured my attention except his Citizens' Council card—frayed at the edges, as though it had been carried in his wallet and sat on for a good many years—and a handful of black-and-white photos: him and my mother waving from their seats on a Ferris wheel, me wearing a black cowboy suit and pointing a silver pistol at the photographer, my grandfather perched on our old Allis-Chalmers.

Just off the den is a long, narrow space dominated by the washer and dryer where I knew he'd been stockpiling junk for years, so I moved in there and pulled the string dangling from the single overhead bulb.

I seemed to remember seeing some fake leather-bound albums on the floor beneath shelves that held a couple hundred paperback westerns and fishing tackle he hadn't used in forty years. I got down on my knees and looked, but all I saw were several rows of *American Rifleman*, the NRA magazine. I pulled one stack back, though, and behind it were several of those albums, and I dragged them out.

They were full of pictures that had to date into the late '40s. There were several shots of my mother at about the same age as my daughters were now, her hair long and blowsy, her face unlined, and there was one of my dad standing behind her and helping her aim a shotgun, both of his hands bracing her right elbow. I laid the albums aside and, hoping there might be more of them, reached behind the other copies of *American Rifleman* to see if anything else was back there, up against the baseboard.

My hand touched something that felt like a spiral ring, and I withdrew a stack of notebooks, some of which were obviously quite old. The one on top, however, looked new. I realized it was the green one I'd spotted back in September on the floor by his chair. I flipped it open and read a few lines, written in my father's surprisingly small script:

He was sitting on the living room floor eating popcorn. He wasn't worried about nothing and I remember thinking that's how it should be, a boy ought not have to worry while he was only a boy.

Safe from the Neighbors

"IF THIS COUNTRY should ever reach the point," the president was saying, while I sat on the floor with that bowl of popcorn between my legs, "where any man or group of men, by force or threat of force, could long defy the commands of our courts and Constitution, no law would stand free from doubt, no judge would be sure of his writ and no citizen would be safe from his neighbors."

All over the South, in living rooms like ours, people were jeering at the image on their TV sets, and my father knew it. But he himself felt no such urge. And it wasn't because my mother, sitting beside him on the couch and culling pecans, thought JFK was right. It was because he'd just recently come to understand something he never would've wanted to admit: he was hardly safe from his own neighbors.

Certainly not from Herman Horton. From 1948, when he began farming with my grandfather, until I left for Ole Miss and he gave up and quit, he had to trudge into the bank and face that old man or another just like him, and even though he always got his furnish, he'd walk out feeling poorer. Nor was he safe from the guy who ginned his cotton, though they attended the same church—if his trailers were standing out in the yard full of cotton as a storm front approached, they'd stay right there while those belonging to people who owned land and had money got pulled under the shed and onto the scales. It was the same with Feed and Seed, Delta Lumber and Allis-Chalmers.

But most of all, he wasn't even safe from Arlan Calloway. They used to ride the same bus into Loring after the one-room schoolhouse at Fairway Crossroads closed down, and when they reached their destination they were given the same treatment. Town kids said they smelled bad and made fun of their clothes, their long country vowels, so they ran off together more times than my father could count and, when caught, took their floggings from the principal in tandem. Later on, they joined different branches of the service two days apart, which was the first time they ever disagreed about anything: my dad said he'd rather drown than get shot, while Arlan, who could barely swim, preferred to face bullets and land mines. They wrote each other throughout the war, letters that surely must have stumped the censors:

I been thinking what we used to do with Ex-Lax.

What about Miss Waters and that old pitcher pump on the Pool place?

Remember that cake on the roof at Western Auto?

Back then, according to what my father wrote in the green notebook I found in the laundry room, Arlan wasn't the kind of person who took. He was the giving sort. He gave the answers to homework if he knew them and you didn't, and he gave you a bite of his sandwich if he knew his was better than yours. During the war, if you confessed to being scared, he gave you to understand that he was, too, probably even more than you. When I finally found a few of his letters, in a shoe box my dad had stashed in the attic, he came across as an affable young man. *I bet I'm going to die before I can get home,* he wrote in one that had several passages blacked out. *If I do I sure am sorry if I ever did any-thing nasty to you. If I don't then I'm not!*

After he came back in one piece and went to work down in south Mississippi, Arlan still wrote my father occasionally, but over time his letters started sounding different. He began to use unusual words and phrases. *Today leaves me bemired in a situation with which I was previously unfamiliar but I don't mean to bemoan my fate for fact is I have found my beloved and she's half a foot taller than me. Kissing her's like climbing that old slash pine at the edge of Daddy's porch.*

In 1962, by which time he'd been back in the Delta for just over three years, Arlan Calloway owned a good car and a good truck and a new house with a swimming pool, not to mention several hundred acres. He had the respect of the same people who used to say he smelled bad and talked funny. And he also had the best-looking wife anybody around town had ever seen. But before long he didn't have her all to himself anymore, and a couple of times—after learning that his friend had placed a bid on our land—my father nearly let him in on the secret. *I figured if I told him,* he wrote in the green notebook, *he'd be so ashamed he'd pack up and leave town. But I couldn't stand the thought of the expression I knew I'd see on his face, it would just about kill him, he loved that woman so much.*

I once heard Dad tell my uncle about riding a train home from California at the end of World War II. He didn't have a seat when it left Oakland, so he stood at the counter in the dining car, treating himself to several cups of coffee and two different kinds of pie while looking out the window and watching the great San Joaquin Valley slide by. Then the train stopped in Fresno and a lot of people got off, and after it pulled out again he paid up and went to find himself a seat.

He was walking down the aisle, looking for an empty row,

thinking maybe he'd stretch out and grab a few hours' sleep, when a man reading a newspaper glanced up and broke into a broad-faced grin. "Say, mate. You just got off a ship, didn't you?" he asked.

My father told my uncle he was wearing civvies he'd bought in a shop on Market Street, that the blues he'd been discharged in were packed away in his duffel bag and stowed in the baggage car. He didn't know how the man could tell he'd been in the navy, and didn't want to be badgered with a bunch of questions about where he'd been and what he'd seen, but it wasn't in his nature to be impolite. So he just said, "Well, sir, what makes you ask?"

The man laughed. "Everybody else that comes down the aisle hangs on to the seat backs for dear life. But you, you're at home on your feet."

I didn't know why that story pleased me so much when I was nine or ten, but it did. And it still does.

On the evening of September 30, 1962, as JFK neared the end of his speech to the nation, my father was decidedly not on his feet. He was sitting there on the couch beside my mother in a house that wasn't his on land he didn't own. Across the room, cross-legged on the floor, I was munching away on the popcorn. I can almost see myself as he must have seen me then, a snaggle-toothed kid with a cowlick, fingernails bitten to the quick. I'm staring at a book that lies beside the bowl, the standard first-grade reader, *Fun with Dick and Jane.*

That's what my father believed I expected from life: fun. Which is what I was supposed to expect, as he saw it, because I was still a boy and was right to think life ought to be fun, that it was a game, and if today you happened to lose, you'd start over again tomorrow with the score tied at zero. My father and Arlan Calloway were having fun when they ran off from school, slipped into the bakery through the back door, stole an angel food cake and ate it on the roof of Western Auto, and they never once regretted it, not even when they got a good whipping. But as for the fun itself, that night my father hardly recalled what it felt like. He hadn't had any in years.

He knew I wouldn't have any myself either, if this winter I had to stand in the yard and watch everything that was mine being thrown into the back of a pickup, as if this were the Dust Bowl and we were the Joads. My boyhood would end then. Even he'd had a longer run than that.

He rose off the couch. Momma, still culling pecans, throwing the rotten ones into the trash can near her knee, asked, "Where are you heading off to, James?" He didn't answer, but she appeared not to notice. She was listening to the president conclude his speech by saying something about how we had to heal the wounds that were within us so we could turn to the greater crises without.

But the wounds within my father could not be healed. The other crises—well, they were a different matter.

Our phone, at that time, was on a party line. You could have a private line, if you were willing and able to pay for it, but we weren't able to and, even if we had been, I doubt Dad would've been willing. He hated talking on the phone and usually wouldn't even answer if it rang when no one else was home.

I imagine that when he lifted the receiver from its cradle that night, he was listening for heavy breathing. An old man who lived down the road liked to eavesdrop, and you could generally tell when he was doing it because he had emphysema. But I suspect he was otherwise occupied that night. He didn't have a TV but was probably listening to the radio, to WJDX down in Jackson, which had been broadcasting the call to arms all day long, urging folks to grab their guns and head for Oxford. Even the operators were probably listening to the radio, but one finally came on the line. "Number, please," she would have said.

"Seven eight four W one."

"Calling Arlan, are you?"

My father couldn't have been sure which operator answered—there were several who rotated in pairs, and all of them, as I recall, sounded generically nasal—so he probably would've just said, "Yes ma'am."

She would consider neighborly small talk well within her duties. "Big mess they're having up at Ole Miss."

"Sure sounds like it."

My father recorded her next remark in his green notebook. "You boys in the Council aim to do anything about it?" she asked him.

So far as he could tell, those boys didn't intend to do shit. They liked to hold meetings, drink bourbon and talk big, and they were probably talking plenty big that evening as they sat in their living rooms with their doors securely fastened. But all the trouble, from what he knew, was being stirred up by folks who belonged to no organization. *Some of them*, he wrote, *probably didn't even belong to theirselves. They were owned by others just like I was and that accounted for a good measure of their meanness.* "I don't rightly know, ma'am," he said, trying his best to sound polite, though it wouldn't have been easy for him that night. "Could you go ahead and connect me?"

"Excuse *me*," she said, and the line must have crackled when she jammed the plug into the jack.

The phone rang four times: both Dad and Maggie remembered it the same way. Four rings, and with each one his resolve grew a little bit fainter. If it rang five times, he told himself, he'd just hang up. And if he had, he would not have called back. On the evening of September 30, 1962, he was still close enough to the man he'd been a month before that he could say with certainty what he would or would not do. He'd say it to himself off and on for the rest of his life: If it had only rung five times, I would not have called back.

But a couple miles away, a little girl was moving through the house in her pajamas, her hand reaching out to grasp the receiver.

For a moment, my father wrote, he couldn't remember her name. Then it came to him. "Maggie," he said, "can I speak to your daddy?"

She knew who it was, she'd told me, but pretended not to. She couldn't say why, except that it hadn't been a good day. Her momma had started drinking around lunchtime, which was normal by then, but her daddy had been drinking, too, which wasn't. They'd been talking in low voices all day long, wandering in and out of rooms, stepping outside once or twice to talk by the pool. He was angry, and seeing him like that had unsettled her. Her dad was the one she could count on. Twice since supper she'd had to run to the bathroom, her stomach in rebellion, and she was heading there again when she picked up the phone. "May I ask who's calling?"

It annoyed my father beyond all reason that she said *may* rather than *can*. *May* wasn't just a word to be spat out by a prissy little girl. It was also a name that happened to be his. "This is James May," he told her. "Can I please speak to Arlan Calloway?"

"Just a moment," she said. "I'll see if he can take your call."

The next thing my father knew, he heard a toilet being flushed. The phone at the Calloways' house stood on a table in the hallway, right next to the bathroom door. He figured Maggie must have taken a leisurely pee before going to summon her father—but in fact she'd barely made it to the toilet before suffering another bout of diarrhea.

By the time Arlan answered, my father was almost out of his mind. He'd been standing there waiting for four or five minutes, just like he always had to outside of Herman Horton's office, until the old man had nothing better to do than grant him a quarter of an hour. He'd been waiting, he thought, for the better part of his life, without even knowing what for. Up till now. "Listen," he proposed, "how about you and me head up the road?"

"Up the road where?"

"You know where," my father said.

"Did, I wouldn't be asking."

"Oxford."

"Oxford?"

"Ole Miss."

"Ole Miss?"

My father heard himself laugh. It surprised him, because nothing was funny this evening. Nothing had been for a month, and maybe never would be again. "What's the matter, Arlan?" he said. "Some wizard turn you into a parrot?"

He'd never said anything like that to his old friend, or to anybody else, either, and his first impulse, after that snotty response left his mouth, was to say *Sorry* and beg forgiveness. But what did he have to be sorry for? He wouldn't have tried to take Arlan's house, because it wasn't his. Nor would he have taken his truck, his car or his wife, not even if he held a lien against them.

"No, James," Arlan said quietly, "I'm not a parrot." Maggie recalled that after he said that, he made a fist of his right hand and whacked himself on the thigh. "You may not believe it, but I'm a person. Just like you."

"That colored boy that wants to go to Ole Miss, he's a person, too," my father said. "But he's not like me, and neither are you. You got a leadership role to play, Arlan. I'm just a loyal follower. Seems like I been following you since I was the size of a

slop jar. And I'm ready to follow you tonight." He could visual-
ize him over there in that new ranch-style house, in those
charcoal-gray slacks he liked to wear when he headed to a gath-
ering at Mayor Finley's or went into town to eat with his wife
and family. Not too long ago he'd started calling supper "dinner," like somebody that'd spent his whole life in a city.

Maggie got a very different view. From where she stood, she
saw a thin film of sweat on her father's upper lip. One corner of
his mouth began to twitch, and the hand that wasn't holding the
receiver rose to his forehead as if he were racking his brain for a
solution to an impossible situation.

Just then, though my father would never know it, Nadine
walked into the hall. She placed her palm against Maggie's
shoulder and pushed her, none too gently, towards her bedroom.

My father couldn't have heard her whisper, "What the fuck's
going on? Who's that you're talking to? Get off the goddamn
phone."

With his angry wife towering over him, Arlan Calloway's
voice assumed the tone of command he used when issuing
instructions to hoe hands and tractor drivers. "All right, now,"
he told my dad, "you walk out to the main road and wait. I'll
pick you up in ten minutes."

At Ole Miss, one of my best friends was another history major
who'd grown up in East Tennessee, not far from the Virginia
line. I went home with him once on spring break, and those hills
they lived in were by no means heavily populated, and it got
pretty dark there at night, especially once you turned off the
interstate onto a winding mountain road. So it means something
that when he came home with me to the Delta and we were sitting in the car one evening, drinking beer on the side of the road
a few miles north of town, he claimed he'd never seen any place
so dark. "Look," he said, gesturing at the windshield, "there's

not a single light in sight. Man, I mean, this is like being in the grave."

My father would've seen a light on that night while waiting for Arlan Calloway. Our house was no more than a couple hundred yards away, and my mother hadn't gone to bed yet. But ours would have been the only light visible, because the only other house you could see from that spot was a tenant shack that didn't have electricity.

The night had turned chilly, the temperature dipping into the fifties, according to weather reports I found in the Memphis paper. To the best of my knowledge, my father never owned a heavy coat, so if it got really cold he'd just put on extra layers. Furthermore, the Colt Python he'd jammed into his pants, under the elastic band of his boxer shorts, had to be cold against his skin. He'd left the house fast, telling my mother not to wait up, that he'd be back late. It seems to me that she might've said his name once or twice and asked where he was going, but I don't believe he ever answered.

This wasn't the first time he'd left the house armed. Whenever somebody ran off from the County Farm, he was one of the people they called up to walk the roads. I once heard him explain how he and Arlan helped corner two escapees in a barn on Beaverdam Creek. He told my grandfather that one of the other men on the patrol—Benny Earl Baggot, who also farmed sixteenth-section land—kept passing a bottle and calling out insults, begging the convicts to make a run for it, because it had always bothered him that he'd never shot anybody. "Over in Europe I shot several somebodies," Dad said Mr. Calloway had told Baggot. "And if you ever do, you'll probably need to start buying bigger bottles than that little one you got now." Before long the runaways surrendered, spoiling Benny Earl's evening.

Waiting there on the main road, my father wondered what

Arlan had told his wife. *I convinced myself he probably fed her a bunch of bunk about fighting for states rights knowing she wouldn't be for it but would still give him credit for having guts. She could forgive a man for a lot of things I imagine but I don't think she ever forgave any person male nor female for being gutless.*

Finally he spotted headlights about a mile away. Later on, he recalled thinking that he wouldn't have been shocked if his friend was about to suggest, "Why don't we just ride around for a few hours, maybe drive down to Belzoni to that truck stop that's always open, and get us some barbecue and coleslaw? I don't have a stake in Ole Miss, and neither do you."

The pickup didn't seem to be in any hurry, but finally it pulled up beside him, and Arlan threw open the door on the passenger side. When the interior light came on, Dad saw the shotgun, its muzzle resting on the floorboard.

None of the five notebooks I found on Christmas Eve have dates in them. But given various bits of information, I can make pretty good guesses about how old each of them might be. The first spans a period from early summer of 1947 to sometime late in 1949: there's a reference near the beginning to his forthcoming marriage, which took place on July 6, 1947, and near the end he alludes to the burning of a Canadian Great Lakes cruiser named *Noronic*, which according to Google happened on September 17, 1949, killing 118 people. The second notebook takes up almost immediately after the end of the first, as if he intended to record his thoughts regularly, but then he must have stopped for a good while, because there are no references at all to the Korean War—an odd oversight, considering his own experiences. Somewhere around the middle he notes his feelings upon learning my mother had gotten pregnant, which would place it near the end of 1955. My birth is duly recorded some pages later, along with the information, new to me, that she almost died in the delivery room. The last entry expresses his joy at his old friend Arlan's homecoming, with his wife and children, and that happened late in the spring of 1959.

The third notebook is the one I'd seen as a kid, in which he ponders that girl in the Philippines. It starts with the death of my grandfather, in the summer of 1965, and ends with me in junior high, when I discarded his advice to concentrate on school instead of athletics. The fourth notebook starts with me about to go to Ole Miss and ends a few pages later, in the middle of a sentence about his new job at the Loring County school bus barn, the remaining sheets having been ripped out. The last of the five, the green one he'd started sometime in the fall, contains forty pages of ungrammatical but frequently eloquent prose, most of it directly related to the events of September and October of 1962—though in the middle, there's a four-page section about driving my mother around in his van, stopping by where our house used to stand, then spotting my car in Maggie's driveway and finding it there again on the same day the following week as well as the one after that. *It's the first time I've wished I was like her and didn't know what I was seeing*, he wrote. *And she don't. If she did she'd start that humming.*

He might have thought he'd have enough warning at the end of his life to destroy the notebooks before anyone could find them, though there's rarely much description and many comments are so cryptic that nobody else could make much sense of them. But in the green one, when he writes about the evening he and Arlan Calloway went to Oxford, there's a remarkable amount of detail—as if, for once, he was writing with an audience in mind.

At one point, as they traveled north that night on Highway 49, a truck with Louisiana license plates swept by them, with a bunch of men in back wearing orange hunting vests. One of them stuck his shotgun in the air and fired off a blast, a cone of fire spewing from the muzzle. Mr. Calloway called him a dumb son of a bitch and predicted he'd be among the next to die.

One person was already dead—they'd heard that on the radio—and the people storming onto the campus could hardly breathe because of all the teargas. A retired army general named Edwin Walker was supposedly organizing an attack on the U.S. marshals, who'd already surrounded the administration building. When Arlan heard that, my father recalled, he shook his head and asked him if knew who Walker was.

"The fellow that commanded the troops at Little Rock Central?"

"Yeah, so I guess he's down here trying to make up for past sins. Except that now, instead of a bunch of besotted rednecks, he's facing some folks that know how to shoot back."

"Whose side you on, Arlan?"

"I'm on my side, James. Aren't you on yours? You'd better be. Because if you're not, who do you think is?"

My father replied that he thought Arlan was. Weren't they members of the same organization?

All that organization amounted to, Mr. Calloway told him, was a fucking civic club. Didn't my father have enough gumption to know that?

Well, he had more than most folks knew. He understood perfectly well that the Council was a civic club. *And like's the case with most clubs not being in it could hit you in the pocketbook and mine was too thin to absorb much of a blow. I said to him hell Arlan I thought we was fighting for racial supremacy. And he says how in the hell is the white race so damn supreme when we live in a place that's got three or four of them for every one of us? I'm just trying to conduct my business in the most efficient way possible he tells me, that the day doing business means saying yes sir to colored folks I'll say it just as sweet as can be. That day's not here yet. He says people have to adapt James and that's what I've been trying to show you. I got half a mind to turn around and head back. We're not going to accomplish nothing up there tonight except maybe getting ourselves killed.*

Heading back was the last thing my father wanted. Or to put it another way, it was the last thing he could afford. If they went back, he said, they'd just look like a couple of windbags.

Nobody would know, Mr. Calloway observed, unless he ran his mouth.

My father lied and said he'd already run it, that the operator had asked if they were going to Oxford and he'd said yes.

Well Arlan says to me like he's being philosophical, that means it's in the public domain.

Highway 6, at that time, didn't bypass the town of Oxford as it does today. Back then it ran straight into the square, with the university off to the right. When they got there, the western edge of town seemed surprisingly quiet, given that a battle supposedly was raging just a couple miles away. My father noticed a rundown gas station on their left, a bunch of used tires stacked up on a spoke where anybody who wanted to could steal them, the door to the service bay wide open and somebody's tool chest sitting on the floor. A hundred yards or so ahead on the right, there was what appeared to be a construction site, a broad expanse of newly poured concrete with absolutely nothing around it—in all likelihood, the foundation of the strip mall where the Jitney-Jungle stood when I was a student.

At first he wondered if maybe the news going out over the radio was an exaggeration. The highway ahead looked empty and dark. Then, over the drone of Arlan's engine, he became aware of the noise: small-arms fire. He rolled the window down, and it got a lot louder. There was a weird odor in the air, too.

"Reckon you know what that stink is," Arlan said. "Navy give you any training with gas?"

The navy had offered gas training, but that was when he'd been in the hospital with pneumonia, about to die, and then they shipped him out without forcing him to make it up. "I know how to put the mask on," he said. "We had 'em on board."

"Yeah, well we ain't got 'em on board now." Arlan pulled to the side of the road, got out and grabbed something from under the seat. While my father sat and watched, he walked around in front of the truck, into the glare of his own headlights, carrying a couple of towels. He stooped down next to the road ditch. Then he climbed back in and laid the soaked towels on the seat.

I told him it looked like he come prepared and he put the truck in gear and said that when folks started shooting it was best to be. I asked if he'd been shot at a lot and he said that a lot or a little it didn't make no difference, it was like fucking, do it once and you get the gist.

Arlan pulled back on the road, and the truck topped a rise. Up ahead half a mile or so, they saw flashing lights and uniformed men running back and forth, hundreds of them. They were members of the Mississippi Highway Patrol, and my father thought, as any sane person would, they were setting up a roadblock to stop people like him and Arlan from reaching the campus. In reality, the police were on the verge of mounting an attack themselves. They'd just decided to storm the Lyceum and kill every last marshal if they had to. The attack was averted, according to William Doyle's book, by a visit from Paul B. Johnson, Jr., the lieutenant governor, who told them: "Don't go up there fighting with those federals."

When he saw all them folks Arlan pumped the brakes but didn't actually stop, he just looked at me and asked what I wanted to do. Said for me to make the call.

This was not, my father knew, in Arlan Calloway's nature. Though he didn't say so in the notebook, he must have realized that his friend was acting out of character, and this, in and of itself, should have given him pause. But it failed to—he must have been pumping adrenaline, his heart pounding, his face and neck hot. In his side-view mirror he saw headlights on the road behind them, several more vehicles streaming into town. They could all get together and try to force the roadblock, he guessed, or a group of them could engage the highway patrolmen while the rest took off through the woods ahead on the right. That would've made a certain kind of sense, assuming anybody felt like doing so that night. But he wasn't much interested in concerted action. "Let's park right up yonder," he said, "and see if we can't slip through them trees."

"I get it—a little flanking maneuver, like Jackson at Chancellorsville?"

I knew damn well he was mocking me and I figured I deserved it like the whole damn state did and that this time next week Meredith would be sitting in school on a campus I'd never seen and probably never would, not that I wanted to because by then I didn't. And I still don't. Yeah I said, like Jackson. So he pulls off the road and says he guessed I knew what happened to old Stonewall a little while later in that battle. And I said yeah, that he got shot by one of his own, a Tar Heel confused in the dark. Then I said what I knew would get him good and I was right. I said if he was scared to go with me he didn't need to. I said I got a lot less to lose than you do. You can go on back home and take care of your kids. And that great big beautiful wife.

He'd known Arlan Calloway longer than anyone else. He knew what his face looked like when he was mad, how his mouth used to get smaller when a teacher embarrassed him or a town kid taunted him, the corners of it drawn together so tightly that it no longer looked like a mouth at all, but more like an asshole. It certainly did that night.

"I can take care of my wife," Arlan said. "Do *not* fucking besaddle yourself with any worries about that."

Besaddle, my father felt fairly certain, wasn't an American word, just a set of sounds Arlan had put together to disguise his despair, and this marked a turning point. Feeling in control for the first time all night, my father opened the door and climbed out of the truck.

Arlan sat there looking across the seat at him while the handguns and rifles kept going off and a column of smoke rose into the black sky. Finally he threw Dad one of the wet towels, then grabbed his shotgun and jumped out.

When he thought back on that night, my father always remembered how he and Arlan lingered at the edge of the woods, each one waiting for the other to take the first step. Neither of them carried a flashlight, a major oversight they normally wouldn't be guilty of. It was as if they both understood that the business at hand could only be transacted in the dark.

My dad tripped on a log or stump but managed to right himself. Undergrowth broke beneath his feet, and when he stepped into a soggy spot the mud made a sucking sound. "Reckon the rattlers are out tonight?" he said.

"They got 'em up here?"

"Hell, I don't know. I ain't even set foot in Oxford and don't know much about this part of the state. If we don't get killed, though, I reckon we could ask old man Horton. He went to school up here. Him and that fellow that runs the newspaper."

Mr. Calloway didn't respond. The woods smelled of ammonia, onions, rotten wood. The gunfire got louder as they moved towards campus, and by then there would have been no shortage of it. My father recalled hearing the droning noise of chopper blades slicing the air, and somebody hollered something over a bullhorn. A moment later a cheer went up, like you'd hear at a football game when the home team scored a touchdown.

"Sounds like maybe they just put a rope around Meredith's neck," my father said, and it occurred to him, once he said it, that this was as far as he needed or wanted to go, that right there in the middle of the woods was where he and Arlan ought to do whatever they were going to. The same realization must have struck Mr. Calloway, because when Dad stopped pushing through the undergrowth, he did too. They just stood there in the woods waiting for something to happen, and before long, my father recalled, it did: above their heads they heard the *thunk* of a stray slug tearing into a tree.

And right then is when he says to me I withdrew my bid on your land last week. Says I guess nobody told you. Or maybe they did and it don't matter. Could be you think that me placing that bid took a few inches off your height or lopped off the end of your dick. I don't know and I don't care. I thought I had to when I did it, but I was wrong. I ain't about to tell you I'm sorry though because you won't believe me no way. You got your mind made up. But he was wrong about that. My mind wasn't made up. It was when I placed that phone call and when I got in the truck and it was still made up back there on the road when I got out and started tromping through them woods into what was sounding more like a engagement between armies. It was not made up now because all I wanted was to keep a roof over the heads of my wife and boy and if Arlan didn't aim to take it away then there really wasn't any big problem. Which was not the same as saying we'd ever be friends again because we wouldn't.

My father's eyes were starting to burn—from the gas, he thought, though later on he wondered if it might not have been something else. "Why'd you do it, Arlan? What in the name of God made you want to take what little I call mine?"

He could see him over there in the dark—his small, trim outline—and the muzzle of his shotgun, which was not, Dad noticed, pointing at the ground. *He was holding that thing waist high with the stock near his navel and the barrel jutting out from his rib cage like a extra arm. And though I didn't know it till then my own right hand had worked under my waistband and wrapped itself around the butt of that Colt Python like it had gone there on its own without no help from me.*

Arlan Calloway laughed. "What you *call* yours? Yeah, that's about right. You might call that house and land yours, but they're not and you shouldn't ever forget it. My land actually is mine, but you don't see a problem with standing in *my* front yard and throwing your arms around *my* wife and telling her, 'Lord, if you ain't something.' "

At first my father didn't know what he was talking about. Then he remembered Arlan dropping him off in front of his house that night after the Council meeting and then going off to check on things, that he'd seen Nadine standing there and made that remark. But Arlan couldn't have heard it. His engine was still running and he was already backing out of his driveway. "Do *what*?" Dad said.

And that outraged Arlan. "Don't you dare say *do what*. Nadine's daddy used to talk like that, and he's a dumb-ass redneck."

It came to me right then that's exactly what the both of us was. Only dumb-ass rednecks would be trying to settle their private scores while half a mile away folks was shooting at one another and maybe even dying to keep a air force veteran from going to school where he wanted to. I knew it was wrong to keep him out and though I didn't want him in I wouldn't of fought to keep it from happening. And it seemed to me then like it does now that me and Arlan had some disease in common though I'll be damned if I know what to call it.

He heard himself laugh. "Is there such a word as *benignant*?"

"I have no fucking idea," Arlan told him. "I have to look all that shit up in a dictionary. And if there is such a word, I don't need it here tonight."

"I'm pretty sure it's a word. I believe it means when something's not dangerous, that it's okay."

"Things between you and me are not okay."

My father probably tried for the jocular tone guys will use when discussing things they think only a man can understand. "My Lord, you thought I was trying to make time with your wife? Why?"

"I knew somebody was, and at the time you were the only one that came to mind."

Somewhere behind them, a bullet pinged off a tree. "Because I said wasn't she something?"

"I wouldn't tell *your* wife that."

"Well, my wife's not exactly the kind of woman that makes anybody want to say that." My father immediately regretted that comment. "Listen, don't get me wrong," he added, "I wouldn't trade her for—"

"I don't give a shit if you'd trade her or not. I got half a mind to shoot you, James. Nobody'd ever know I did it, not with all this hell that's breaking loose. I could say we got separated in the dark and the marshals or the National Guard or somebody else must've shot you. But you know that. It's why you wanted us to come up here in the first place. You meant to lead me out into the woods and shoot me, James, and that plain ain't right. I might've taken your house—hell, there's no might to it, I damn well would've if I needed to—but I wouldn't have tried to kill you."

I wasn't safe from my neighbor but my neighbor, he was safe from me. I might of used the Python fifteen minutes earlier or fifteen years later if I ever needed to to protect my wife and boy. But I couldn't use it then and there was nothing I could do but hope that Arlan knew it.

Evidently, he didn't. While my father stood there suddenly awash in sweat, Arlan Calloway brought the muzzle around.

The sound, when Dad heard it, was right behind him where, as far as he knew, no living creature ought to be. A quick rustling followed by a couple thumps—of feet whacking the ground?—and then something dark and frantic darted past. Arlan swung his shotgun in that direction, and my father expected the night to explode, but it didn't. Whatever it was had bolted through the woods towards the road—the dark form leaping forward, rising four or five feet into the air—with both of them staring after it.

And then Arlan looks at me and says I wish I'd shot that goddamn deer. You've sure made me want to fire this gun tonight.

Driving back to Loring they kept meeting cars and pickups, hundreds if not thousands of folks bound for Oxford. Arlan had turned the radio down low, but my father could still hear it. Someone else had been killed, and the 108th Cavalry was moving into position to assault the campus. Helicopters hovering near the administration building were constantly being shot at by the rioters. One reporter claimed the marshals had run out of teargas, that the Lyceum couldn't be held much longer. Nobody seemed to know where Meredith was, even whether or not he was still alive. There was speculation that the marshals might have airlifted him back to Memphis.

This would prove false. In just a few hours, accompanied by the chief U.S. marshal and an assistant attorney general, Meredith entered the rear door of the Lyceum and registered for classes, becoming a junior at the University of Mississippi. On August 18, 1963, he earned the college degree that my father never dreamed of.

None of that would have mattered to Dad had he known it that evening. What mattered, as he and Arlan rode together through a night as dark as any he'd ever seen, was that this time next year he and my mother and I would be right where we'd always been, the three of us eating around the table in a home that belonged to the county. It wasn't an especially good place to be—most folks, he knew, would consider it pretty awful—but at least it was familiar. We wouldn't be undergoing any big changes. And, on some level, he was grateful to Arlan for putting him to the test. Now he knew something about himself that he'd never known before, and this could only be a good thing. You need to know yourself. You need to know what you'd be willing to do in the service of those you love.

When Arlan stopped on the main road to let him out, it was a quarter till four on the first of October. He could walk the two hundred yards to our house and maybe get an hour or two of sleep before heading off to the fields to pick the rest of his crop. And the moment his feet hit the ground, he felt strangely buoyant. He looked into the cab at a man who'd been his best friend for as long as he could remember, a little guy with a hard face and tired eyes. He had a lot that my father lacked, and almost anybody assessing their relative merits would say that his future was a whole lot brighter. But my dad wouldn't have traded places with him even if the opportunity arose. "You take care of yourself, Arlan," he said.

There was no reply. So my father shut the door and Arlan Calloway drove off down the road, heading home to his kids and his wife.

When Ellis rang the bell that Christmas Eve, I didn't open the door. He knocked a few times, too, but then had the good sense to leave. It was cold outside, the snow falling heavily now, and he didn't intend to stand there with that ham and bottle of wine under his arm and freeze. I apologized later on, and of course he understood once I told him I'd been sitting on the laundry room floor with my father's life spread out across my knees.

In the months since I've thought a good bit about what we know and how we know it and have concluded that I know a lot more about some things than I realized and much less about others. Some of what I know involves facts, some of it doesn't, and even the part that does isn't as dependent on the facts themselves as it is on my own capacity to believe and accept truths that might be painful. I've also spent time thinking about how one event can lead to another and have come to understand that while *cause* might well be, as I've long thought, the most frequently misappropriated term in our language, its properties are nevertheless real and more than a little mysterious.

The day I asked Dad what he meant when he said he'd been out looking after my interests that night in 1962, he replied, "I'll tell you this: the answer won't never be found in no book." But about that, and no small number of other things as well, my father was wrong.

ACKNOWLEDGMENTS

During the writing of this novel, the following sources were invaluable: *The Most Southern Place on Earth: The Mississippi Delta and the Roots of Regional Identity*, by James C. Cobb; *Local People: The Struggle for Civil Rights in Mississippi*, by John Dittmer; *An American Insurrection: James Meredith and the Battle of Oxford, Mississippi, 1962*, by William Doyle; *Speak Now Against the Day: The Generation Before the Civil Rights Movement in the South*, by John Egerton; *Ever Is a Long Time: A Journey into Mississippi's Dark Past*, by W. Ralph Eubanks; *Sons of Mississippi: A Story of Race and Its Legacy*, by Paul Hendrickson; *Let the People Decide: Black Freedom and White Resistance Movements in Sunflower County, Mississippi, 1945–1986*, by J. Todd Moye; and *The Negro in Mississippi, 1865–1890*, by Vernon Lane Wharton.

Thanks to Linnea Alexander, David Borofka, Steven Church, Bill Doyle, David Anthony Durham, Susan Early, Alex Espinoza, Ralph Eubanks, Lillian Faderman, Connie and John Hales, Coke and James Hallowell, Kristyn Keene, Beverly Lowry, Emily Milder, Todd Moye, Samina Najmi, Vida Samiian, Tim Skeen, Liz Van Hoose and James Walton for their advice and support. I remain indebted to Sloan Harris for being the best agent any writer ever had, and to Ewa, Lena and Tosha for being the best family anyone could ever ask for. Last, as always, my special thanks to my friend and editor Gary Fisketjon, who has no peer.